Big Game

THE V V INN SERIES:
BOOK THREE

C.J. ELLISSON

Red Hot Publishing
P.O. BOX 651193, STERLING VA, 20165-1193

First Print Edition May 2012

Copyright 2012 C.J. Ellisson
All Rights Reserved

ISBN 9781938601002

Without limiting the rights under copyright reserved above, no part of this publication may be reproduced, stored or introduced into a retrieval system, or transmitted, in any form or by any means (electronic, mechanical, photocopying, recording, or otherwise), without the prior written permission of both the copyright owner and the above publisher of this book.

PUBLISHER'S NOTE
This is a work of fiction. Names, characters, places, and incidents are either the products of the author's imagination or are used fictitiously, and any resemblance to actual persons, living or dead (or undead ;-), business establishments, events, or locales is entirely coincidental.

This book is dedicated to my readers, especially the ones on Facebook. Without you, there'd be no point in writing. Thank you for your continued support—you forever honor me with your interest.

Acknowledgements

I knew all along how I wanted this book to unfold. Getting the vision down on paper proved to be more challenging than I bargained for! Some writers churn out a book a month, others finish one a year, and still more—one every few years. I'd eventually like to be in between the monthly and yearly bunch, producing a few novellas and one or two novels per year, but I'm not there yet.

My health has always been my Achilles' heel, but it is also what brought me to this new career, so I can't complain.

Above and beyond the dedication on the previous page, my readers need to be acknowledged here as well. The emails, Facebook comments, status updates, and reviews... gosh, I could go on and on... it has all been truly awe-inspiring. Thank you!

When I had a set back (again) with my health this year, I was in a funk for months, unable to get my mind focused on writing. But as the deadline approached, the energy from my readers carried me through 'til the very end.

I had a fabulous group of alpha readers on Facebook, who tuned in every few days to read my unedited pages while I created *Big Game*. Thank you, each and every one of you, who made it to the end. Your support and desire to see the story unfold made all the difference in the world!

I had a new editor on this book, **Tina Winograd**. Damned if she wasn't the best editor I've worked with to date. She tightened my prose, made the story pop, and really pushed my writing abilities to the limit, demanding quality work from me no matter what. Thank you for the hours you poured into the manuscript, it wouldn't be where it is today without you.

A big thank you to my supportive children and family. **Justin Monson**, my nephew, read the first two books and had nothing but great things to say -- thanks, Justin! **Asa Monson** is still on my shit list for not reading them...perhaps I'll torture his character in a later book.

Last, but never least, the biggest thanks of all goes to my husband for his continued support. Pete, I know we're no where near that dream of a lake house, but maybe one day soon, after the medical bills end. Love you, hon.

Contributors

The following individuals inspired names for characters. They either thought the name up, volunteered the use of their name, I stole their name because I liked it, or they supported me so much I wanted to thank them:

Andy Lipshultz: It started as an April fool's joke, but then I twisted things and named a character after him (and basically stole his name, too).
Angie Linne: I named a character after her.
Asa Monson: My nephew, whom I based a character on and stole his name.
Brett Monson: My sister-in-law's ex, and my nephews' father in real life. You knew you couldn't escape the love, right?
Cali Blackadder, aka Julie Jewell: I based a character on her Second Life persona, and named the character after her.
Cy Whitfield, aka Michael Stern: My brother, whom I based a character on his Second Life persona, and named the character after him.
Debi Singleton: I named a character after her.
Dalton & Flavia Luz: An incredibly nice Brazilian couple that I based characters on and stole their names.
Deneishia Jacobpita: I named a character after her.
Diane O'Neill-Mason: She volunteered to have her name used.
Donald Swanson, Sr: I named a character after him.
Eric Monson: My nephew, whom I based a character on and stole his name.
Elsa Cisneros: I named a character after her.

Frank Natsuhara: I stole his last name for a character.

George "GJ" Marko: I named a character after him.

Helena Gardella: I named a character after her.

Jerry Stern: My dad, whom I based a character on and stole his name.

Justin Monson: The oldest nephew of the three. I based a character on him and stole his name.

Patrick Larson: I gladly wrote him into the story, with his permission, so he and Eric could continue to have adventures together forever.

Paul Ocker: I named a character after him.

Lori Anderson: I asked to use her name and her nickname Lor-Lor: she graciously agreed.

Margery Cook Stern: My mom, whom I based a character on and stole her name.

Michelle Pazdan: I named a character after her.

Miranda Blevins: I stole her name.

Nkotsana: Waiter at Cheesecake factory. I stole his name and took off the silent "N" to make it Kotsana.

Rolando Ray: He thought of the name Ivan, which won in an online vote—and I stole his name.

Romeo LoGiurato: I stole his name.

Stan Logan: I named a character after him.

Stephanie Groot: My friend, who gladly volunteered to be a character in the book.

Stephen Grantham: I named a character after him.

Theresa Dowd: I named a character after her and she picked Dria/Vivian's original first name, Ceara, which won in an online vote.

Vikram Savkoor: I stole his name; his only request was his character be cool ;-)

C.J. Ellisson

Vivian

CHAPTER ONE

Vivian

The soft hum of the jet fades into the background noise of the small cabin. Rafe exits the cockpit and locks eyes with me across the tight space. His rugged face carries a tired grin, and his blue eyes look weary. He's been flying through the daylight hours as we make our way down the globe to Argentina, where our final destination is a small private island off the southeastern coast.

His muscular form, encased in well-worn jeans and a snug black t-shirt, looks as delicious as ever. Worry pinches my husband's expression as he heads back to my location opposite the plane's bar. Chelly, lounging on a brown chenille couch, shifts her attention from her eReader—more than likely trying to catch a last glimpse of Drew who took over flying duties. Her long blond hair hides her expression from me, but I'm sure I'd see a hint of longing on her face. She deflates when she sees Rafe and goes back to her reading.

She and Drew, the one-hundred-and-fifty-year-old vampire who came to our resort as a guest last fall before joining our seethe, began dating this winter. Now he only feeds from her, taking bagged blood for extra nutrition when needed. To my knowledge, he hasn't yet claimed her by exchanging blood to make her his servant. He does treat her better than a simple blood donor, more like one does a companion. His old-fashioned ways make for a cute courtship display, but I doubt Chelly can take much more of the long tease. When Drew invited her on this trip, she nearly jumped his bones on the spot.

Bob, one of our ground crew, plays cards with Tommy — our imported Aussie who usually mans the inn's front desk— and Paul, our fledgling vampire. The three men crowd around a small table set between four plush seats, each wearing an intense look while examining his own cards. Their voices are pitched low, but every so often their excited chatter fills the cabin. Tommy glances up as Rafe walks by. The sandy-haired young man folds his cards and slips into the aisle behind my husband.

Rafe leans down and kisses my cheek before settling into the club chair next to mine. A half-glass of red wine sits before me on the round cocktail table bolted through the cream carpet. In honor of our destination, I've changed to South American wines instead of the Alaskan vampire favorite of hot coffee. To appear uncouth at Tribunal gatherings holding a mug instead of a crystal goblet filled with bloodwine would be an unacceptable *faux pas*. But I admit, I do miss the mild caffeine jolt.

"Tired, darling?" I ask.

"Yeah." A heavy sigh escapes him as he runs a hand across his forehead and back over his short light-brown hair. "Flying through the last storm was a challenge. Head winds slowed us down quite a bit."

On our right, Tommy stands behind the glistening marble-topped bar. "Can I get you something, sir?"

"A Yuengling, thanks."

Vivian

The young man pours beer into an ice-cold pilsner glass and sets it on the low table. After a nod of appreciation from Rafe, Tommy heads back to his cards.

Rafe stares at the amber liquid but doesn't drink. "I'm worried, Dria."

"I know."

"The talk with the seethe about your manipulator abilities went well, but it won't be the same with the Ancients."

"Yes, our group took it surprisingly well." I stifle a smile at the reminder of that night after the hunt. No one will ever forget Paul's confusion and mini-freak out. Asa, our ex-military vamp, only nodded as if confirming something he suspected, and Drew listened in stony silence. I haven't quite pegged him yet, but he pledged his loyalty again with the others easily enough, showing no hesitation.

Glancing at the shaded window blocking the night sky, I debate on raising it to view the stars. "The idea isn't to tell the Ancients; I'd never risk that. The plan to arrive earlier than in previous years is to surprise them—find out who knows or suspects what I can do."

"And then what? Slip into their minds and alter what they know?" He shakes his head. "Too risky."

"The alternative is to kill them." I stare at Rafe and see the concern he never tries to hide. "Depending on how many of the Inner Circle we're talking about, that might not be smart—or plausible."

Rafe grips the chair arms, his frustration and anger quickly outweighing his previous concern. "Twenty-two members of the Circle and eleven Ancients, not to mention an unknown number of powerful gophers and lackeys on the fringe doing their bidding. Too many variables. I prefer a concentrated and planned attack."

"We've gone over this before, love. What choice is there? Let them come to us in Alaska where we have over a hundred humans in our care?" I shake my head. "I won't put them at risk. Not an option. Besides, we normally head down south when the season changes, making it impossible to run the inn for vampire guests. This early fact-finding mission in Buenos Aires is the best way to go."

"Yes, yes, your 'beard the lion in his den', crap. I get it." He reaches for his beer and drains half the glass before setting it down. "I worry there's more than the three members you've speculated on."

Bitter resentment and rage coil in my middle. For years I've hidden my ability and ran from certain death, only to find I'm now cornered in a remote location with twelve dozen lives at stake. Fight or flight. That's what any predator would do when left with no options.

"I don't plan on running again." Anger leaks through my tone and the tension in the cabin rises. "The only option is to infiltrate and bring a stealthy battle to them."

"Won't they be expecting that? Coraline visited back in January. It's foolish to think they haven't done anything in three months."

"If it were me," I say with a deadly smile, "I would have attacked immediately."

"Agreed. So why didn't they?"

"Coraline could be the main force driving the entire witch hunt after me. With the alterations I did to her psyche, Cora's cohorts will need a while to bring her back up to speed —maybe even weeks to unravel what I did and how I did it. I'm not sure they could repair the damage if they weren't able to slip into her mind, as well."

"What about that damn charmed brooch? Someone made it for her. Maybe the person is a strong magic user and has countered what you did?"

Vivian

I speculate on his suggestion for a bit and focus on letting go of my fury. I try to center my thoughts and picture myself mentally moving through a few sun salutations. The yoga moves work for mental balance, even while sitting still. The anger deflates, and I focus back on Rafe's suggestion, again.

His idea is possible, I suppose, but I've never met a witch or wizard who's that powerful. Most of them can do what Diane, Dr. Cook's witchy daughter, does back home. She can cast minor spells and contrive complicated charms, given enough time and the right ingredients... but a witch with mind powers or the ability to cast a complex spell to counter my mind altering? Not likely. Could it be a wizard? They are known to do more mental damage, but the spells are quite intricate, and having no innate elemental powers like those a witch is born with would make it unlikely a wizard could pull it off.

"I don't think so," I finally answer. "But, you're right. It could be an option."

Paul, our undead head chef, saunters toward us. He's become a sleeker version of himself, thanks to the liquid diet, and is now able to keep up with his kids and slim wife much easier. He nods to us on his way to the lavatory in the rear of the plane.

After emerging from the tiny room, Paul leans against the bar. "Smooth flying, Rafe." He brushes a lock of dark wavy hair off his forehead. "Will I ever get to add 'pilot' to my growing list of super-cool things I know?"

"Ask Drew to teach you," Rafe answers with an easy-going smile. "The facilities are better in Alaska, but you could probably start on the basics while in Argentina."

Paul sighs. "This trip would have been great to share with Bunny. I'm still bummed she and the kids couldn't come."

"We don't know what we're walking into, Paul," I say. "Bringing them wouldn't be wise."

"Yeah, I know. Doesn't mean I have to like it. And why are there only male donors for me, Viv?" At my sly smile, he laughs. "What, you thought I didn't notice Tommy and Bob were guys?"

"Bunny asked me to make sure you were loyal. No temptations for you while I'm on watch."

Paul looks stricken as he faces away from the passengers in the cabin and leans in, speaking low. "What happens when the men become tempting?"

"You close your eyes," I whisper, "think of your wife, and jerk off when they leave."

The smile is absent from his usual jovial face. He nods like he's received a death sentence. "Okay."

I flash him a wink. "There's also a large supply of donated blood on ice coming with us. You'll do fine." I reach out and grab his sleeve before he leaves. "You're gaining control, Paul. Getting stronger each day. Don't let the urges get the better of you."

"Put the shoe on the other foot," Rafe says. "Would you want Bunny spreading her legs every few days when she got hungry?"

Anger colors the cheeks of the good-humored vampire. "No!"

Rafe drains his glass and stands. "Then keep that anger front and center in your brain when you get horny for another person." He slaps Paul on the back then moves to the bar.

"How do you do it, Vivian?" Paul asks. "Do you ever crave another lover?"

My mind flashes to Jonathan, my hunky werewolf servant with the compact wrestler's body who tastes like dark chocolate. I've stashed ten pints of his blood for the few months in Argentina. Yum. "You channel it back into passion for your mate. You can't control what your body craves, but you can control what you do with those cravings."

His shoulders slump. "Why is it so hard?"

"Most vampires want the sex and the blood together. It's only as we age we can channel the blood-lust into pure sexual lust." Beeps and a whir come from microwave in the bar area.

"You mean, someday I might want sex from everyone rather than their blood?"

I laugh. "We're talking centuries, Paul. And maybe not sex from *everyone*, but some days it may feel that way."

"Won't I still need blood?"

"Of course, but not as much. As time passes our kind can feed from other means, like sexual energy." My thoughts turn inward, remembering some of the old vampires who fed on fear and pain. When their appetites overtook sanity and too many humans were terrorized, the Tribunal of Ancients would send an enforcer to end their madness. I pull my mind away from those horrible years and pat my fledgling's cheek. "Trust me, Paul. There are a lot worse things than sex and lust to crave energy from."

The smell of corned beef wafts our way, teasing me of times long past in Ireland. Rafe sets a large plate holding a Rueben and chips on the cocktail table then eases into the chair. "Paul, thanks for making this for me. It heated perfectly, not soggy."

Paul smiles at the praise and heads toward his card game. Bob and Tommy look up at his approach and then back to their hands. I wonder what they are wagering to make them so serious.

I lean closer to my husband. "Do you think Bob and Tommy will do okay on the island?"

Rafe nods, swallowing a bite of his sandwich. "They're good guys. Tommy will make sure everyone stays in line; he's pretty good at herding cats and managing without being overbearing. And I trust him to anticipate Paul's needs before Paul does. Bob can help when Paul decides to cook—which you know he will—and maybe work with the gardener during the day." He swigs another long drink and a few harsh lines of exhaustion soften from his face. "Our main issue will be the housekeeper's barely-legal daughter, doubling as a maid this year."

The ends of my lips curl up as I recall the dark, good looks of Rosia. Her eyes snap with life, and she knows exactly how to sway her hips to attract a man's eye. "Dalton might exert his fatherly protection and insist his daughter work in the gardens with him while we're in attendance."

"Last we spoke, he said his wife called her younger twin sisters to help out this season."

Picturing the women we've met before, I can't help but feel amusement. They're all as pretty as Dalton's wife, Flavia, and will provide ample distraction for the two men, not to mention a major temptation for Paul after Rafe and I leave for Buenos Aires alone. Chelly's light hair and full curves will stand out like a beacon compared to the small-breasted, exotic-looking brunettes.

"Paul might have a hard time resisting Dalton." My eyes dance with humor, teasing my spouse. "He's a suave and sexy guy."

Rafe wipes his mouth with a cloth napkin and tosses the fabric onto the empty plate. "You've managed to resist him for almost two decades." A warm palm lands on my thigh, caressing the leg through linen trousers. "However did you cope?"

Vivian

Heat fills me, burning a path from Rafe's hand to my privates. "I've got this big stud of a husband I ravish daily. Thankfully, the old man doesn't need Viagra yet."

Rafe's laughter booms across the cabin. The four other passengers glance in our direction, then back to their interests. "All thanks to you, dear—and those magical sips of blood I have every now and then."

My lids lower, and I gaze at him through my thick lashes. "Surely, it can't all be just me?"

Rafe leans in, and our lips meet. His soft mouth molds to mine, the tip of his tongue gently begging entrance. I open, and he deepens the kiss, plundering my mouth like a starving man at his first meal in weeks. A throaty growl escapes one of us. Could have been me—I've been known to growl once in a while.

A soft, electric tingle enters my mind as my husband telepathically speaks to me through our mate-bond. *The day I need a pill to be ready for you is the day you need to shoot me.*

Put the old dog out of his misery, eh? You'll not get rid of me that easily. A warm hand caresses the back of my head and holds me in place while Rafe pillages my mouth. When I hear a throat clearing, I pull back. *No need to put on a show. Should we retire to the bedroom?*

Rafe ends the kiss and stares into my eyes. *Sixty-five years together and you still have to ask?* Heat fills his gaze, as a predatory grin curves his lips. *Get your ass in there or I'll pull a cave man and throw you over my shoulder and carry you back.*

I rise from the chair and sashay toward the bedroom cabin at the end of the narrow hallway, feeling the burning gaze of my lover on my backside the entire time. The cell phone clipped to my waist vibrates, with its usual horrible timing. I answer while opening the privacy door and hear the

17

gruff tones of my werewolf servant across thousands of miles.

"Have you landed?"

In man-speak that means, *I'm worried you haven't called.* I try to swallow the humor in my response. "No, we haven't."

"What's the hold up? Problem at one of the refueling spots or weather?"

A sigh escapes me as I climb onto the queen-sized bed and recline against the upholstered headboard. A feral look in his eyes, Rafe closes the door with his foot, hands already pulling off his shirt.

"You guessed it," I say. "We hit several storms, and the winds were against us."

A muffled "hrmph" reaches me from the other end of the line and I stare at the flesh slowly revealed by my spouse. The hard sculpted planes of his chest slip into view, and he tosses the shirt at my face—his not so subtle hint to get off the phone.

Rafe stretches his arms over his head, bending at the elbows to avoid hitting the aircraft's low ceiling and then leans right and left working his cramped muscles. God, that man has delicious abs. Saliva fills my mouth at the thought of licking the hard stomach ridges.

"The werewolves will be landing in two hours."

What? Oh yeah, I'm still on the damn phone. Jon's referring to the inn's summer guests, who plan to hunt Alaska's native game during their stay. The upcoming arrival must be what triggered his call; he'll be tied up for the rest of the day. Rafe reaches for the button on his pants, and I track every movement of his supple fingers. "Good. Any last minute questions for me, Jon?"

"No. Our mind connection is getting fuzzy. I can't feel much of you in my head."

Vivian

"I think it's the distance." He should count himself lucky—I doubt he'd want to see my husband getting naked. Then again, knowing Jon's conflicted emotions regarding Rafe and me, he just might enjoy the view. "You'll do fine this summer. We're only a phone call away if you need us."

"Yeah, and including stops, you're over a full day via plane. I'm not reassured. And for the record, it's not me and the pups I'm worried about—or even Asa, for that matter."

Jon loves teasing Pat and Eric, our new permanent werewolf members, by calling them *pups*. Makes the two grown men squirm in their desires to correct him—but both are pretty smart and resist his goading well. "I'll be fine, Jon."

"This is your first year in seven without me there. What if you need me?"

Rafe's vampire-sharp hearing listens to both ends of the conversation. He snorts his disagreement on the likelihood of needing Jon and thrusts his jeans down past his hips, taking his tight boxer briefs with them.

My mouth dries at the sight of my husband in all his aroused glory. I clear my throat to hurry the phone call along. "This year we've got Drew and Paul here. Things will work out."

Rafe steps out of his clothing and leaps onto the bed, straddling my body. His muscular arms bracket my torso propped against the headboard, and the heat of his breath fans my cheek.

"Okay, gotta go. I'll call you when we land."

"Wai—"

I click off the phone and toss it to the floor before wrapping my arms around the man I love more than anything in the world, including my own semi-immortality.

Chapter Two

Jonathan

The line drops. I can picture, all too well, why Vivian ended the call—a half-naked Rafe. Her husband distracts her way too easily. My worry of being so far from the couple's side grows, gnawing at my stomach.

Will he be quick enough, strong enough, observant enough to protect her and keep them safe in Argentina? *I should be there to make sure her enemies don't get to her at a weak moment.* A sigh escapes me as I slip the thin cell into my flannel shirt pocket. Time will tell—but for her sake, I hope they made a smart choice.

An ache in my chest has me knuckling a fist and rubbing a sharp circle. The sound of banging pots and pans pulls my attention from the quiet foyer to the activity in the dining room. Eric and Pat, balancing loads of cookware, move toward the side door leading to the hot tub grotto.

"What the hell are you two doing?"

Pat looks at me—his crooked nose hanging over an infectious grin. "Dude, we're setting up a cooking station by

Jonathan

the spas. Good idea, right? It'll be a great party spot for the Weres."

A glance out the window reveals they've already set up a large drum-like grill and three folding tables. I love the thought of grilling outside now that the weather is bearable—not warm, but not below freezing all the time either. I grunt my approval. "You won't need all the pasta pots and such. They'll be easier to use on the stove in here."

"Jerry lent us a grill station with three gas burners. We're setting that up next."

I nod, suppressing a laugh as Eric's broad shoulders ease sideways to squeeze through the doorway with his arms loaded full of supplies.

"Fine. But take care of everything yourselves. And no drunken cooking mishaps like last month, understood?"

Pat's face sobers at the memory of burning half their cabin's kitchen after passing out while boiling water. A Were has got to be pretty damn drunk not to wake up at the smell of melting cookware. Thankfully, they came to when the flames started and put out the fire before they lost any of their limited possessions.

"Yes, sir," Pat says in a serious tone. "Count on it."

I can never tell if the crafty little bastard's telling me what his new alpha wants to hear, or if he's genuine. Next time I catch the bugger in a lie, I'm going to pound on him a bit so he knows I won't take his irresponsible behavior like many before me. Eric has a harder time lying to my face and comes clean when caught. I think watching a whoop-ass session will work fine for him.

I shudder realizing the implication of my thoughts. My musings seem, dare I say, permanent in their tone. Christ, the little fuckers are growing on me.

Wanting to push any complex concepts out of my brain, I follow my ears toward the back of the kitchen where the buzz of a Sawzall rips the air. Dirt and dust on the once-clean tile floor scratch under my step. Maybe it is best not to cook in here for a while. Good thing werewolves aren't picky and will probably gorge themselves while in wolf form, if they catch anything.

I open the door to the small storage room next to the walk-in freezer and weave past the pushed-aside metal shelves and stacked boxes. Temporary work lights on hooks hang from the ceiling and illuminate the windowless space to a near-blinding brightness.

Asa angles the power tool blade through the exposed subfloor plywood. Within a week, the new spiral staircase leading into the basement command center should be completed. Framing a secure closet around the stairwell and installing locks will be the tedious part. But now, it's time for demolition. I rub my hands together, ready for some good, old-fashion destruction. Glad I didn't miss it.

The whine of the jagged saw shuts down when the young vampire sees me. "You need something, Jon?"

"Yeah, I came to help with demo. Where are the sledgehammers? Don't we get to bust through beams and shit?"

Asa's stoic face doesn't crack at my attempt of humor. "If you want to ruin the structure and create more expense to repair the damage, sure. But this isn't a wall we're tearing down—we're building inside a room we'd like to keep intact."

"Just kidding, man." I smile at his deadpan look. Guess my joking is lost on the undead bastard. "Did you clear the drywall and insulation from the basement side, and check for wires and pipes before you started cutting? Oh, and remember to turn off the power in that section?"

"No, I'm a complete idiot who didn't build out the entire command center and five basement rooms with you this past winter."

Jonathan

"Good. Glad to see you only need to cut through live wires once to learn your lesson."

Asa gives me a flat stare and raises one eyebrow toward the smooth bald expanse of his shaved head. "Can I get back to work, now?"

"Wait—did you print the file on the new arrivals for me?"

"Yeah. It's on the kitchen table in Rafe and Viv's apartment."

We've been using the suite in their absence, and I'm debating on temporarily moving in when the guests are here. I wouldn't have to trek from my cabin in the woods every morning.

I curb the longing to smash my bare hands through the subfloor Asa's cutting. The release of strength and call to action would drain the tension coiled in me... but might reveal my frustration from being away from her. Apparently, the eight-mile run this morning wasn't enough. God, I feel a syringe of adrenaline pricking at muscles below the skin, just waiting for the right moment to explode into movement.

I exit the construction site and enter the couple's apartment via the key-carded security door located in the rear of the kitchen.

The warm tones and bright jewel colors accenting the living room always projects a warm welcome. The scent of the happy lovers wraps around me, pummeling my gut with a boxer's right jab. Damn, I miss them. Our mind connection had strengthened since the hunt, but weakened when they were a few hours away on the plane.

Could I push and try to reach her? Should I? I need a break from them, mentally, but losing complete touch with her, even for a few minutes, makes me queasy. After I almost died when Vikram attacked me in the gym months ago, they've brought me much closer. I feel what they feel when they look at and think of me. They love me, and in Rafe's case, he hates me a little, too. I can't blame him, after all, for years I wished him dead and wanted his wife for myself.

When I pledged my loyalty to Vivian over seven years ago, I never expected any relationship between the three of us to evolve. That's what I get for jumping in with both feet without a backward glance. Granted, at the time, I was hoping she wasn't too attached to her human husband, but that didn't prove to be the case.

While sinking onto the cushy couch, I grab Vivian's favorite lap blanket, bringing the soft red knit to my nose. Images of our trio relaxing for another of Rafe's movie marathons fill my head. It took over two months until I felt comfortable joining the love birds on the couch, previously isolating myself on the chair closer to the TV.

I never would've believed we'd all let down our guards enough to build a connection. But damned, if those two didn't somehow pull it off. No sexual tension, no innuendo, no handholding—just pure admiration of the films and heated discussions of the plots. The pack bond grew strong among us, I felt content.

Content for the first time in years.

I'd lean next to where Vivian snuggled into a deep cushion, and our calves or thighs might touch. The comforting weight felt like a deeply loved friend, but not a lover. I never experienced that before, even during my time in Romeo's group.

Sexual undertones pervade most wolf packs. Unmarried partners are often swapped as young wolves try to find mates. Anger and resentment run close to the surface, fueling the blinding animal passion. I never understood the rationale—how were they supposed to pick a mate when they only wanted to bed hop? Love doesn't blossom instantaneously, for most.

Jonathan

The movie marathons allowed me the freedom to get past the mental hang-up of "all or nothing", and let my mind carve a place where I belonged in Vivian's life. Her intense love for me burns inside my core, and even though I know these emotions will never cross a physical line, I can't help but want them to.

My cock stirs at the familiar dreams of Rafe and me both taking Vivian. Too bad Diane took the summer to visit friends in the lower states. The witch had always been a willing bed partner and often helped me escape from my overwhelming fantasies with her blocking charms. I shift my eager erection to a more comfortable position—not going to happen. Might as well get some work done.

After pushing off the couch, I search for the files. The lingering aroma of coffee fills the air, once again, reminding me of Rafe holding his steadfast coffee mug. I grab a bottle of water from the fridge and settle at the worn round tabletop with the folder Asa prepared.

There's a small number of guests for the opening week—only sixteen wolves. With all the rooms and cabins, we could easily handle sixty or more. The season will reach full capacity when daylight hours increase and the bigger animals migrate north. Right now, in early April, we're at ten hours of darkness and fourteen of light, almost a normal day—although, *normal* never lasts long up here.

I sift through paperwork and notice Romeo and Elsa are coming with half of their Manitoba pack. I recognize several of the names that joined before I left eight years ago. It'll be nice to see how some of the ladies turned out. Damn, thoughts of randy female werewolves aren't helping to calm my raging boner.

A mental weight lifts when I note Lori's name is not on the list. Considering her friendship with Eric and Pat, I wasn't sure if Romeo would acquiesce and allow the angry bitch to attend. She's attractive, but after our last encounter, I have no desire to tangle with her sour nature again. Wonder if Vivian requested they not bring her? I wouldn't put it past the vampire to try to spare me any awkwardness, if she could.

Thinking back to my last meeting with the pack, I realize the pups have now been with me longer than they had lived with Romeo and Elsa. Both of them were attacked in early October last year and came here in January with a smaller portion of Romeo's pack. Having Asa to help Eric adjust to his new way of life has helped. Occasionally, Asa needed to slip into both Eric and Pat's minds to calm them when wolf instincts rode them too high after a kill. Certainly easier than me corralling them—I'd likely have to wrestle them to the ice, causing damage.

While studying the list of attendees, the lovely ladies inspiring my tight-pants problem leap to mind. Katrina, Naomi, and Ruby were scrumptious co-eds attacked in their senior year of high school after a football game. They were still wearing their cheerleader outfits when Romeo and I strolled into the emergency room to break the news of exactly *what* attacked them. Best friends, the three brunettes struggled together through the change and the subsequent lifestyle alterations.

They'd be twenty-six, now. All three were long-legged and athletic. One of Russian, one of Jamaican, and one of Latina descent. Huh... maybe there's a reason Lori isn't coming. Elsa wants me to have a fresh shot at these gorgeous young ladies. Hot damn, I love a meddlesome female alpha with good taste in women.

With a spark of hope swelling in my heart at the prospect of getting laid by a hot-blooded, good-looking Were, I zip through the other pages containing the rest of the visiting pack: A couple I kinda know—Kotsana and his wife

Jonathan

Deneishia, two females I don't know—Lilli and Tricia, three other couples I vaguely recall, and Spike. Do I really need to study these sheets as carefully as Vivian always does? It's not like we're with a bunch of vampires and need to worry about hidden power plays and intrigue.

Pretty simple when you think about it—wolves hunting big game animals. Running free with no cities, roads or too many humans nearby. What could be better than that?

A soft contented sigh seeps out, dispelling some of the pent up sexual energy. I'm looking forward to partying and hanging out with fellow wolves. Racing through the forest after the scent of prey will be exhilarating—having it possibly end with sex would be the icing on the cake. Wonder if the three girls are close enough that I could talk them into a *ménage a quatre*?

A painful lurch in my pants makes me realize I need to stop this line of thought, or I'll be sporting a woody all afternoon. A little under two hours until the first plane lands. Better tell Asa to clean up and do a last minute check. Knowing him, he finished his routine before starting with the tools, but I'm telling him to quit just the same.

From the corner of my eye, I see a whoosh of flames shoot skyward outside the window and quickly die. Loud voices holler from the hot tub grotto. Perhaps I'll detour outside and make sure Pat and Eric haven't set the whole place on fire.

Chapter Three

Rafe

A soft beep from the plane's intercom system jars me from a light slumber. Dria slips under my arm, and presses a button on the com box near the cabin's door. "Yes?"

"We're landing in twenty minutes."

"Thanks, Drew."

She pads lightly to the bed and leans over me. A whisper soft kiss lands on my lips. "Time to get up, love."

"Yeah, I heard." I stretch, allowing the sheet to fall away from my chest. Dria's eyes lock onto my revealed stomach muscles. Mouth slightly agape, her tiny pointed tongue brushes a lengthening canine. It's so fun to tease her. She's like a caged tiger living next door to the butcher, and I'm the raw meat parading past her bars. "Let me pull on some clothes and grab our overnight bag."

"My turn to pilot. I'll fly the seaplane from the marina hangar." Dria draws back from the bed and snatches a jumpsuit from a nearby chair. She deftly steps in and zips the dark blue coverall up her naked form, wiggling her round ass to torment me. The lined fabric hugs her curves and hides the fact she's not wearing underwear.

She gently pulls out her long hair from under the collar and gives her head a sexy shake. Just like when she teased my cock an hour or so ago. The glint in her eye reveals she knows I'm watching and the gesture was intentional. The little minx.

The next couple of hours proceed without a hitch. Minutes after a smooth water landing, workers from our private island taxi the plane through the cove to return to the hangar to retrieve the rest of our luggage from the jet.

"Holy cow!" Paul stands on the large dock, staring up the gentle slope of the island. "The house overhangs a freakin' cliff? I don't know why I thought 'tropical' when I pictured Argentina."

I look at the large crest Paul called a cliff. Shadows and crags hide in the dark recesses, showcasing the brightly lit stucco house at the rocky pinnacle.

"Flip your thoughts when you pass the equator," I say. "Buenos Aires is three hours north of us. Right now, it's like the difference between New Jersey and northern Florida during the fall in the U.S."

Drew grabs Chelly's hand. The couple steps in line behind Dria. My wife leads our merry band toward the small parking lot a hundred yards up a gently sloping hill. The rolling landscape here is much greener than Alaska was when we left. Lots of short grasses and manicured shrubs.

"It's fall?" Bob comments from the dock. "Who ever heard of fall in April?" His shoulders shrug. "Makes no sense, I tell ya."

Paul shoves the large man playfully, encouraging him to walk behind the others. "Dude, didn't you hear him? We crossed the equator. Southern Hemisphere is opposite the northern one in seasons."

A "harrumph" comes from the larger man, but he dutifully trails along with the rest of us. "So that means it gets colder the more south you go, too?" Bob shakes his head. "Right when I think I get to understanding how the world works, I get thrown a curve ball and visit the other side of the globe."

Tommy smirks, "God-forbid you step out from the comfort of your living room and explore beyond the flat screen TV."

"I always wondered where you guys went in the summer," Paul directs to Dria and me. "Should have guessed you'd follow suit and go someplace where the nights are long."

Drew leans close to Chelly's ear. "That Vivian," he whispers in a faux conspirator-like tone, "she's a smart one."

My wife grins. "I've owned this small island for seven decades. It's come far since I first brought Rafe here."

I laugh recalling the two-room shack my wealthy wife so humbly lived in. It was dank, dark, and cold. I don't know how or why she lived in it for as long as she did. To hide from her enemies, I suspect. She never ceases to amaze me. "It took a team of engineers and gardeners to make this desolate island into what you see today. Not many trees, anyone notice?"

"Yeah," says Chelly. "I was wondering about that."

Drew asks, "Remember the Falkland Islands pictures I showed you?" She nods. "I had a feeling the terrain here would be the same." He glances to the sloping ground. "Looks like something cleared most of the vegetation."

"No," I answer. "It may look that way, but the rock under the surface makes it very hard for roots to form, making it a natural terrain for grasses."

"Still," Bob says, "I hoped for palm trees and bright flowers." He eyes up a grouping of two-toned ornamental grasses. "It's pretty, don't get me wrong. I just hadn't pictured grassy hills when I thought of visiting an island off Argentina."

"Reminds me a little of Ireland," Drew says. "From the pictures it didn't seem as green, though. Now that I'm here it's colder, and much windier than I expected."

A two-foot tall black-and-white body waddles by, heading back to the cove, and I wait for the expected exclamations.

"Holy crap," says Paul. "Did I just see a penguin?"

"Bet they don't have those in Ireland." Chelly leans into Drew and kisses his cheek. He whips around to gawk at the bird, and the group continues in this fascinated vein for a bit while we walk.

By their expressions, I'm betting only one or two of them even vaguely researched where we were going. Typical ignorant Americans. They really do make the rest of us look bad. Hell, Tommy is Australian and Drew is older than I am —there's no excuse for the lot of them, really.

Vivian continues walking, ignoring the inane chatter from the group. She looks regal as she carries herself over the crushed stone drive, even in a jumpsuit. The lighted trails remind me of the winding pathways in Alaska, without the snow and different plants. I wonder if that was subconscious on our part when we directed Dalton to install them down here.

We gather on the terraced parking area near a group of electric utility and transport carts. They are larger and nicer than golf carts, but the principle is the same—compact, not built for speed, but designed to shuttle people and things for short distances.

Chelly looks around, the strong breeze whipping her long hair about while she takes in the many small buildings and road leading to the main house. "I'm getting the feeling like I'm walking through an episode of *Fantasy Island* more and more as the months go by."

Drew laughs and squeezes her hand. "Vivian as Mr. Roarke?"

Before Chelly has a chance to clarify, Dria jumps in. "But of course, darling," her eyes flash in a rare show of amazing good humor. "I'm proud to say you're the first in a while to make the connection."

The young blond woman straightens under the attention and smiles. "Classic TV. 'Da plane, boss. Da plane'."

We toss our bags in the carts and motor up the winding drive toward the main house. Bob, Tommy, and Paul make a big show of driving the cart while acting like fools. All in good fun and we've been cooped up in the plane, so I don't correct their idiotic behavior. Dria must be thinking the same thing since she rarely suffers fools.

The largest grouping of buildings we pass look like old English country farmhouses, a style Vivian detests, and one most prevalent on these islands. She never lived in the houses here, flat out refused, making a rustic cabin instead. Said the old design reminded her of the homestead Mikov locked her in for over two decades. Can't say I blame her for disliking it.

Dalton and his wife remodeled the dilapidated structures when they hired on. By then, the first portion of the main home was built and we didn't have to field questions on why we lived in the crappy cabin. I've gotten used to my wife's idiosyncrasies, but that tiny shack was never my favorite—like living in a windy coffin.

"Is that the caretaker's house?" Drew asks from the cart behind us. "Where are they now?"

"Yes, it is," I say. "Dalton and Flavia await us at the main house. Dria dislikes them crowding around the dock to say hello." I slide a warm palm over Dria's jumpsuit-covered thigh, snagging on a zipper pull. I tickle the edge of it and resist. The multiple fasteners make me want to open up *all* the zippers and explore.

"Well," Dria says, "their daughter fell in the cove that one time. I felt so guilty when she cried for her ruined dress."

"That was fifteen years ago, dear. She's no longer a four-year-old wearing frilly pink dresses." No sooner do the words leave my mouth than we round the last bend to see Dalton standing on the cobblestone circular drive flanked by four delectable beauties. Poor Paul, he's going to whimper when he gets a gander at them.

A stifled intake of breath comes from one of the stopped carts. I suppress a smile as I picture the poor sod trying to calm his raging vampiric tendencies to seduce and feed from anything attractive.

I lived through it when Dria changed Cy, but his fledgling stages progressed so very quickly it was maybe only a week where he walked around being led by his semi-mortal cock. There's not as much temptation for Paul at a job worked for ten years and they all know your wife.

"Welcome," Dalton steps forward and shakes my hand the moment I disembark from the cart. "How was your long trip?"

"A few storms," I answer. "Uneventful, otherwise." The wind slashes across the driveway, hitting us harder at the hilltop.

"Good." He withdraws his hand and kisses Dria on both cheeks. I note the dark haired, doe-eyed beauty of his wife still looks as lovely as ever. Flavia's full lips part in a small smile and she greets me with the traditional show of Argentine hospitality, double cheek kisses and a short hug.

Their daughter, Rosia, stands near her two aunts Carmella and Carmina. The trio could've stepped off the set of a South American telenova—glossy, dark-brown hair, fully made-up faces, dressed to the nines, and exuding a sexual air combined with a womanly confidence one doesn't often see in the States.

I nod to the ladies, but wisely keep my distance. Dalton is a protective man and already the frown forms between his brows at Tommy and Bob's slack-jawed appreciation of the single women. Thankfully, with a shove from Chelly, they close their mouths and manage to keep quiet.

I'm guessing Flavia's younger sisters are in their mid-twenties, the perfect age for sexual experimentation with exotic strangers. This could be a very good trip for the two bumbling fools if they play their cards right, and avoid Dalton's watchful eye. Although, I think I'll mention something to them about not hitting on his daughter. Dria would be pissed if we lost a good caretaker over their exploits.

After Dria introduces the group to our traveling companions, we make our way to the large, modified Spanish-style hacienda. All of the lights have been left on inside to welcome us, and the effect is grand. A warm glow spills from each pane of glass, inviting the weary traveler indoors. The red tile roof compliments the creamy stucco beautifully, even years after flying in craftsmen from northern Argentina to do the work.

The many exterior balconies have been enclosed with high-tech glass that tints to block the sun at the press of a button. From every side of the house the gently sloping terrain does not hinder observation of the ocean, but prior to the conversion it was not cozy viewing this time of year. The central courtyard of the home is enclosed as well, with high-arching atrium panels spanning the open area between rooftops.

Maintaining the sparsely-wooded twenty acres closest to the home takes up a large portion of Dalton's time in the summer. But since Jon didn't join us and we plan on heading to Buenos Aires soon, his efforts won't be as appreciated this trip.

With a welcoming gesture, the couple ushers us into the home so we can get out of the wind. The foyer is much smaller than the one at the inn, but it makes up for its lack of size with homey warmth. Terra cotta tile covered with boldly designed rugs stretch off in all directions, spilling into the rooms on the ground floor.

Pieces of art from around Central and South America decorate the walls, rustic wrought iron scones highlighting their beauty without being harsh. The kitchen and dining rooms lay to the right, leading away and bending around the corner to bracket the central courtyard, and the various living room areas lay to the left, also wrapping around the courtyard. The bedrooms lay above, on the second floor, with the hallway to all the bedrooms overlooking the green interior.

The mouth-watering aroma of seafood and fresh bread drift from the kitchen wing to greet our weary group.

"Oh, something smells good," Paul says, earning an appreciative smile from Flavia.

"You like to cook, sir?" the housekeeper asks, deftly guessing from his pale complexion, so like her employer's—that he probably likes to cook more than eat.

"Yes, and I can hardly wait to get in your kitchen. I'd love to learn the local dishes if you don't mind sharing. My wife and kids always appreciate new cuisine."

Dalton's face relaxes at the mention of Paul's family, and Flavia's smile grows even broader. "Come back to the kitchen with me." She gestures for him to follow. "I'll show you what I've made for tonight." As they walk off, she peppers Paul with questions about his wife, the ages of his children, and where he learned to cook.

Dalton approaches Dria and bows slightly at the waist. "Dinner at nine? Is that acceptable, ma'am?"

My wife's face softens as she looks to him fondly. "Call me Dria, please. You know I don't stand on ceremony."

"As you wish, Dria." He smiles to show he's agreeable, but I can still tell he'd feel more comfortable calling her *ma'am*. It's not only a generational sign of respect, but manners from his upbringing. We do this same dance every year when we arrive. "Is nine still good?"

"Yes, thank you." Before we left, we emailed the sleeping preferences. Tommy and Bob will share a suite next to Paul, and Chelly and Drew will be alone in their own room. "Dalton, would you mind showing our guests to their rooms? The luggage will be a while, but I'd like them to get a feel for the place."

"Certainly, ma'—Dria. Right this way, gentlemen," indicating Tommy, Bob, and Paul should follow him. "Carmella, would you mind showing the couple to their room?"

Carmella casts a lingering glance at Drew, raking his body from head to toe. Chelly sees the look and steps closer to Drew, slipping an arm around his and glaring back at the honey-skinned brunette.

It figures. Carmella's more interested in the man who has a woman than the available single ones drooling at her feet.

Dalton clears his throat and Carmina, caught staring at Drew as well, scurries off toward the kitchen.

I wonder what's going on there? I say to Dria through a slight tingle of connection.

She shrugs and motions for Drew and Chelly to follow us to the staircase, trailing after the men and Carmella. "Come, your room is just past theirs, she'll show you the way." Drew,

Rafe

oblivious to the entire female power exchange, smiles warmly and looks to us to follow.

Looks to me like the ladies want to bag a vampire lover, Dria says. *Should prove an interesting few weeks for Chelly, that's for sure.*

Chapter Four
Asa

The dull thud of my footsteps echo back off the smooth walls of the dimly lit, narrow tunnel. With the twist of a key and a hard shove from my shoulder, I open one of the heavy steel doors placed every hundred yards or so in this complex warren of underground passages.

Vivian said it took ten years to build the subterranean basement and intricate tunnel system, but I didn't fully grasp the magnitude of the project. Seeing and walking the maze, is a whole 'nother level of awe.

There is no map, and according to Vivian, there never will be one. Only the seethe and our small werewolf pack know of its existence and I swear, even after five months, there are twists and turns I don't think I've discovered. I wouldn't put it past Vivian to have designed hidden rooms on purpose, hence there being no map. The slim dimensions of the tunnel make it easily defensible by one person, denying fighting space and blocking any enemies farther down.

There are hidden stores of weapons, which frankly alarmed me when I saw how old the stuff was. It's like a bomb shelter for an extremist group—except the food stores

Asa

are sadly lacking. I've come across canned goods, which I bet must have been intended for Rafe and Jon, but I think this place was designed more to confuse an enemy than defend against one. Make them chase their tails single- file underground while Viv and Rafe escaped safely.

A chill creeps up my spine. The cold of the surrounding permafrost never lets you forget where you are. The sub-zero temperature seeps past the two-foot-thick walls, and grasps every inanimate object it touches. I may not fully understand the reasoning behind such an elaborate and expensive design that is off limits to guests, but I can certainly appreciate it now that I need to get around while the sun is out.

It's almost three and darkness won't descend for several hours. The newly arrived Weres plan to gather and strip in the hot tub grotto before transforming to hunt. I grew up where hunters routinely received the license to hunt bear by lottery, so the concept of big-game hunting isn't lost on me, but doing it in animal form is.

After making two more lefts, three rights, and passing through six more steel doors, I approach a metal ladder identical to the other half dozen I've seen. Nothing is labeled. You must learn the means of access by rote memory and not leave a mark when passing. Vivian was quite emphatic on her wishes if we were to start using the network of tunnels. And even though there are no cameras down here, I don't doubt that she patrols them every once in a while to check that her requirements are being met.

Thankfully, I haven't gotten lost yet. Turned around once or twice, but not lost. The humiliation of having to call for guidance has proven a terrific incentive to pay attention when exploring.

Not a trace of dirt or dust is anywhere; a smudge might reveal a location or turn to a pursuing enemy. Who cleans it? Maybe it's one of the tasks Vivian takes on when she's not taking a daily restorative sleep, like I still need to do. I ascend a ladder into a tight tube leading to the surface and open the submarine-like hatch at the top, taking a step down two rungs to allow it to swing inward and settle against the tube's wall. It works opposite as a normal submarine hatch would, which took some getting used to on my part. A thick, wooden trap door lays over the hatch, with no trace of light leaking around the seams.

I press a secret panel to the left of the seam, which triggers a hidden latch on the other side and the lock springs softly open. Easing the heavy floor piece up, I carefully lean it against the closet's interior wall that houses the escape hatch. I scramble up and return it quietly to its original position. Once it's closed and locked I knock on the closet door leading into the cabin.

"Yo! Asa, is that you?" comes from the room beyond the thick wood.

"Who the hell else would it be, Pat?" I say, trying to keep the annoyance from my tone. Sonovabitch knows it would only be me, but he still asks every freakin' time. "Is it safe? Have you dropped the window shutters down yet?"

Unknown to most of the guests and employees, all the cabins are equipped with light-deterring, steel hurricane shutters. To say Vivian planned for every possibility would be putting it mildly.

"Oh yeah, let me do that."

Prick. I'm betting he's hoping to catch me one day to see if I really will burn from the sun's rays.

A metallic whir and the clickity-clack of the descending exterior shades soon follow. A glance over at the fire extinguisher mounted in the closet leaves me wondering what safety precaution the rustic-looking cabins could possibly lack. No vampire, young or old, needs to worry about the sun burning them during the rare hours of twilight the winter does see or, thanks to the sprinkler systems, concern themselves with a candle mishap torching them while they sleep.

"It's cool, man," Pat calls. "Come on out."

I enter the pristine cabin and glance around, once again amazed at how clean the place is. Two beer bottles sit on the table. Eric and Pat are spread out on the couch and recliner like they haven't a care in the world. *Sons of Anarchy* is paused on the television, the surfer-boy, relaxed-but-messy looks of Jax in black leather are frozen in mid-grin.

No dirty dishes, no open food containers, no dirty socks under the coffee table, just the two beers they are currently drinking. The young men were complete slobs when I left for the Army eight years ago. The government whipped their asses into shape and taught them what it means to be a man —one key point being that you pick up after yourself. You'd never know two guys in their early twenties lived here.

"Haven't you seen this episode already?" I ask, knowing they have watched the entire series at least twice.

Eric nods and picks up his beer. "Yeah, but there's nothing better on, and we needed to kill time before the gathering."

"I'm really surprised you're not hanging out with your old pack-mates," I say while heading into the room. "Jon was smiling and grinning like a jackass over something he read about cheerleader chicks."

"They're hot as hell, sure," Pat says. "But they want nothing to do with us." He lets out a gut-wrenching burp. "Stuck-up bitches."

I look to my brother, who proceeds to shrug his wide shoulders. "I think he's just bitter they shot him down... over and over again."

A smile lights my face as I join Pat on the couch, forcing the younger man to sit up and make way for me. "You were with Romeo's pack, like, what—two months? You couldn't help yourself from hitting on everyone there?"

Pat flashes me an indignant look. "No, not everyone."

Eric laughs, "He managed not to hit on the guys or Elsa, Romeo's wife."

"Glad to see you have some sense," I say.

"Fuck off, both of you. One of them might've said yes." He sniffs and looks back to the TV. "And hell, you don't know unless you try."

Typical of most guys, our conversation peters off after the ribbing is over. We watch the rest of the show in silence, each lost in our own thoughts. The peace of being near my brother never ceases to soothe me. It was never like this with our other brother, Justin. Our mom poisoned him to us long ago, using him to shield the world from her many flaws. He grew up being her staunchest defender, but was still too young to escape her selfishness when she took him and fled the country.

It's been ages since I've thought of him. Hell, before this winter I didn't think I'd ever get to see any part of my family again. If someone had told me last year where I'd be at this moment I'd have thought they were smoking crack.

My attention drifts from the show I've already seen, to the modifications made on the resort for the werewolves this summer. We've got an outdoor shower area set up in the hot tub grotto to wash off the bloody hunters fresh in from the chase—with strict orders from Vivian to not allow any wet wolves into the main building while in their furry form.

My nose wrinkles in slight distaste. It would be hard to get their distinct odor out once they shook like wet dogs all over the carpet and furniture.

Pat thumps his bottle on the coffee table. "I'd offer you a beer," he says with a sneer in his voice. "But you being a bloodsucker and all, you couldn't enjoy it."

I allow my fangs to descend and smile menacingly at my old friend. "I could drink it if you opened a vein to mix in."

Pat pales and launches from the sofa, masking his unease by turning the movement into a stretch. "Not funny, dude." He flips me off and downs the rest of his drink. "Shouldn't we be heading out soon?"

Eric glances at the clock and brings the recliner to an upright position.

"What did Jon tell you guys to do during the hunt expedition?"

"We're to hang back and not interfere," Eric says. "Even though we know the wolves attending this first week, we're no longer a part of their pack and need to respect their limits while in animal form."

I nod, already aware of Jon's instructions, but wanting to hear it straight from them. Well, straight from Pat, truth be told—or at least within his hearing with a witness. He could very well pretend to not remember later if it suits his needs.

"Do you miss the larger pack?" I ask.

Pat barks out a laugh, "Aww, hell no!" He pulls off his shirt and tosses it on the couch. "Lots more willing ladies here." He smiles as his own irony hits him. "Who woulda thought I'd be saying that about Alaska?"

Eric shakes his head and likewise, starts to disrobe. "More like the women in the pack just didn't want to be with 'puppies'. We have better chances here, with the single female employees."

"Assuming they don't mind when you shed," I add with a grin.

He smiles one of his rare full-toothed smiles, revealing a jagged tooth he's been self-conscious about for years, and reaches for his waistband. "Yeah, there is that."

Wanting to get the hell out before they're both buck-naked, I make my way to the closet. "Don't forget to open the door this time *before* you shift." I don't hold my laughter in. Damn, it was funny as hell when they had to dive through a window after a change last month.

Jon didn't find it too amusing when he first found out, but it has gradually become an event to razz them about. Vivian was not pleased when she heard. She gave them both a terse look and said, "Plan better next time."

Needless to say, there hasn't been a reoccurrence—yet. They've been changing more, several times a day, to be able to master the skill. Apparently, the frequent transformations require a lot of energy, and they've each been eating like a family of six on an all-protein diet. And damn, that's a lot of food.

As I shut the tunnel hatch behind me, a soft whine and scrape meet my ear. Eric must be scratching at the closet, following my scent. While the idea of howling wolves running through the tunnels sounds cool, and straight out of a movie, I'm betting the ladder would be a difficult obstacle to overcome. I knock twice to let him know I heard him and slip into the tube to head back to the main building.

Within ten minutes, I close the heavy steel door in the north wing of the basement. The large concrete foundation runs the entire length of the large T-shaped hotel. We constructed six rooms and still have a huge amount of unutilized space under two of the wings.

The conference room won't get used much with most of the seethe away. This summer I could have occupied Paul's safe room during the day, but I chose to make a bedroom suite for myself out of two of the other unused rooms. It felt nice to personalize the space and make it my own.

Easy access to my rooms and the SCIF is another reason I'll be glad to get the new entrance into the kitchen

Asa

storeroom completed. The spiral staircase in the large closet next to my bedroom will be much simpler than trekking through the owners' apartment.

One time of walking in on Rafe and Viv getting busy is enough for my entire undead lifetime, thank you very much. Not like I had the right to tell them they shouldn't be doing the nasty in the living room—after all, it is their apartment. It felt like I walked in on relatives—kind of creepy and very uncomfortable. Made me want to bleach my eyes afterward.

I settle into a swivel chair in front of the large command center desk. A press of a keyboard button reveals three views of the hot tub grotto, courtesy of a few of the cameras we installed all over the property before the hunt this past January.

Four LCD computer monitors each have the ability to show six different views at once, rotating between camera locations on the screen. The system lets an observer quickly scan an area or monitor a preprogrammed set of views, like outside entrances, for example. Not sure how helpful the cameras will be once the wolves venture into the raw area of the property, though.

The sun won't set for about four hours, allowing the werewolves to get the joy of hunting in daylight and darkness on their first trip out. The plan is for me to help with manning the grilling area when darkness hits. Eric and Pat did a good job with setting up the outdoor kitchen. And with the dust from the construction project it was probably a good idea they moved the kitchen.

The regular day shift cook, Stephanie, left to go visit her family once the high season ended, as did a lot of the regular employees. We're down to less than half staff right now, about fifty, but that's not bad considering Vivian normally likes to have more people here than I think are truly needed.

A silver-gray wolf, with a white left foreleg, bounds into the monitor's view of the grotto. I'd recognize Pat's playful manner even if I didn't know his markings well. Eric meanders in a moment later, his larger form and charcoal tones blending into the sparse greenery better. Jon's reddish-brown coat comes into view and the alpha nips playfully at the heels of Pat, sending the younger wolf into a yapping whirl. The three of them seem to get along well, and I haven't noticed any overt clashing from either side.

In another minute the clearing between hot tubs explodes with furry forms. With the crowded and chaotic movements, I can't be sure if the whole pack is present or if maybe one or two bowed out from this first excursion.

From what Jon told me earlier, the Weres will head off into an undeveloped portion of the property and see what trails they come across. According to my research, it still seems a little early for there to be anything worthy of a wolf pack this far north, maybe a stray caribou and that's about it.

Do they perhaps just want a place to run that is different than their own territory? Could they be here to scout the terrain for real hunting later on in the season? Jon seemed a little baffled by it as well. I hope they find something to make the journey worthwhile.

Four or five smaller wolves circle Jon, nudging him to join them when the pack begins to head out. One or two lick his jaw and rub shoulders with the larger male. Huh. Wonder if this could be some elaborate set up from Romeo and Elsa to find Jon a suitable bitch. After Jon reviewed the files, he said it looked like they brought every eligible female they had in their pack.

Poor guy is in for it if those ladies are looking for an alpha to start a new pack. I can't believe Vivian would go for this. I wouldn't put it past her to hand-pick Jon's mate herself. She must not have any idea what his old pack leaders

Asa

are doing. Hell, I'm seeing it right on the screen in front of me, and I'm still having a hard time believing it. Matchmaking for a werewolf? Poor bastard. Then again, he might get laid this week, so it's not all bad.

Finally, after much tail wagging and what appears to be happy yips, the remaining wolves race out. I toggle the screen and watch the group tearing down the paths toward the empty family cabins. The group splits and before you know it, there are three groups barreling through the trees into the wilderness.

I spent some time this winter researching wolves and watching lots of nature films. Observing these wolves with human intelligence is downright scary. I notice an almost military precision with how they move and spread out. Not quite the same as the natural wolves behaved on TV, and rightly so since they aren't real wolves.

Their forms sprint across the screen and within minutes, I run out of cameras to monitor them. I toggle quickly between all the viewpoints in the region, but come back blank. Damn, I'll have to keep switching and hope something comes into view.

I reach for the phone, doing a mental calculation in my head. Should be close to ten p.m. in Argentina right now. I wonder what Drew and Paul are up to?

Chapter Five

Drew

I **hang up the phone** with Asa, grinning at his description of the subtle matchmaking by the pack alphas. We're six hours ahead of the crew in Alaska, so while our human travel mates have just finished a late dinner, Asa and the wolves still await sunset back home. Overall, sounds like the Weres have settled in and things are off to a smooth start.

I'm not used to hopping so many time zones in such a short span of time, but will enjoy the increased darkness here with the change of seasons. The stinging wind I could do without, but for now, I'm content.

From the moment I heard about the island, I've been excited about this trip. When Vivian moved up the leave date by a month and said we could bring guests, I thought maybe she was off a few days on an April Fool's joke.

There's more to this than meets the eye. Viv explained she wants to surprise the Tribunal by arriving early, in the hopes to ferret out her enemies, but I wonder if there is more we don't know. Why leave her werewolf servant and military vamp behind? If she's expecting trouble, it'd be wise to keep the seethe together and strong.

Drew

With the council being a hidden ruling class for my whole existence, I've never attended an event at the Tribunal headquarters—but I do recall hearing stories from the masters in Chicago. They said the Ancients stick to the old ways and tend to treat humans like pets. Could that still be accurate in this ever-changing world? After *True Blood*, *Blade*, and Anne Rice is there anyone left who doesn't have an inkling of our existence?

Surely the Ancients have evolved like the rest of the undead? *Adapt or Die*, isn't that one of Vivian's favorite sayings?

I shake my head at the puzzles rattling in my brain. It'll all work out, and eventually I'll see her plan; I just need to think on it more. Never once have I thought of questioning her outright. It's simply not done. I could get a major ass chewing or smack down, depending on a master's mood. Sure, I spoke out at our meetings during the hunt with Emiko, but making a habit of it would be dumb. *Pick your battles wisely* is more than just advice for a teenager's parent.

Chelly enters our suite from the connecting bath, an excited expression on her cherubic face. "I'm done!" She strolls toward me sitting on a club chair in the bedroom sitting area. Her tousled blond hair looks wild and sexy draped over her shoulders, framing her freshly scrubbed face. Ample cleavage is on display, and her round hips stretch the gossamer material of her baby-doll nightie.

I raise an eyebrow to indicate I have no idea what she's talking about. Actually, I'm having trouble focusing on anything except her pert nipples pebbled beneath the pale pink fabric.

"I unpacked, silly. Nothing like getting all your clothes hung up and placed in drawers—not to mention your toiletries laid out—to really make you feel like you've settled in."

She ignores my look of feigned interest and turns to the enclosed balcony. "Have you checked out this area yet?" She fiddles with the drapes covering the glass doors, fingering the thick blackout fabric firmly affixed over the panes. The sheer negligée reveals bare skin underneath and the full globes of her bottom jiggle slightly as she works the latch. My fangs itch to descend, and my cock surges to life in my pants. Perhaps I should move my seduction plan to tonight. I don't think I can handle a whole night by her side while she's wearing that delicious concoction.

Unaware of my internal debate, Chelly opens and folds the glass doors against the wall then strides into the small, enclosed space. The floor tile extends into the balcony area, making it feel like a natural addition to the room.

"Nice," I say, rising from my seat. I'm staring at her butt and not the view, but I mean it nonetheless.

"Oh," Chelly exclaims while gazing out into the starlight. "We've got a distant view of Puerto Santa Cruz. The lights are pretty. How far away is it?"

"Hmm?" I approach her body with an outstretched hand ready to cup her buttocks. She must know what she's doing to me prancing around in such a flimsy getup.

A knock at the door whips us both around. "Who do you think that is?" Chelly races to the closet.

My cock deflates slightly at the interruption. "I'll send them away, not to worry." Before I reach the door, Chelly emerges from the closet wearing a thick white robe.

I swing open the heavy carved door to reveal the twins, Carmella and Carmina. They're dressed in short, black terrycloth robes hanging open over gold string bikinis. Sparkly wedge sandals decorate their slim, tanned feet. Each woman carries two glasses and a bottle of champagne. Long,

Drew

wavy dark hair spills down to tickle their barely-covered breasts and sultry brown eyes hold an invitation no one could misread.

"We'd like to offer you a tour of the house..." Carmella says. "With maybe an end at the hot tub... if you're interested."

Chelly pushes forward, a nasty expression on her face until she counts the glasses. "Oh, I see." Her cheeks flush a deep scarlet and I'm tickled by her shyness when I know she's a bold creature of passion.

"Perhaps," I say, while staring at my blond temptress wrapped in her fluffy robe, "simply a tour for tonight?"

Chelly's eyes meet mine, and the heat in them at the mention of the hot tub is unmistakable. "That sounds fine. Let me get my slippers."

She retrieves the shoes and we follow the sashaying hips of the twins to the staircase. I find it quite telling that the pair approached us and not the single men. One of them must prefer Chelly.

While I've had my share of group sex, I'm positive my new girlfriend hasn't. Considering this trip will be our first time consummating our union, and where I plan to make her my vampire servant, I doubt we'll explore any ideas the twins might have. A wistful sigh escapes me, and Chelly shoots me a heated look.

She's thinking about the women. Interesting. I slip my arm around her waist and then casually lower my palm to rest on her ass. We reach the end of the hall, having passed the rooms Bob and Tommy occupy, and descend the stairs. Back in the main foyer two sets of French doors stand open, allowing the scent of the hot tub to drift in.

Chelly squeezes my hand in a signal I have no clue how to read. Does she want to get in the hot tub with them? I'm happy to oblige, but I have no intention of sharing her just yet—despite the mincing, sexy walk of the twins, and the waft of their arousal tickling my senses.

We enter the formal dining room, and the inclusion of a fireplace combined with the heavy wood furniture lends a historic Spanish feel to the space. Thick beeswax candles burn brightly on the rich mahogany table and mantle, releasing a faint sweetness into the air.

"Oh, this is pretty," says Chelly.

We skipped the sit-down meal with the men, and Paul, ever the conscientious chef, brought Chelly a plate to our room. I nod while taking in the rich red drapes and dark buffets pushed against one wall. The lingering odor of the fish dinner prepared with lemon is detected as we walk further into the room.

A wide archway leads into a true gourmand's kitchen. On the far end of the room away from traffic, stands a wet bar complete with full-sized wine fridge. Six stools line the long kitchen island, indicating my masters planned for more visitors down the line—as the numerous upstairs suites and large dining room would suggest, too.

Bright yellow, blue and red tiles decorate the back splash and counters, conveying joy and life with their vibrant designs. An industrial-sized Viking stove, freestanding freezer, and stainless steel fridge nestle together on the other side of the island. "Wow," says Chelly, "and I thought the inn had a nice kitchen."

"The difference, my dear, is that one is commercial and this one is in a private home."

Carmina runs her hand along the tile counter, staring at my blond companion the entire time. "Yes, it is lovely, no?"

"It is," I respond, trailing a hand down to cup Chelly's ass, letting the other woman know she's very obviously taken. Chelly smiles over her shoulder at me and Carmina's mouth turns up at the corner, seemingly amused by my show of possessiveness.

"Is there more to see?" Chelly walks to the doorway near the bar, beside Carmella.

"The game room is through there." Carmella puts her glasses and bottle on the bar counter and takes Chelly's hand. The moment their skin touch, sexual tension spikes. "This wing wraps around the back of the building and leads to the large living room that takes up the wing on the other side of the courtyard."

Arousal of all three women coats my senses like honey. It's a heady experience, and one I'm not sure what to do with. Are they trying to seduce Chelly to get to me, or are they truly interested in women? This strong show of attention within hours of our arrival is discomforting.

Carmina moves to Chelly's other side and takes her free hand. "Come, we'll show you."

A nervous laugh escapes the blond. "Which one are you again? Carmella?"

Carmina shakes her head, tossing her long dark hair back and encouraging her robe to slip off one shoulder. "Call me Mina. It's much easier than the silly matching names our parents gave us."

The two lovely twins walk my girlfriend into the game room, and I follow close behind. We walk through the Spanish-themed room past a pool table, Ping Pong and card tables, arcade games, darts... there might be more, but my mind is focused on the two sirens corralling Chelly between them.

If I speak up I'll look like a jealous sod, and yet, that's exactly how I feel. Definitely the odd man out. Carmella's hand drifts out of Chelly's to rest on the blond's lower back, in a gesture to usher her forward. Or at least, that's the way it's supposed to look, but I'm thinking it's just another excuse to touch my girlfriend more intimately.

Mina looks over her bare shoulder at me, her heated stare perhaps meant to inflame and bring me into the magic of their seduction. We walk through the large, plush living room. The rest of the downstairs doesn't quite register in my mind, as my peripheral vision spirals in on the threesome.

The two slinky brunettes clatter across the tile in their gold wedge sandals, leading Chelly toward another set of open French doors. The courtyard's small trees and plants spread before us. The hint of bromine and fresh earth assail my senses. I step onto a cobblestone path and glance up.

Lights twinkle on the vaulted atrium glass ceiling, reflecting the flickering tiki torches dotted throughout the courtyard. Gotta hand it to Viv and Rafe, this is some set up. It's similar to the pool wing in Alaska, but smaller and greener, with in-ground plants rather than pots around a pool.

The three ladies venture to the hot tub and I see another body lounging in the water, awaiting us—Rosia, the owners' nineteen-year-old daughter. Warning bells sound in my head. Whatever fun the twins were hoping isn't going to happen now, not if I can help it. I have a feeling Rafe and Viv would have my head if Rosia were involved, right after Dalton tried killing me in my sleep.

I quicken my pace to pull alongside the twins as they shrug off their robes. Rosia stands to greet us, the water spilling off her topless body, droplets glinting in the torchlight. "Come, join me. The water feels perfect."

Chelly catches her breath at the sight of the younger woman's perfect palm-sized breasts. A seductive smile spreads over Rosia's face as she reaches for a drink on the edge of the hot tub.

Drew

The twins hang their robes on a nearby hook then focus all their attention on Chelly, sashaying forward with their arms extended to help my girlfriend out of her robe. I slip my hand into Chelly's and draw her back to my side. I push my awareness out to the three women, sliding into their minds to take control. One by one, they look to me, and our eyes briefly lock. Mina and Carmella's arms drop to their sides.

"Thank you for the tour ladies, but I think we're going to turn in for the evening." Chelly lets out a slight mew of protest, but says nothing. She fidgets from foot to foot, and I smell her arousal on the air. I stroke a thumb across the back of her hand, reassuring her that she's forefront in my mind.

Should I plant a suggestion in their mind or dig to see what has brought on the sudden interest in us? It could simply be they are lonely on the island. I know how protective Vivian is of the humans in her care, so it might be best to leave this group link as unobtrusive as I can.

I tip my head in acknowledgement of their loveliness. "Enjoy yourselves. Perhaps we'll join you another time." I let go mentally, pulling my will from coating their minds, and the twins react as if nothing happened, changing direction toward the hot tub and climbing in. Rosia gives us a playful little pout, but otherwise she looks fine, too.

"What just happened here?" Chelly whispers to me in a low voice. "Did you do something?"

"We'll discuss it in our room." We turn and head down the path we came, entering the large living room wing of the house and head silently for the stairs together.

Once the door closes Chelly pounces, unbuttoning my shirt and latching her heated mouth onto mine. When I saw her leave the bathroom in her negligée, I'd thought tonight would be the night we'd consummate our relationship, but now I'm not sure. I want to drive all thoughts of the sexy women from my lover's mind, demanding she focus solely on me and the pleasures I can give her—not what might have been at the hot tub.

She spreads my shirt open and runs her hands across my chest. "Drew, those ladies were hot. Do you think they were hitting on us?"

I chuckle and decide now is not the time to analyze, but to act. I untie her robe, sliding the soft terrycloth off her shoulders to pool on the tile. The bra cups of Chelly's sheer nightie hug her luscious curves and the sight drives the blood back into my wilted erection. Running my thumbs over her aroused peaks pulls a gasp and shudder from my lover.

Never one to stand still, Chelly boldly unzips my fly and pushes my pants past my hips, springing my cock free of its confines. She grins. "I think they were hitting on you in a round-about way..." Her voice trails off as she pumps my cock. "Bet they thought if they won me over, they could get at your man meat." She snickers at her crude phrase and squeezes the head of my cock harder.

"Am I all yours?" I ask, guiding her slowly toward the bed.

"Hmph. I'm not sharing until I've had every bit of you inside me—repeatedly."

Her sexy innuendo could lead to more down the line, but right now, all I care about is the here and now. Chelly's legs hit the edge of the mattress, and she scoots toward the padded headboard.

I remove my shirt and step out of my pants before climbing onto the bed. Chelly pats the covers beside her, motioning for me to sit next to her. I stop instead at her knees and push her legs apart. Her mouth parts in a little "O" and heat fills her cheeks.

"How about we start this trip with my tongue inside you first?"

Drew

Chelly nods enthusiastically and settles on the pillows. I plant my first kiss along her thigh and the warm skin above her knee prickles in gooseflesh. We've touched and fondled for months, but our dates have been every two weeks when I can safely feed from her, and have not included oral sex, despite the vixen's many attempts to get down on her knees and gobble me whole.

The scent of clean woman and tangy arousal wraps around me as I slowly work my way closer to her center. I slip my hands under her full bottom to tilt her up and open, encouraging her to spread her legs wider. With a moan she complies and the delicate flesh along the crease where thigh meets torso is exposed to my eager lips.

Her shaven pussy quivers under my attention, silently drawing my eye and focus to the delicate folds of flesh. Moisture gathers at her entrance, glistening in the soft light, inviting me to bend and taste. I resist for a moment longer and spread her outer lips open with my thumbs.

The flesh here is swollen, eager for coupling. The dark pink color tells me blood has rushed to her arousal like mine does to harden my prick. The pulse pounds through my raging erection at the sight of her readiness, and I have to physically resist the overwhelming urge to thrust inside her as my body demands.

Instead, I nuzzle her privates, dipping my nose near her mound and move my face around gently to coat myself in her delicate scent. I continue to plant soft kisses and lightly lick the heated skin. She squirms and thrusts her hips up, begging for more pressure and more attention where she wants it—right on her clit.

A rumble of satisfaction comes from me as I gently press her onto the bed. I plan on controlling this ride and want her screaming my name before I'm done. My cock weeps onto the covers, my own arousal at her pleasure like fire to my senses. Focusing on the outer lips, I gently lick, nibble and tug until the wetness from her opening flows down to coat her tiny pink ass pucker.

My pointed tongue dips to her center and trails up from the dripping opening to her hard nub peeking from its hood. "Yes! More like that," she calls out while thrashing back and forth on the pillows.

I know exactly what she wants and don't intend to give it to her yet. At the top, I change my tactic and caress the inner folds with my tongue, skimming the sides of the clit where the nerve endings extend. "No, no, no..." she pleads, "back to the middle, you tease."

Spreading her legs even wider, I take one hand from holding her lips and tease her opening by pushing a finger in up to the first knuckle. I'm worried she might not feel it with all the wetness, but she immediately bears down and tries to force it deeper.

"Oh, yes. That's it. Get that finger in me."

Steadily I pump back and forth, working in the entire digit and curving it up as I pull out the stroke. I keep my licking focused to the right and left of her sensitive clit, not wanting her to peak. Soon, I'm able to double finger and this time apply pressure with both to the spongy spot at the top of her vaginal wall, curving up toward her clit from the inside.

I stroke in a circle as her moans become louder and her squirming on the bed, more intense.

"Please, Drew! Lick my clit, dammit! I want to come."

A smile forms on my face as I pull away from her succulent flesh. "As the lady wishes."

Without further direction, I amp up the pressure and speed of my fingers inside her, while zeroing in on the hard button above her pussy with my mouth. I rotate between

Drew

sucking the heated flesh between my lips and flicking fast with my tongue.

Her body bows off the bed and quivers beneath my hand and mouth. "Oh God, this feels different. Oh, God. I'm coming. Drew!"

The ripple of her pleasure wraps around my fingers, squeezing them tight and pulling them in. The pulses through her body vibrate out from her spasming clit as her cries of pleasure bounce off the bedroom walls.

I ease the pressure as her orgasm continues, not wanting to over rub the sensitized flesh. After a moment she relaxes on the bed, to stare down at me winded and flushed. "Holy crap. What did you do with your fingers?"

A satisfied grin curves my mouth as I rise and lay down next to her, my own throbbing cock bobbing with each movement. "That, my dear, was your G-spot."

"Wow," she says, wrapping her hand around my long cock and stroking. "Is there an equivalent for a guy? 'Cause man, I'd like to return the favor. It was mind blowing."

I settle back on the pillows while my lover pumps my shaft up and down, exactly as I like. "Yes, there is." My hips rise off the bed as my need to come tingles at the base of my prick. "But I don't think I can handle it, right now."

Chapter Six

Jonathan

The scents of mud, dead grasses, and woods fill my lupine nose. I slow to a trot, making sure I don't come up behind Romeo's pack too closely. While there is no worry the wolves will get lost, I want to know how this scouting expedition turns out.

The single females from the pack rallied around me and gave me more attention than I was prepared for. I'm not complaining, but getting a woody in wolf form isn't like human form. *Everyone* can see, and when the bitches nuzzled the area, the wolf urge to mount was almost overwhelming. Damn, I knew I was horny, but I have no desire to hump like a mongrel my first time with a woman.

Flashes of taking Ruby doggie-style whisper through my brain—thankfully, in my vision we're both in human form or I'd be in real trouble. This is what happens when you hold back your desires too long, you wind up getting a boner like a teenager the moment a woman pays you any attention.

A black body zips across my peripheral vision and turns mid-leap to plow into me. The weight of another werewolf slams my shoulder and Spike's confusing scent wafts

Jonathan

through my brain. We tumble to the ground and spring up to face one another. His dark fur has a glossy sheen and his muzzle hangs open in a playful manner with a long pink tongue dangling.

What the hell does he want? I snap my jaws at his shoulder when he approaches, telling him to keep his distance. He bounds away, pulling his tongue in before closing his mouth. His head lowers, dipping slightly onto his extended front paws.

In a split second, he charges and I rear up to meet his advance. We clash together, our front legs tangling—his mouth an open maw, angling for my throat. No tense growl of tension comes off him, and he playfully nips my lower jaw to show me the clash is all in fun. We bound apart and I lower my head, ears down, but in no way pinned back in a submissive show.

What the hell? Since when do werewolves play like a bunch of puppies? A low rumble vibrates my chest—my way of letting him know his playful antics are not welcome right now. The flesh pulls back from my teeth and the snarl has the desired effect.

Spike lowers his head, curves his back, and tucks his tail, pinning back his ears back while looking away to show he understands I'm not game to play. I ignore his show, looking into the brush, to let him know his apology is accepted, and he can stop the self-deprecating display.

Apparently, I came across a little strong. The black wolf leaps forward, eagerness pouring from his exaggerated wiggle, and licks my jaw. To say I'm confused is putting it mildly. Weres don't normally mimic our counter parts so closely while in animal form, but sometimes it's the only way to convey intent.

I walk away from the unwanted submissive show only to receive a wet, sniffing nose in my ass and balls. My furry form quickly whips around, and I snap a warning at Spike's face to tell him to *cut this shit out.*

His tongue once again lolls out in laughter, and he bounds away. What is it with that guy? If I didn't know better, I'd say he was flirting with me. Is he a gay werewolf and thinks I am, too?

With a snap at my flank and a playful yip, Spike darts into the sparse woods, to be swallowed up quickly by the low-growing underbrush. I continue along the scent trail left by the pack and focus my ears forward to catch any hint of when I might be getting too close. Eric and Pat were supposed to stay behind, but I hear them crashing through the woods behind me about half a mile back.

In a few hundred yards, the scent of fresh blood carries on a breeze. The animal desire to rend with my teeth and feast on the flesh of prey clouds my mind. Steady. Don't want to approach the others when their own feeding instincts will be running high, as well.

As I pick up my pace, the aroma strengthens, and I hear the unmistakable growls of a feeding pack. Keeping my distance, I edge through bushes until I see Romeo and Elsa off to one side licking blood from their paws and muzzles. Further off, there's a mass of other wolf bodies surrounding a carcass. From the underlying odor I'd wager they downed a caribou. Way luckier than I would've guessed.

The ten wolves who attended this first hunt aren't eating from hunger. They're allowing their inner instincts to come to the surface and enjoy a few moments as true animals, acting and savoring their place in the pack.

In a little while, I hear the unsubtle movements of Eric and Pat approaching. The three of us haven't hunted much due to the lack of winter game. This early spring kill has to be strongly tempting their inner beasts. They follow my trail, approaching my spot in the bushes. At a glance from me,

Jonathan

they settle down, lowering to the ground and putting their heads on their paws, ears perked and staring toward the feasting wolves.

The pack moves away, having its fill, with no sign of Spike joining. In fact, he's been absent since I last saw him streak off. Romeo walks to our location twenty yards away from their kill, head high and ears forward. He looks to the carcass then away, letting me know his pack no longer has an interest in it. In a final show, he turns his back on our group of three and trots into the woods, toward the inn.

I have no desire to feed from the caribou. I plan to keep my wolf tightly leashed during this week to ensure no conflicts between Romeo and me. A small whine issues from Pat, as he holds his tightly coiled body, ready to pounce on the bloody remains. I wait until the others have trailed after their alphas before giving the two young pups their freedom.

With a soft snort from me, the two leap from the bushes and race to check out the hull of the carcass. I pad over to the fleeting pack's exit route and settle down to ensure no one backtracks to harass the young ones.

Eric gnaws on a rib while Pat drags a leg bone to the edge of the clearing. A loud pop echoes in the distance, northeast. Recognition whips my head around. Gunshot. I raise my nose to the breeze, scenting for a precise location. Two more pops echo and a yip of pain sounds nearby.

I burst forward, the instinct to protect my pack overriding common sense to run away from gunfire. Pat limps toward me, head down, ears back, favoring his back right leg. Eric circles the kill, lost as to what to do. I race, past Pat, toward the dark gray wolf and nip at Eric's haunches. On my way to the hobbling, silver form of Patrick, I look over my shoulder to make sure Eric follows us.

The urge to race toward the shooter, discover our assailant—and rip them limb from limb—pushes against my will like a living beast. My current job is not to hunt, but to protect the wounded in our small pack and find safety. *Protect! Protect!* I scream into my mind, trying to override the hard wiring within to search and attack.

Eric follows me as we trot in a weaving pattern away from the kill site. Ahead, Romeo's pack barrels through the woods toward us. A few try to approach Pat, scenting his bloodied wound, but a show of teeth from Eric and me keeps them back. I don't think they'd do him any harm, but I'm not willing to risk his safety further.

Romeo sees I have the situation under control and takes off in the direction of the gunfire, Elsa and the others on his heels. I'm betting they plan to fan out and catch the shooter in a wide net.

Eric and I flank our weakened packmate, setting a fair pace to the inn and medical attention. At a mile into our trek, I angle toward one of the outermost cameras, still quite a distance from the inn's developed area. We pause for a moment and I circle around to sniff Pat's wound, hoping Asa is monitoring the cameras and can see the torn skin and blood on the black and white image.

Time moves slowly, but we arrive at the hot tub grotto with no further incident. Pat's lost a lot of blood, often needing a nudge to keep going when he wanted to lie down and instinctually make the shift to human form. After the first step onto the paved walkway, he collapses and the change slams him.

Screams rip from his throat as his body convulses and thrashes, trying to reshape. The transformation is more painful if injured and have fought the inner need to change, which will normally heal mild damage. The good news is he'll soon pass out and won't feel it anymore. Calling my will, the change flows over me, 'til I'm human once more, and scooping up the still-transforming Pat.

Jonathan

He's blacked out and doesn't feel the crack and snap of his bones melding forcefully back into place. I've coached them to change more frequently because it becomes easier with practice—but practice doesn't help when he's unconscious from pain.

I carry the semi-furry, semi-naked form to the outside shower set up for the Weres. After wrestling Pat's weight to free a hand, I adjust the water and soon the worst of the past hour is washed away. Eric walks nude to the kitchen door leading to Viv and Rafe's suite, as the unflappable Dr. Cook opens it, coming out to assist us.

"What happened?" she calls out, hustling over with clean towels.

"Pat was shot." I step from the shower stall and the doctor drapes a towel over Pat's middle and dries his limbs with another.

"Let's get him inside and see the wound," the older woman says. "Take him to the basement."

Eric emerges wearing a pair of sweatpants to take Pat from me. "I'll carry him in so you can dry off."

Dr. Cook tosses me the last towel, and I follow their retreating forms into the building.

"No, no, you fool. Not their couch." The doctor calls out to change Eric's direction. "The basement. He's not going to die for crying out loud and blood is really hard to get out of furniture fabric."

I push aside the angry retort clouding my mind. No need to fight when she's right. He won't die from a leg wound. Asa stands in the hallway going down to the basement stairs, carefully avoiding the fading sunlight from the kitchen windows. "Can I help?"

"Just move," Eric says. "The doctor wants him downstairs."

"I set up the medical table and laid out supplies."

"Good boy," the auburn-haired doctor pats Asa on the arm as she goes by. "That's a big help to me. I'll be able to start right away."

Eric makes his way down and through the halls, then carefully sets his injured friend on the examining table. The towels come away and it's clear the wound is deep, but there are entrance and exit wounds, two rounded holes.

"Holy shit," Asa barks, trying to hold in a laugh. "I don't know which is funnier, the fact that Pat got shot in the ass or that he has a fat chick tattooed on a butt cheek."

Eric gives him a shove, but the comment is just what we needed to diffuse the tension.

Dr. Cook shakes her head while examining the injuries. "You young people today. Thinking you invented sex and anything interesting. Tattoos last for life, you idiots! I have no idea why this handsome young man would want an unattractive woman on his butt for all eternity."

"Well, now it's a torn-up fat lady, to boot," Asa remarks. "That's one grisly-looking bullet hole."

The doctor motions to a cart nearby. "Hand me that bottle, Eric."

He steps into the room to fulfill her request, smiling when he turns back to his brother. "You're not going to get all vampy on us and lock your mouth on his ass, are you?"

"Hell, no!" A look of true revulsion crosses Asa's face. "I don't think I've ever been that hungry."

Dr. Cook dabs at the wound with a cleansing agent and Pat comes screaming back to consciousness.

"Fuck! That burns!" He glances at the doctor. "Hey, could you go a little easier? It really hurts."

The doctor harrumphs under her breath while readying sutures. "Almost as much as that tattoo?"

"What?" Pat looks confused. "Oh, that." His old smartass expression races across his features. "Keep your comments

Jonathan

to yourself, thank you very much. How about you focus on the bloody holes giving me horrible pain?"

Asa laughs. "Man, all you do is bitch and moan. Do you have anything positive to say, ever?"

"Yeah, okay. How about *'aint it nice I got shot in the ass and not that stupid vampire'*? Is that better?" Pat lets out a howl of protest when the threaded needle punctures his skin. "Damn it woman, don't you have drugs? This isn't how a real hospital treats a patient."

"Drugs will slow down your werewolf ability to heal faster," she replies in a soft voice. "We wouldn't want that."

Another yowl erupts from the enraged Pat. "You've got to be lying. That sounds like bullshit to me. I want drugs, woman!"

I shake my head and wander toward the command center. The kill zone was off the camera grid, but I wonder if Asa saw anyone on the property who shouldn't have been.

Pat's cries of pain and complaints continue until Eric offers him a leather belt to bite. Asa makes his way to my location, still cracking up over Pat.

"Shot in the ass. Damn, that's funny." He looks up and meets my stoic gaze.

"Yes, except you're forgetting this wasn't friendly fire. Someone is on our land. I want to see all feeds from the last few hours, right now. We need to figure out what the fuck happened."

Chapter Seven

Paul

Muted gray light seeps past my eyelids. I stretch in the king-sized bed and wonder what everyone is up to. It's late afternoon, and I'm always the last one in the seethe to rise from my forced undead sleep. In Alaska, Vivian stays up almost non-stop, but I bet even here she'd succumb to the pull of rest whether she wanted to or not. If I asked, would she tell me or give me one of her usual enigmatic smiles?

The heavy drapes and tinted glass of the enclosed balcony ensured I wasn't fried in my restorative siesta during the sun's highpoint. A shiver steals over me, underscoring that I prefer to sleep in a basement where there is no accidental risk of exposure when defenseless. Maybe this place has a basement? I'll have to ask.

I rise and pad to the bathroom to get ready. I'd love to spend time in the kitchen working on some dishes. Flavia gave me a tour before she and her husband departed for the evening. They'd stocked the pantry and fridge well for our arrival.

I pull on a faded pair of jeans and an old "Bite the Cook, He Likes it Al Dente" t-shirt before cracking open the door to the hallway. The darkened passage looks safe, no stray burning beams of fading sunlight. I ease out and shut the

Paul

door, thankful I'm not sharing a suite with Tommy and Bob. They're nice guys and all, but in a weak moment they could become my unexpected dinner.

I travel the lit stairwell and emerge on one side of the foyer. Blackout fabric covers the many doors leading to the enclosed courtyard, preventing any chance of injury. Hmm... Vivian has thought of everything. Well, in half a century, I guess you'd learn a thing or two—or died long before.

Canned laughter from a television issues from the living room wing, and voices drift from the opposite side of the foyer, indicating more people are gathered in the kitchen. The scent of fresh coffee fills the air and the ending sounds of a sputtering cycle means a new pot has finished brewing.

In the kitchen, Rafe sits at the long island, laptop open in front of him. Dressed in dark jeans and blue top, his face shows deep concentration as he examines the screen. Distant laughing brings my eye to the retreating forms of Drew and Chelly, arms wrapped around each other's waist while they disappear into the game room.

I head straight for the coffee pot across the room, snagging Rafe's empty mug as I go by. "More joe, boss?"

"Good afternoon, Paul. Thanks, I was just going to get a refill. New pot if you want any."

"Think I'll prepare a carafe of bloodcoffee in case anyone wants a cup besides me." I pour Rafe's mug and then proceed to heat water to pre-warm the carafe.

"How was your first night?" Rafe asks.

"Not bad. The guys and I watched a movie. Jet lag was a bitch for Tommy and Bob. They crashed way before I turned in." A phone rings on the other side of the French doors leading into the courtyard. "I wandered outside in the dark for a bit. Explored the property a little. Windy as all hell."

Vivian's voice carries through the glass doors. She opens them and steps inside, closing the doors quickly. Weak light spilled in, somehow looking more like twilight than late afternoon. Must be nice to be outside while the sun's still up. She's wearing a blue-patterned wrap dress, tied at the waist, and matching heels.

"What do you mean someone shot Pat in the ass?" Vivian's voice is raised and Rafe and I clearly hear both sides of the conversation. Viv absentmindedly waves at me, but doesn't shoo me off, so I'm guessing it's safe to stay and listen. I continue in my task, hoping to be as unobtrusive as possible.

"I meant just what I said," replies Jon from the other end. "Why can't I feel you in my thoughts? You promised we'd stay connected."

"It's the distance, Jon. Nothing more. Tell me about Pat's injury. How bad is it?"

"The shot went clean through, no bullet was found. But it sure as hell seemed like someone was shooting directly at us."

"Did you go after the shooter?"

"Romeo's pack did. Eric and I got Pat to safety first, unaware of how bad the wound was or if the bullet was still inside." Jon chuckles a bit. "Bastard bled like a stuck pig and cried the whole time Dr. Cook stitched his butt cheek."

"Well, I'm relieved he's fine, but I don't like the sound of this. It's too early for hunting season. Our employees wouldn't be after skinny caribou or reindeer right now."

"Yeah, I thought of that."

"Could someone have been after one of your wolf-dogs?"

A snort comes across the line. "Someone who? It's not like we're easily accessible up here."

"Yes... yes..." Vivian trails off, looking to Rafe. They remain quiet for a moment. I'm betting they're talking mind to mind. Kind of rude with someone else in the room, but damned if I'm stupid enough to point that out.

Paul

"Viv?" Jon prompts.

"I want you and Asa to question the employees. One-on-one if needed. It could have been an accident, but I'm not taking a chance. We need to find out what's going on."

"Calm down, your highness. We're not dumb and helpless just because you and Rafe are gone. Asa has already started questioning them. He's doing it alone so he can slip into their minds with no witnesses."

Tension leaks out of Vivian, and she settles onto a stool next to Rafe. "Good. I meant no offense, Jon. I'm just worried."

Facing my task at the counter, I raise my brows over her almost conciliatory tone—she's much more gruff and short with the rest of us. Must be that whole "vampire servant" status that makes her not as bitchy to him.

"He's gone through about forty people already," Jon says. "I waited to call in the hopes I'd have more news for you."

"What did Romeo's pack report?"

"Lots of confusing smells. Like heavy odors of synthetic deer and elk musk. Messed up their noses for the most part."

"Hmmm... could mean someone was really hunting."

"Yeah, maybe."

"Okay, keep us posted."

"Sure thing."

The call ends as I remove the heated blood bag from the microwave. I pour the red, salty goodness into the warm carafe and fill the rest with fresh coffee.

"Does anyone working for us hate Jon's dogs that much?" Rafe asks.

I turn to the couple, raising the pitcher to see if Viv wants some. She shakes her head, and I pour myself a steaming mug.

Viv takes a small sip out of Rafe's mug of plain coffee. "Not that I know of."

A rich chocovine-colored liquid tumbles into my ceramic cup, filling my head with the delicious aroma of delectable coffee and blood. Yumm... my fangs descend, causing me to sputter in embarrassment. Stupid. Stupid!

Rafe smiles over my *faux pas,* and a wrinkle of concern flits across Vivian's brow. I whip around to face the sink, hoping to hide my slip. The clatter of her high heels echoes across the tile, and in a second I feel her cool hand rest on my arm. Calmness seeps through me, and my fangs retract, removing the awkward "kid with a boner" feeling.

"Don't beat yourself up, Paul. You're doing fabulous. It's the added stress of a new place and jumping all the time zones."

I relax my shoulders, unaware my body clenched in anger over the involuntary reactions. "Thanks. I still feel like a dork when it happens like that."

Vivian walks away, removing her soothing touch as she goes. "Make sure you get enough bottled blood today, Paul. It might help you adjust." She looks my way as she climbs onto the stool near her husband.

I raise my bloodcoffee and nod before turning my attention toward cooking. Maybe Bob will do a tasting for me tonight? I rummage through the cupboards, checking out the equipment and ingredients I have to work with.

"What are you looking at, love?" Viv directs to Rafe.

"The Tribunal's website regarding a big party tonight."

I rear and bang my head. "Did you just say the Tribunal has a website? What the hell?"

Vivian glances at the laptop screen. "It's probably Rolando's doing. The crafty bastard is always thinking of ways to pull vampires from all over the world. The site is password protected from what I understand."

Paul

"Really?" I turn back to the cabinets. "Why would they do that?"

"Whatever their reasons," answers Rafe, "they've got a huge spread going on tonight. Even posted a program of the night's activities and a 'menu.'"

I make my way to the laptop. I can't deny, he's piqued my interest with the mention of a menu.

" *'Fall* into Blood Lust', eh?" I read the glowing red letters dripping blood on the screen. "I don't know—looks a little cheesy to me."

Vivian walks over to the house phone and flips through a small book nearby. "I'm betting the cheesiness is on purpose so it would look fake."

"Could be considered 'camp' by some," Rafe says.

I look over the dishes listed on the screen. "Blood pudding? Is it even possible we could eat it?"

"They'd use a thickening agent and serve it chilled." A shudder ripples across his broad shoulders. "Ugh... I remember from years past the stench in their formal dining room from all the blood. We usually avoid being in it for long. Just plain nasty."

Vivian picks up the phone and dials some numbers. "Which is why you used the coroner's gel under your nose, if I remember correctly."

"Look at this," I say, pointing to the computer, "Blood soup, blood cocktails, blood fountains, 'live meals'.... What the hell is that?"

"Just what you think. Live donors ready for feasting."

My slow heart skips a beat at the thought of such abundance. Thankfully, the coffee took the edge off, and I don't go all "bustafang" again.

"Hello, Dalton?" Vivian speaks into the phone. "Get the seaplane ready for travel in one hour. Call the hangar in Puerto Santa Cruz and make sure the Gulfstream is fuelled and ready to go. Have a flight plan submitted for Buenos Aires."

"Whoa!" I say, scrambling to figure out if I brought fancy enough clothes to attend. "We're leaving to go, just like that? We just got here."

"No, darling." My boss gives me a sad little smile. "It will only be Rafe and me. Surprising them early at this party is perfect."

"Perfect? How is that? Don't you need an invite or something?" I gesture to the laptop. "Says here it's formal."

"Rafe and I have plenty of clothes." She walks out, ending the conversation when she leaves the room. The clatter of her heels across the tiles softens as she strolls further away.

"Really—just like that?" I flail my arms and go back to the other side of the island. "She walks off and doesn't say another word?"

Rafe languidly stretches and looks my way with a raised eyebrow. "What were you thinking, Paul? That she'd call us all together and talk it over?"

I temper my behavior in the face of his relaxed sureness. He's right, of course. Did I really think my boss would talk over her decision with the lowest member of her seethe and possibly include me in going? My disappointment surprises me.

"No... er, I... I guess not."

"Listen, old man. The place is full of political maneuvering, backstabbing, and the occasional killing. It's not the type of event any master would bring a fledgling to. At least, not one they valued."

His last words help take the sting off my feelings, childish as that sounds. "Yeah, I suppose."

The French doors to the courtyard open and vague half-light spills in. One of the exotic twins glides in. She's dressed

Paul

in a clingy dress, dark hair spilling down her back, and spiked heels on her bronzed feet.

My tongue freezes in my mouth and an image of drinking from her neck until she writhes in pleasure beneath me fills my mind with desire.

"Hi," I stammer. "I'm married." What the hell did I just say?

The brown-haired beauty smiles at me like a sticky-fingered toddler holding a drawing covered in mud. "Yes, you're Paul, no?"

I nod. She looks to Rafe, thankfully ignoring my slack-jawed stupidity. "I thought I'd come in to see about turning the tint off on the atrium ceiling. Is that acceptable, sir?"

Rafe looks at his watch. "Yes, the sun has dropped past the horizon. Thank you for checking with me, Carmella."

"Yes, sir."

She turns to leave, not even glancing my way, and I'm left scrambling to regain the shreds of my dignity. Redirection might work. "So... what was that she said about tint?"

"All the windows in the house, even the atrium panels, are tinted to block out light. Vivian figured we might have others here who couldn't handle even the slightest bit of sunlight, so we planned it in the recent remodel."

"Makes sense. But then, why the blackout cloth under the designer drapes?"

"Because the tint still lets some light in, although it's muted and very filtered." Rafe closes up his laptop. "Drew?" he raises his voice, pitching over the infrequent clink of pool balls from the game wing. "Can you come here, please?"

Drew arrives, and leans in the doorway. "You need me?"

"Vivian and I are leaving for Buenos Aires—alone."

Knowing where this is going, I step to the window and pull back the drapes, peering out at the lovely Carmella as

75

she picks up what looks to be an eReader, a notepad, and a pen. When she bends at the waist I get a view of her perfectly-rounded, heart-shaped butt. Man! I heard the South American trend was more hips and ass than the U.S. preference of big breasts, but I hadn't realized all of them would have such gorgeous derrieres.

Rafe's voice continues behind me while I stare. "You'll be in charge, Drew. Keep an eye on everyone and make sure we don't have any... mingling... with the caretaker's daughter." My head whips around, sure his pause was directed at me. "Vivian would be most displeased."

"Hey, I'm married," I reply. "Don't need to worry about me. And that one out there is not the daughter."

"Uh-huh." Rafe's look doesn't match his neutral tone. "Let's keep it that way."

"No harm in looking." I walk back to the island and deliberately turn my back on the fuckable ass outside.

"How long will you be gone?" Drew asks, ignoring my entire exchange.

I reach for the fridge doors and mentally catalog what's inside, trying my best to not think about the twin. *I'm happily married. I'm happily married,* plays over and over in my head.

"Not sure. Come, walk with me." Footsteps sound and Rafe's voice grows fainter as the two disappear into the dining room. "We can always buy what we don't take with us. I have no idea if this will be a two or three day trip or something longer. We'll call twice a day to check in and keep you abreast of what's going on. Let me go over security protocols and systems...."

"Hey, Paul." Chelly's lyrical voice pulls my attention from staring blindly at the vegetables and meats I can no longer consume. "Whatcha doing?"

Paul

I beam a radiant smile at her, glad to have someone here I can call a friend to get my mind off of the luscious strangers I must learn to ignore. "Thinking about cooking dinner. Care to help?"

Chapter Eight
Asa

The sun feels high, not quite at full strength due to the time of year, but it's certainly kill-worthy for me. A short, restorative sleep helped relieve the mental strain from questioning the employees, but I really need bagged blood to feel better. I don't drink much from live donors anymore after learning how painful my bite is to humans. I haven't heard of another vampire whose feeding causes such agony and I've often wondered why mine is so off. I waited to confess my aberration to Vivian, wanting to put it off as long as I can.

The dull quiet of the basement is welcome after the last few hours listening to Pat bitch about his gunshot wound.

It took me all night to question the employees one-by-one, and it drained my strength, causing me to fall into rest like the walking dead. Still no answers. On the surface, it seems like none of them is responsible for hunting off-season. No one held Jon or his wolf dogs in particular disregard, most exhibited an indifference to the well-trained animals and the head groundskeeper.

Could someone have gone on leave recently and not be on my summer staff list? That would make sense. Someone

Asa

sneakily taking vacation time and staying behind to wreak havoc... but it doesn't add up. Surely, I would've encountered at least a twinge of hatred during questioning to indicate someone knew something?

I settle deeper into the swivel chair in front of the desk and stare mindlessly above the four monitors. Things could have been far worse for Pat. The bullet could've landed higher and shattered his spine, paralyzing him. Would that have led to a follow-up kill shot?

My slow-moving blood runs cold at the thought of being so close to losing an old friend. Even a shock-jock like Patrick has his good moments. What if they had been aiming for Eric? It could easily be him the doctor stitched up on the med table.

This morning, Jon issued a no-hunting policy on the property while guests are in attendance. The new restriction seemed to be received well, as if the majority figured that was a given when we had paying clients and jobs to do.

Who could have done this and was it truly a mistake?

Then why were three shots fired?

Eric walks in. "Pat's ass doesn't look good."

A snort of laughter escapes me before I have a chance to clamp it down. "What did you expect with a ripped-up fat lady tattoo?" I swivel my chair around to face my brother. "It didn't look great to begin with."

"Nah, that's a given. I mean the wound. Neither of us has been shot before, so I have nothing to compare it to. But hey, how long do you think a compound fracture would take to set?"

"Are we talking about a human or a Were?"

"Were."

"You tell me, dog-boy. I'm the vampire." I smile at the absurdity of my own words.

"Speaking of which, have you eaten since you did all that mesmerizing and questioning? You look like pale vomit."

"Gee, thanks." I stand and stretch, realizing he's right—I do need to get some blood in me before the stinky dog smell coming off him and Pat no longer repulses me and I decide to snack on them. "Back to the broken limb?"

"Yeah. While in Romeo's pack, I fell out a window."

I raise an eyebrow as I walk past him into the hall, heading for the mini-fridge and microwave set up in the conference room.

He continues talking while following me. "Don't ask. Lots of alcohol and a stupid drinking game. But after the bone was set, I could use my arm again in a few hours."

Eric trails behind me and then sits in one of the leather office chairs. I take a bag of blood from the fridge. "Sounds a little slower than vamp healing abilities, but yours could get stronger as you age." I pop a small vent valve and place the bag in the microwave. The whir of the machine causes an almost Pavlovian reaction and my fangs start to itch.

"My point is, I think Pat's stitched wounds should have stopped weeping blood and started healing a long time ago."

"What does Jon say?"

The stocky wolf in question answers from the doorway, "What does Jon say about what?" He's wearing a scowl and appears to be taking the shooting of Pat very personally. Which I don't blame him for—either someone purposely tried to shoot his packmate or one of his dogs. Hard to not take that personally.

"Pat's injury," Eric says when the microwave timer dings. "It's not healing."

With my back to the men, I pour the dark red liquid into a travel mug. A rich copper penny smell fills the air and I know their sensitive noses can pick it up easily. I slap the cover onto the tall stainless steel container, hoping to cut down on the released odor.

It's one thing to be a vampire and quite another to open a vein on someone whenever hungry. I much prefer the more civilized bagged blood approach Vivian provides for the guests, but still feel creepy when drinking in front of an audience. I down a long slow drink before turning around, not wanting to look like a greedy bloodsucker.

Jon continues, hopefully ignoring my actions. "Sometimes these things take time. Healing can depend on the Were's strength reserves when they were shot. I didn't think he was worn out or hungry, but he could have been. Has Dr. Cook looked at it again?"

"Not that I know of," Eric replies.

After my second long pull, I face them and sit a couple of chairs down from Eric.

"Could a fragment of the bullet still be inside?" I suggest.

Jon shakes his head. "No, the doctor did an x-ray to confirm no metal remained."

"He's sleeping, now," Eric says. "We could go and check it out if you think that will help."

"No, thanks," Jon says. "I already have Pat's lily-white, tattooed flesh emblazoned on my corneas for the rest of time. Who the fuck gets a fat girl tattooed on their ass, anyway?"

Eric doesn't rise to the bait. I shift in my chair and take another sip of blood. "A guy with exceptionally high standards who thinks it's easy to get laid?" I smile as a thought occurs to me. "And then he moves to Alaska and realizes real women who like frequent sex don't look like they're starving to death."

Eric stands and walks to the door, his movements stiff and jerky. "I think I'll call Dr. Cook again. You guys can sit and make fun all you want, but I think something's wrong."

Jon grabs Eric's shoulder as he goes by. "You're right, man. I'm sorry. I've been so wracked with anger over the shooting, I let a little bad humor creep in when I shouldn't."

Jon drops his hand and Eric's tension eases a bit. "What could cause this? I'll be the first to admit I'm still getting used to being furry and sure as hell don't have all the answers. But the holes won't stop weeping blood."

Jon's complexion pales. "You mean it's still bleeding after twelve hours?"

"Yes. I guess you missed that earlier part of our conversation."

Jon pushes past the taller, broader wolf and bolts down the hall toward Pat's room. Eric and I follow. Pat thrashes in his sleep, sweat covering his forehead.

"He looks like he's getting a fever." Jon says. "Which would indicate an infection—highly unlikely in a werewolf."

He whips the sheet off the lanky Were, revealing a blood-soaked gauze pad. He pries the adhesive from one end and exposes one stitched hole. A bead of blood swells up as we watch and slides away from the ragged seam.

"Shit!" Jon tears off the bloody pad in one sharp jerk. "This is not good."

Panic edges into Eric's voice. "What is it? Some kind of poison?"

"Yes, but not how you think." With fresh gauze, Jon cleans the wound's edge. "He was shot with silver. We missed it because we don't have the bullet. The damage is done and his system will fight the slightest trace of contamination."

Color drains from Eric's face, looking like he might get sick. "Can it kill him?"

Jon grabs scissors and cuts away the careful stitching. "If the silver remained inside or was injected into his blood stream, yes. I think this wound will just be a bitch to heal.

He'll lose a lot of blood while his body fights to expel every last trace."

"Then why are you cutting his sutures?" I ask.

Ignoring me, he continues with his task of opening the wound. "Eric, call Dr. Cook. We'll need her to close this when we're done."

Eric leaps into action, looking grateful to have something to do. He grabs the wall phone and punches numbers.

"What can we do?" I try again, hoping to get an answer to the madness swirling from his energy permeating the air. "Why the hell are you opening it back up?"

"To pour in a cleansing agent to flush out the traces of silver."

"Okay, what do you need me to grab—peroxide?"

"No." Jon reaches into his boot and pulls out a silver dagger. "I need to cut your wrist."

I stare at the werewolf in confusion. "Did you say you want to cut me?"

Eric hangs up the phone and whips back to us. "She's on her way. What can I do next?"

"Grab your slack-jawed brother and haul him over here." Jon motions toward me where I'm still standing at the door staring at him, trying to figure out why he'd need to cut my wrist. "We need vampire blood to purge the silver."

"Oh," I say, stepping forward and placing my mug on a side table. "Why didn't you say so in the first place?" A rush of apprehension slides through me when I glance at the silver edge of the sharp blade. Eric hovers nearby, looking willing to grab me if I resist. "Relax, Eric." I take a deep breath and shove my own inner fears to the back of my mind. Humor usually helps when three grown men are tense. "You're sending off so much tension it's enough to make me worry you plan on sticking me like a virgin at the prom—fast, furious, and without a moment's thought to the young woman."

He cracks a smile. "Not my prom, man. Maybe yours."

I reach Jon and pull my left sleeve up. "Hand me the knife." The werewolf rotates the handle to me. I slice open a shallow cut and blood wells in the gap. "What do I do? Let it drip in?"

He nods, pinning down Pat's legs with his knee. "We're more sensitive to the silver than you are. Once it's inside our bodies it can circulate quickly and do more damage than expected."

I hold my dripping incision over Pat's torn and ragged flesh. When the crimson drops descend into the wound, Pat settles, his body relaxing into the bed.

Jon releases his hold, watching my blood mix with Pat's to staunch the flow. In a few seconds my wound seals and I look to the worried alpha with a question in my eyes. "Again?"

He examines the injury—some of the jagged flesh has puckered at the edges, starting to heal. "Looks like once was enough."

Eric wipes a wet cloth over the clammy sweat on his friend's face. "Is vampire blood the only thing that works?"

I hand back Jon's knife and saunter to my travel mug for a sip.

"No," he says. "There are several herbal compresses that work. But they take longer and should be used right away. His fever told me we already had an issue brewing."

We tidy up the room and change the sheets under our patient, anticipating what the doctor will have us do when she arrives. In a few minutes the soft form of the aging medic joins us and Jon explains what happened.

We leave her to the task of re-stitching the unconscious Were and step into the hall. Anger radiates off Jon in an almost palpable wave. "Asa, did you question Jerry last night?"

I think back to the dozens of employees, rather sure the cagey engineer was not among them. "I don't think so."

"We need to find the old man and see what he knows."

"What's wrong, Jon?" Eric asks. "You really think that nice guy tried to shoot one of us?"

"I think someone using silver bullets to hunt werewolves was no mistake—they were gunning for supernatural. We need to find out if any other employees know how to make their own silver ammo."

We head into the command center where I scan employee leave notices on the terminal. "He was on leave for a few days and due back tonight." Jon reads over the list as well. "Do we tell the visiting wolves?"

"Of course we do," says Eric. "Right? This is too important to keep from them."

Jon's face clouds over and he slams a fist into his thigh. "Dammit! They already left an hour ago. I told them our results with questioning the employees and issuing the no-hunting policy. Romeo and Elsa felt it was safe to proceed."

"Shit!" Eric runs a hand over his short hair. "What do we do?"

"What choice do we have?" Jon says dashing for the stairs. "We find them and warn them."

Chapter Nine

Vivian

The **dark sky spans** before the windshield, making the private jet feel like an insignificant bug in the huge expanse. I don't sense Jon in my mind anymore, having slowly and carefully dwindled our connection until almost severed. He needs the break from me, whether he admits it or not. It would be terrific if he found a mate in the batch of frisky females parading back and forth in front of him this summer... time will tell.

Allowing Jon to worry about me, my safety, and my subsequent approval of a potential partner day in and day out is not healthy to his wolf or human psyche. I worried seven years ago that taking him on so young would have its drawbacks, but I never bargained on his love and devotion clouding natural instinct. An alpha wolf needs an alpha mate. That's the order of things. Balancing a new love with his duties as my servant and loyalty to the seethe may be tricky, but not impossible.

I have no doubt whomever he chooses will despise me on some level. Making sure the two have their own intimate bond, separate from his bond to me, will be crucial for his happiness. A small pain pierces my soul at the thought of losing him—but, if he continues as he has, his obsession over me might destroy any daily peace he enjoys.

"Why are you shielding so hard right now, Dria?" Rafe's smooth voice breaks me from my thoughts. "Worried about the evening, or something else?"

"Combination of things, really."

"Hmm.... That suspiciously sounds like an evasive answer. The furball again?"

I look away while examining the dials and readings on the control panel in front of us. "Maybe."

"I haven't felt his pull in my mind since we left. He might buy that crap about our distance being the reason, but I know differently. What are you planning?"

A sigh escapes me as I gaze at my lover. "No actual plan this time. Just a hope."

"Does it have something to do with the huge amount of female wolves coming to the inn this summer?"

I shrug my shoulder and look away.

"Did you think I'd miss the fifty percent discount you offered to packs bringing three or more unattached females?"

"Hey, it worked, didn't it? You saw some of the guests' dossiers? Gorgeous women."

Rafe pats my forearm. "You're a good bitch, Dria. I don't care what the others say about you."

"Wiseass," I remark with a smirk. "Why don't you read the coordinates and leave me be?"

It's full dark by the time we approach the private airstrip inside the city limits. Buenos Aires sparkles like a glittering jewel, bringing back my love of the old city in crystal clarity.

Rafe's hand caresses my thigh through the jumpsuit, our earlier snipe forgotten. "Why do you insist on wearing these things? The zippers drive me to distraction."

A slow smile inches across my face as his hot palm slides closer to my hip. "That's precisely why I wear them, darling."

Rafe shifts in his seat, casually adjusting himself under his slacks. "Think we'll have time to visit that Simpson's shop I love?"

My grin broadens at his attempt to distract himself from his growing arousal. I smell his interest in the confines of the small plane; it's impossible to hide from my sharp senses. "The one with the tacky Homer and Marge merchandise all over the walls?"

"No, that store is good, but not the one I mean. The one named Cowabunga, with the specialty Duff beer?"

I shake my head at his obvious enjoyment. Men will be men.

"What? Is it my fault Buenos Aires is the Simpson capital of the world? How can I resist?"

I laugh and he continues. "I need some new talking Homer bottle openers, too. Hey, pay attention to the runway, it's coming up fast."

In a few minutes we touch down and taxi into a waiting hangar. We grab our wardrobe bags and head to a storage room at the back of the building. Changing quickly, we hustle into our evening attire.

My strapless purple gown plunges deep in the back and I shiver when cool air in the unheated building touches my skin. I gather my hair loosely at the base of my skull, shoving pins in with a precision gained from decades of experience. The elegant style doesn't look too formal and allows some of the curlier tendrils to cascade around my face and down the nape of my neck. I pull on the matching satin gloves, tugging the material up to my biceps, and turn to Rafe.

He's finishing the last touches on his black bowtie, pulling the knot tight. "How does it look? Crooked?"

Vivian

I stare at his well-muscled body, encased in the custom-made, silk and cashmere blend black tuxedo. Light from the overhead fixture glints off the fabric, catching on the diamond studs running down the pleated white shirt. I retrieve the gray silk scarf from his bag, then lift his collar and slide it around his neck, draping the fine material down the jacket's lapels.

"You look divine. And the tie is perfect." I run a hand down his chest and below, slipping a warm palm over his pants to cup his cock.

"No teasing," he says, pulling his hips away. "I'm not walking into a group of bloodsuckers with an erection."

"Fair point." I sashay to the door and zip my hanging wardrobe bag. "I hear an engine outside, must be the hired car."

"Do you want a wrap?"

I shake my head and step into my glittery heels. "I'm fine. I'll touch up my makeup in the car. Let's get on the road."

Rafe unbolts the outer door and a moist breeze pushes my hair from my face. The driver stands at the ready and opens the rear car door. I slide into the long limousine, across the soft leather seat, while Rafe stows the bags in the trunk and speaks to the driver. He's a private hire not associated with the Tribunal. The two men speak in Spanish and in no time we're rolling through the darkened city streets.

We cruise past ornate, older structures, skyscrapers, the capitol building and the miniature Washington Monument known here as *El Obelisco*, which marks the 400th anniversary of the city's founding. Buenos Aires has changed much in that time, and I've enjoyed seeing it grow over the centuries. The area is a gorgeous mix of culture and European architectural styles.

Finishing the last touches to my makeup, I snap my compact shut, slip my red lipstick into a handbag, and check the time. Almost nine. We should arrive before the party has truly begun. I fiddle with a glove and stare out the window at the various lights racing by.

Worried, dear? Rafe's soothing mental voice fills my head.

Concerned would be more accurate. Best we stay on our toes tonight.

A soft snort comes from the seat next to me. *Yeah, you think? I dread these events at the best of times, but after Coraline's Alaskan visit... who knows what den of vipers we could be strolling into.*

I rest a hand on his arm in reassurance. *Nothing will be blatant or outright. Vampires are subtle in their steering of events, especially when dealing with their own kind.*

After twenty minutes, we pull in front of an opulent townhouse. Its stone veneer, intricate railings, and high arched windows are reminiscent of old, large London townhomes costing millions of pounds. Warm light spills from every window of the distinguished structure. The Tribunal owns the entire, very expensive, block and their underground lair below the street surface far exceeds the footprint of the buildings above. A lone doorman stands outside with no indication of a party going on through the windows.

Rafe opens the car door and exits, offering a hand to me. As I emerge from the sleek black limo a shiver steals down my spine again. Is that apprehension I'm feeling or a tinge of excitement? I shake it off and pull my aura in tight, not wanting to broadcast, if I don't have to.

My rhinestone-encrusted spiked heels flash in the street lamps as I step to the curb, glancing up and down the sidewalk. A couple walks arm and arm from the next house

Vivian

down, and two more figures beyond them stroll in our direction. I brace myself and plaster on a smile to my perfectly made-up face.

Show time, darling, I project to my husband. *Be sharp.*

Rafe's warm hand glides down my bare back, stealing some of the chill that's settled at the base of my spine. *Never you fear, liebling. I've got your back. We'll do fine tonight.*

Fear? I wouldn't call it fear.

No, of course you wouldn't. How silly of me.

He's trying to draw me out, but that shiver really surprised me. Was it intuition?

It's called 'you should have worn a coat', Rafe quips while motioning for the doorman on the steps to come to us. A younger vampire around the age of fifty saunters down, looking unsure if he wants to listen to a human or not. I turn to face the pony-tailed wall of meat and wait for him to recognize me. It only takes a second. His goateed visage shows genuine happiness at my arrival.

"Alexandria?" He bows deep and takes my hand, delivering a perfunctory kiss to my gloved fingers. "I had no idea. You weren't on the list tonight."

"Surprise, George," I say, pushing fake warmth into my tone. "Think they'll have room for two more?"

To his credit, not a reaction is revealed as he smiles. "You know they always do."

By this time, the closest couple has reached us, and George nods for them to proceed us up the stairs. I keep my back to them, not wanting to engage anyone here on the street. Rafe grabs the bags, and the car pulls away.

"Any remaining accommodations in the main building or will we be forced to one of the other Tribunal homes tonight?" I ask.

91

He takes our luggage from Rafe and climbs the steep stairs to the ornately carved wood double doors. "There's always a room for VIPs, Alexandria. You should know that."

I smile, following him up. "One never knows what favor one might be in when arriving unannounced."

George's amusement rumbles from deep in his broad chest and spills into the night air. "If I treated you poorly, I think Rolando would eat me for breakfast."

We enter the main hall, and the interior warmth banishes the last of the night chill from my skin. Honest-to-God burning torches line the walls of the tapestry-covered walls, with reflections of the dancing flames shimmering on the highly polished marble floor. Scenes of harvest and goodwill are depicted on the wall hangings—the Tribunal's only nod of festive adornment to the fall season on the main floor. I'm betting downstairs there will be a more elaborate theme for their autumn gala.

"Shall I put your things in a room upstairs?"

At my nod of thanks, the doorman ascends the curving, black-carpeted tread. "I think the Edwardian room is free. Will that suit?"

"Anything is fine, thanks. We're going down to the party."

Rafe takes my elbow and directs me after the couple, who entered ahead us. Closed doors line the long hall, and at the end of the foyer sits a large freight elevator spruced up with wood panels and inset with tile, but the size leaves no doubt it's not a regular elevator car.

I don't know the couple, so thankfully we're not forced to engage in conversation while descending into the pits of hell—known as the Seat of Darkness among the undead. The elevator doors *ping* open and the subtle stink of death rolls in to greet us. The scent isn't overpowering like decaying flesh or rotting vegetation, but it lingers on the back of my

Vivian

palate, reminding me why I hate associating with fellow vampires for too long—the more we congregate, the more the odor builds. The others must be used to it, that's all I can think as to why no one is hurling in a corner.

Rafe swallows a gag. *Dear God, I forgot how much this place reeks.*

Good news is, in ten minutes or so your nose won't even register it anymore.

The couple next to us takes a deep breath, seeming to draw pleasure in the cloying aroma and disappears into the crowd before us. Pale, primped bodies mill about, all dressed for a formal evening.

This main reception room is large enough to hold a hundred or more people comfortably, and looks to be set up in a cocktail hour sort of gathering. The twelve foot high ceiling is festooned with grand crystal chandeliers every ten feet. Tall tables dot the area, draped in orange, red, yellow and rust-toned silks—no chairs to clutter the stream of the mingling undead.

An ornate champagne fountain sets in the middle of the room. A bubbling mixture of blood and champagne fills the air with an enticing hint of copper and dry wine. Rafe immediately steers us to the right, out of the line of sight from the open elevator, hoping to avoid our discovery as long as possible.

A human waiter approaches with a tray of non-blood drinks. He's dressed in a forest spirit type of costume, someone's idea of a pagan mix to the fall theme. His skin sparkles with glitter and a leaf vest frames his dark chest hair. "Good evening, can I offer either of you a drink?"

Rafe takes a flute, and I reach for one as well, leery of drinking anything with blood under the Tribunal's roof. Do I honestly think they'd poison their guests? No, not really. But since I'm not hungry, no need to risk it.

The waiter grins at me, a seductive light coloring his brown eyes. "Would you prefer to quench your hunger directly from the source, madam?" He tosses his longish black hair back from where it skimmed his shoulder, baring the pristine flesh of his neck.

Rafe tenses beside me, angered some strange boy-toy would offer himself freely to his wife.

"No," I answer with a bland look. "Thank you." I pat my husband's thick bicep. "I brought my own."

The waiter hustles to another group of people and Rafe relaxes. "Cheeky bastard. That was rather bold, don't you think?"

I shrug, not wanting this to turn into an issue. "You never know what compulsion the party organizer may have placed on the staff. Could be normal."

I scan the room, looking for familiar faces. I see several people I'd like to avoid, but Coraline's supporters certainly won't be discovered if I play the wallflower, so I resign to the fact we'll have to circulate.

We step into the milling throng and I brace myself for the fall-out. We'll be spotted, and the whole room will know in minutes we crashed the party. Several heads turn our way, and I see a spark of recognition in more than one set of eyes.

It won't be long now before...

"Dria," an oily voice detaches itself from a nearby shadow and saunters up to us. "What an interesting surprise." The slicked back dark hair and petulant smile belongs to Lucas, an ex-lover to one of the pedophilic Ancients I killed centuries ago. Crap, he would be the first we run into.

"Yes, it is, Lucas. You remember my husband, Rafe, don't you?" I smile pretending not to hate the sonovabitch. If I ever find he has tastes for young boys like his old lover did, I'll make sure he walks into the sun at high noon as well.

Vivian

Rafe shakes his hand and nods, while sending me calming energy through our mental link. *Relax, liebling. You're stewing for a fight. Never a good sign this early in the evening.*

Lucas smiles and shoots me an evil look. What? Like I should apologize for killing his lover and own the deed? Yeah, fat chance in hell of that ever happening. I'm not stupid. Sensing no further conversation coming from our way, Lucas slips into the crowd, scampering away like a rat.

Leave it to you to point out when I'm feeling bitchy, I say, while threading my hand around Rafe's arm and walking deeper into the party. *I have my reasons to hate him.*

Looks like he's running off to report your presence.

Won't matter anyway, once Ro—

"Dria!" Rolando's smooth tones boom across the open space and all heads swivel in our direction. Flamboyant ass has the nerve to grin. He knows I hate being the center of attention when we visit.

Well, if you didn't want to be noticed, you shouldn't have worn that gown, sweetheart.

I pinch Rafe hard through his suit sleeve. *Are you trying to set me off?*

One hand snakes down and cups my ass as the dashingly handsome, dark-haired, dark-eyed Rolando descends on us both. *I'm trying to help you shake the tension. It's boiling off you in waves.*

Realizing he's right, I clamp down my mental walls, effectively shielding any escaping tendrils that might reveal my distressed state to the surrounding undead.

Rolando's eyes mirror his obvious delight at our appearance. "Naughty girl." He kisses both my cheeks and reaches for Rafe's hand. "Why didn't you call first?" His powerful voice glides over me, the subtle Spanish accent adding to his charm.

"After the lovely visit from Coraline and her enforcers in January, we thought coming in under the radar would be smarter."

The tall, elegant vampire nods sagely and turns to usher us deeper into the gathering. I can't help but notice his own power is leashed tightly. It almost feels like there are a bunch of fledglings walking around in the Seat of Darkness. "Yes, that woman does hate you. Whatever did you do to her to earn such wrath?"

I shrug one pale shoulder and follow alongside, still firmly attached to Rafe. "As far as I can tell, I beat her kill record as an enforcer, and she's held it against me over four centuries."

A flash of humor crosses his sharp features. "Some ex-enforcers are eager to forget their long terms of service, and others wrap their achievements around them like a cloak of honor." He pauses and eyes me sideways. "You never struck me as the latter."

Rafe clears his throat when it becomes obvious I'm not going to respond. "Only the soulless could speak callously over the loss of life and disregard the scars left by years of killing."

Roland stops and looks Rafe full in the face, as if seeing him for the first time tonight. "And you believe vampires have souls?" He arches an eyebrow. "You'd be one of the few humans in this room to share such an opinion."

A naked woman walks past us, trailing after a large male vampire in a tux. She appears dazed, and her body bears the mark of many fresh punctures. She locks eyes on Rafe and smiles. A dulled expression, due to drugs or blood loss, colors the effect of her beauty. The vampire holds a gold

Vivian

leash hooked to a velvet collar around her neck, and gives it a gentle tug when her pace falters.

A look of disgust shows briefly on my husband's face before he slips his reaction carefully behind a mask of distance. "When you treat them like pets, how can you expect anything more?"

We stop in front of the blood fountain, and Rolando tilts an empty glass into the flow. "Dria, may I top off yours? Looks like you haven't had any blood, yet."

"No, thanks," I sip from my glass. "I'm driving." He laughs and fills his own glass.

Live music spills from open doors at the far side of the reception hall. The lively beat of Spanish rhythms thrum the air and one of my favorite tango songs fills the night. I straighten and Rolando notices my reaction.

"You should dance." The crafty bastard winks at Rafe. "We can continue this interesting discussion about vampire souls when you return."

Rafe takes our glasses and hands them to a passing semi-naked harvest priestess holding a tray. *It's been a while since we've danced, my love. Maybe it will help chase away the spirit riding you tonight.*

I follow his lead to the rich music pouring from the adjoining room. A large parquet dance floor occupies the middle of the area and faux trees line the room's edge—plastic branches decorated in vibrant fall colors. He shoves my tiny handbag in his suit pocket and drapes both over an empty table at the edge of the dance floor. Bright gowns and black suits encase the pale forms of dancing, whirling vampires, quite distinguishable from the few humans dancing among them.

My husband unfolds a knife from his pocket and kneels at my feet. He places the silver coated blade near the top of my left thigh, drawing the material away from my body and meets my eyes. With one tilted eyebrow he seems to ask "Well?" He's asking permission to slit my tight dress. We won't be able to tango like the music calls for unless he cuts the beautiful fabric.

What the hell, I smile down at him, excited to have some fun. *It's only a dress. Go for it.*

With a devilish grin he proceeds to slice the material in one fell swoop, from my hipbone to the hem. Cool air hits my leg, and one hot hand slides from my knee to thigh. I stare down into my lover's bright blue eyes and the room disappears.

He tightens his grip and returns my gaze, wearing the most seductive look I've seen on him in ages. His thumb creeps up and brushes in close to my bare pussy, sending a tingle to my middle. "You're the naughty one now, aren't you?" I whisper.

"When am I not, liebling?"

Before I can blink, his free hand holding the knife whips down and he's repeated the cut on the other side, altering my expensive gown into suitable tango attire.

I hear the blood pounding through his veins as the pulse of the music takes him. One cannot be in Argentina for long and not be affected by the dance that was born here.

He stows his knife and sweeps me into his arms to whirl us among the other dancers. The music seeps into my bones, washing the vile aftertaste of the room's occupants from my essence. Quickly, I'm lost in the steps, the intoxicating beat, and my husband's experienced lead.

"I needed this." My head snaps right and left as my feet mince and kick, encased in their sparkly heels. We're locked in sync, gliding up and down the dance floor like sensual marionettes, bending to the rhythm and sexual pull from one another.

Vivian

Rafe's hand skates down my back to lower me into a provocative dip, trailing his hot lips along my neck. *If I stay close enough, your perfume blocks out the rancid smell of death coming off these parasites.*

Laughter bubbles up as he sweeps me high above his head, gradually allowing my body to slide down his chest. My calf hooks his leg, slinking around his well-formed muscle before sliding down to rest my foot on the floor. He steps away and twirls me again, bringing our bodies together then apart as I back-kick my calves on every step.

Each time he steps between my legs my hot core presses against a hard muscled thigh, reminding me of the last intimate moment we shared, tangled together on the bed in the plane.

You want me again, don't you? I ask through our mental connection.

He smiles and kisses me briefly when we come together in another move. *Only if you've got that coroner's gel in your little handbag. I need to block out the stench or my parts may not work right.*

I laugh as he spins me again—picturing my virile husband with un-working parts for any reason strikes me as impossible. *Didn't you stop smelling it after ten minutes or so?*

You'd think, right? He heaves a dramatic mental sigh, trying his best to get me into a good mood with his humor. *But sadly, no. Your deadly compatriots really reek. I'd say it's enough to off-put even the most ardent of admirers.*

For a few seconds I'm lost in the moment, allowing the beat of the music to soothe my soul and my husband to guide me through the moves. Am I up for the intrigue and the political maneuvering this trip will take?

The vampire bodies around us shimmer in quick movements. The energy level on the floor rises to meet our own, spurring the others into faster and more complicated moves. The sexual tension becomes too much for a couple and they break off, locked in a sensual kiss.

It takes a lot to get a vampire's blood pumping, and right now, mine sings through my veins, almost matching that of my spouse's. Is it any wonder vampires like to tango?

We continue for two more songs, gathering an audience among my peers. As the strains of the last song die, and Rafe lowers me to the floor in the deepest dip yet, a spark of the Tango burrows deep inside me. It wraps my heart in warmth, making the upcoming greetings awaiting us more bearable.

Rafe slides an arm around my waist and guides me off the dance floor. A group of pale faces approaches us, smiling a welcome they don't mean. *You knew they'd spot us sooner or later, liebling. Might as well get the worst of it behind us.*

Honey blond hair appears from behind a taller, tuxedoed vampire, and the snide tones of Coraline squash the remaining joy I hold from the dance. "Alexandria, aren't you here early this year?"

Jonathan

CHAPTER TEN

Jonathan

The late afternoon sun glints through the thin trees, catching my eye while I sprint across the property in wolf form. Brush and dried grass snag my fur as my paws sink into the thawing tundra. I've left Eric behind, worried he wouldn't be able to change fast enough to explain to the wolves why they need to return to the inn.

Ice fills my gut at the thought of one of my old packmates being hunted with silver bullets. Who's out here, tracking wolves when they come to play? Has Jerry, the crafty sonovabitch, fooled us all?

A series of muted pops sounds in the distance. I push myself further, stretching my body into longer strides. A low wailing howl reaches my ears followed by a chorus of tortured yowls, a sense of loss hanging in lingering notes.

Werewolf blood floats in the air, along with the loud steps of a human crunching through last year's dead growth. The dark-skinned form of Kotsana looms in front of me, carrying the still body of his wife in his arms. Tears pour down his face, and rage billows from every pore on his well-muscled body.

Three Weres flank him, still in wolf form, herding the man toward the inn, away from death and closer to safety.

"Why?" He weeps into the stillness. "Why would someone shoot Deneishia with silver?"

The wolves around him show teeth, telling me to keep my distance. I have several choices—I could hunt the shooter, find and warn the others, or lead this group to the inn and see to helping the injured wolf. I make a snap decision, bounding off in the direction the survivors came from, anxious to keep everyone from danger.

I race across the sloping hills of the vast Alaskan tundra, skirting the edge of the of Arctic National park. My paw snags in a jagged crevice of ground and momentum tumbles me into a shallow ravine created by frost upheaval. As I pick myself up, I notice I'm not alone.

The distinct gray and brown flecking around Naomi's nose distinguishes her from the rest of her pack. Her whiskey-colored eyes meet mine, but she doesn't move from her prone spot in the mud. I give a soft woof to encourage her, and she glances at her right rear leg. She's caught in a trap. Shiny jaws clamp over the delicate bone, digging deep furrows welling with blood.

The metal is too bright for a traditional bear trap, and judging by Naomi's inability to change back to human and pry the jaws open herself, I'm betting the tooth-like spikes are silver-coated. I push my will to the surface and shift, making the change in lightning speed.

Naked, I crouch next to her and soothe a work-roughened hand down Naomi's back, trying to calm her raised hackles. "Shh, honey. It's just me. I'll have you out of this mess in no time."

Anger boils low inside me, chasing the chill from my bare skin and fueling me to grab the silver-coated metal

Jonathan

without hesitation. Pain singes my fingertips and palms as I pry the trap apart.

A small whine escapes the wolf as Naomi limps forward out of the jagged clutches. "We don't allow traps of this sort —never have." I snap the device in half, ensuring its destruction. Blisters rise on my exposed skin, but I ignore them to examine the gaping wounds on Naomi's shifting leg.

Forcing a change to either form will usually heal minor injuries. Transformation takes longer due to the silver taint, but in a few minutes she's back to normal, standing with blood trickling down the deep mocha skin on her calf. She shakes her head, sending long, skinny black braids in a silky tangle of movement. "The trap was hidden under leaves at the bottom of the ravine. I tripped like you did and went sailing into it."

"How's your leg?"

She tests her weight on it. "Not bad. I think I can run." We climb the sloped side of the fissure, staying low to scan for shooters. "Jon, what the hell is going on up here? First we have one of your guys shot yesterday and now one of ours?"

"Were you there when Deneishia was shot?"

"Nope. They were a few miles away, but I heard it and the pack howls afterward." She scans the horizon before turning to me. "Coast looks clear. Should we sprint for the trees?"

The slender trunks won't offer us much cover, but they are bound to be better than walking the open tundra like sitting ducks. "Yeah, can you handle it?"

Naomi lowers her eyes to take in my dangling junk. "Can you run with that hunk of meat banging against your legs on every stride?"

Heat burns in her gaze and my body instantly responds to her attention. "I'll take that as a 'yes'," I say and playfully smack the toned and well-rounded woman on the ass. "You first, so I can watch you run."

She smiles and meets my eyes, well aware I won't leave her behind and want her in front of me to keep her safe.

We take off and the experience of running combines with the jolt of adrenaline to leave my mind curiously free. I don't feel Vivian's weight in my thoughts and the gorgeous werewolf in front of me starts to look sexier by the second. We make it to the trees without incident.

Naomi eyes my growing erection. "I'm betting whoever squeezed off the shots that hit Deneishia is long gone."

I do my best to stop staring at her pert nipples and ignore the light sheen of sweat making her skin glisten like lickable chocolate.

"Has it been that long Jon?" She smiles to take the sting from her next words. "I would have expected better control during a situation like this from an alpha of your caliber."

I turn my face to the side, refusing to talk about what I can and cannot handle as an alpha. It's a little too late to hide my arousal, so I do my best to think unsexy thoughts and will the blood away from my growing dick. "You're the one eyeing me up and talking about my 'meat'. I'm just a poor guy trying to do good when he sees an old packmate in need of help."

"Uh-huh, sure." Her eyes roam down my body.

"Hey, if you keep looking at me like that, it will continue to grow."

We walk in silence for a few minutes. Which is good. I can't keep up the banter and not get a woody.

Naomi glances sideways at me, to see if I'm under control. "Who could have set that trap if it wasn't one of your employees?"

Her question douses the rest of my arousal and I'm able to focus my attention like I should—scanning the nearby

Jonathan

trees to search for a glint of metal or glare from a scope. "I don't know. That's something we're going to need to talk to everyone about."

"You think it could be one of us?"

"Not everyone has gone on both expeditions, have they?" She snorts her disagreement on my path of reasoning.

"Is your leg holding up?" I refuse to look at her well-muscled calf again when she's naked or I could very well embarrass myself with another half-mast here in the woods.

"Stings, the bleeding has slowed. But I can run."

"Good. We're not safe here. Let's get you back with the others at the inn."

We take a circular route, jogging at an easy pace. We come across another group of four wolves and relay what happened while they stay in wolf form. I don't recognize these by sight and Naomi tells me when they leave that they were two of the three married couples I didn't know well. Now that I think of it, besides Spike, all the lone wolves Romeo's group brought are female. I'm surprised more single men from his pack didn't want to try their luck at big-game hunting, but then again, they may plan on coming later in the season when more large animals are around.

By the time we reach the first family cabins, Naomi is limping. Without a word, I scoop her up and toss her over one shoulder in a fireman's carry.

"Hey!" she squeals in an indignant cry. Quickly, her tone changes. "No, we're good. I've got a great view of your ass from this angle. Forge on, my wolfman!"

The blood rushes to my cock again with her shapely ass mere inches from my face. Damn, maybe this wasn't such a good idea.

Naomi starts to wiggle. "Put me down, now."

"No." I don't want her to see my arousal. Even the smell of her healing wound isn't cooling my interest.

She drives her knee into my chest, loosening my grip to allow her to slide off my shoulder. I try to turn my body to the side so she can't feel my erection, but it's too late, she slides a strong thigh over it on her way down.

In a flash she's wrapped her hot hand over my length and starts to pump me. "Oh, what do we have here?" She reaches her free hand up and pulls me down by the neck for a slow, lingering kiss. Her tongue delves deep into my mouth, and the scent of her own arousal permeates the air.

I pull back. "Naomi, not here." I look wildly at the empty cabins, wondering if I should break down a door to give us privacy. "In a bed, please." My breath comes in pants as she pulls my erection. "When you're bandaged and not bleeding...." A gurgle of sound bubbles in my throat, indicating I'm close to losing what little control I have left. "Where I can treat you right."

She places a finger against my lips while continuing to stroke my aching cock. "Now it's your turn to shush." She shifts her weight, proving she's feeling okay. "What a miracle, I don't feel my wound at all." She amps up the speed of her hand and twists her fist at the end, slicking my own pre-come over the swollen head. "If I don't ease you right now you'll be of no use to me later."

I cup her head with my hands and kiss her deeply. She smells like the forest and green living things, and her grip feels like heaven. No visions of red hair, no lingering thoughts of threesomes.... No dreams of fangs sinking into me when I come. Geez, I better shut down my mind or I'm going to ruin this. I break the kiss, gasping for air. "Oh God, Naomi..."

"That's it, baby, let yourself go."

She returns her mouth to mine and latches onto my bottom lip, tugging it between her lips, sucking. Heat burns the base of my cock, building pressure under her tight grasp.

Jonathan

A rustle sounds to our right, but I ignore it, too close now to care about anything else. Two more solid pumps and release rips from my body, shooting white ribbons of come into the late afternoon air.

My hips jerks with her slowing strokes, each pass a gentle milking of sensation through my attention-starved body. "Christ..." I rest my head on her shoulder, wrapping my arms around her in a loose embrace. "I needed that."

She laughs low, a seductive sound full of promise. "You don't say, huh? That was one of the fastest orgasms I've seen in quite a while, Mr. Alpha."

A guttural growl issues from a scrub brush, pulling us around. Black fur rushes forward, a snarling muzzle showing sharp teeth stops six feet from where my ejaculation hit the ground.

Naomi makes a shooing motion with her hand. "Go away, Spike. We had our fun. You and I have been done for a while."

Spike's golden eyes don't rest on Naomi long, but hover over me instead. "You and he were an item?" The unique smell of the werewolf floats up to tickle my nose. I am not gay, dammit. There is no reason he should smell good to me. Has being tied to Vivian for so long somehow fucked up my sense of who I'm attracted to? Then again, I had no problem getting hard over Naomi's glorious ass, so that can't be it. Maybe I'm bi and didn't know it? Attraction is attraction; no reason to place a label on it. I must be doing it now to ease my own confusion.

Naomi turns her back on Spike to show what she thinks of him and tugs me along to walk next to her. "I wouldn't say we were an item. But we had fun once or twice."

Spike trails behind us and growls again when I glance sideways at Naomi's impressive rack. "Was it once or was it twice? And did you dump him?" I look over my shoulder to see the snarling form pacing us about four feet. "Back off, old man. You had your chance."

She huffs and pouts a bit. "If you must know, last fall he licked my pussy like he couldn't get enough. He visits here in January, and then poof, comes back distant. Now he's just interested again because I'm not. Typical jealous werewolf shit."

January was when Spike locked eyes with me and I could have sworn he looked like a woman for a split second. What I really need to figure out is whether Spike's growling his displeasure at my actions or Naomi's? Or maybe he's more annoyed at our timing? After all his packmate has been shot, and I'm the one getting jerked off without a care in the world.

Stupid fool, that's what I am. Alphas don't get a break. Especially when those they're supposed to protect are injured. I straighten my shoulders, slightly disgusted by my own behavior. I wouldn't stop Spike if he decided to bite me instead of just growling like a fiend.

The fun and diversion of the last few minutes melts the moment we enter the hot tub grotto. Tension from the shooting pulses back to life and our little moment of happiness is over. Naomi looks wistfully at me and whispers, "Our time will have to wait, Jon. We've got much more pressing matters, now."

I nod and pat her shoulder as I walk away; grateful she's got a good head on her shoulders and isn't clinging to my side like we're now a mated pair or something dramatic like that.

The sun hasn't quite set, so Asa won't be able to come outdoors yet. Eric and Pat mill about the cooking area near the dining room entrance, handing out sweat pants and towels for showering werewolves. I stroll up to them, hoping the smell of my own release is hidden by the press of furry

Jonathan

and non-furry bodies in the area. And if it isn't, fuck it. Neither of them have the balls to call me out on the inappropriate timing on my part.

Hey, she grabbed my cock. Not like I asked her to. Why does it sound as if I'm trying to convince myself my behavior a few minutes ago wasn't reprehensible? Why is Spike walking close enough to get his nose in my ass? I turn and swat the wet snout, telling him succinctly to back off.

"How is Denieshia?" I ask the pups. "Any word?"

Eric hands me a towel, raising an eyebrow when I don't take it right away. What can I say; I'm comfortable being naked. Once I take the towel he answers, "She lost a lot of blood. I'm not sure how she's doing."

"Where are her alphas?" I ask, scanning the changed forms in the patio area for signs of Elsa or Romeo. It doesn't look like everyone from their pack is here.

"Romeo hasn't come back. Elsa is downstairs with Kotsana and the doctor."

"Deneishia's husband is one large scary dude," Pat says "Kind of reminds me of The Rock." At my blank stare he continues, "You know Dwayne Johnson? The *Scorpion King* dude?"

"Uh-huh, yeah. I'm sure he gives a shit about celebrity look-alikes when his wife has just been shot." Pat flushes slightly at my chastisement. "If she doesn't make it we're going to have one really big, grief-crazed guy. Think about it like that instead."

"Is that why Asa has a big tranquilizer rifle?" Eric asks.

I nod and head toward the owners' apartment. "Yup. He and I wrote down a bunch of protocols in case things went south this summer. Although, we certainly didn't bargain on someone shooting the wolves when we thought up problems."

109

A gut-wrenching howl of pain echoes from the house, and the massive form of Kotsana's half-changed werewolf hurls through the window over the kitchen sink. He growls and slashes at everyone close to him then charges at breakneck speed through the winding paths of the landscaped area.

"Oh, shit," I say, fearing the worst. The tired wolves near us race off, in the hopes of tracking down their packmate before he harms himself.

A window on the second floor opens. The barrel of the tranquilizer gun slides out and aims in the direction Kotsana headed. A small puff of sound sends a brightly colored dart zipping after the rampaging werewolf.

Asa leans out the window wearing a ski mask despite the beginning of twilight and yells, "His wife is gone. Drag him back here so we can restrain him before the tranqs wear off."

Chapter Eleven

Rafe

The overpowering odor of blood in the banquet room has diminished thanks to the strong coroner's gel under my nose. I thought I could take the stink, but after tangling with Coraline and her henchman, my senses were alert to danger and the added adrenaline running through my system made the aromas impossible to ignore.

We've sat through three courses of vampire dishes and regular food served together. To be safe, Dria declined all of the blood concoctions. And I'll admit, I've had a hard time eating with the dark red offerings sharing the same table space with my meal.

"No, thank you," she says to a waiter offering a lumpy looking, disgusting blood pudding.

I stifle my gag reflex as our two undead dining companions dig in, excited by the extravagance and expense shown by the Tribunal. Their dates ignore the red glop set close to their own place settings and enjoy the cheesecake served to the humans.

My stomach gives a heave and Dria rests her hand on my sleeve. *Settle, darling. It would be uncouth of you to vomit right here at the table.*

A queasy smile crosses my face as I try to turn my attention solely on her rather than the feasting vampires surrounding me. *I don't know why it's bothering me so much this year.*

Could you be pregnant? She says with an amused lilt to her tone.

Gee, thanks.

Maybe it's because in previous years we've skipped these tiresome meals and gone off somewhere to fornicate like horny teenagers while they're served.

Even thoughts of sex can't turn my mind away from the revolting dishes circulating during the dinner. Blood soup? I think I spotted some congealed lumps and clots in there. A spasm clenches my stomach, and Dria rises from the table.

"Excuse us," she says to our unknown table companions. "We're off to enjoy other entertainments for the evening." My wife grabs my hand and leads me to a curtained alcove off the main foyer, outside the dining room.

I ease onto the red crushed velvet chaise while she closes the curtains. Dria turns to me, concern filling her face. *Are you okay?*

Yes. Just not myself with all the dishes and the eating. Really grossed me out tonight for some reason.

This coming from the man who can watch a Saw *marathon while eating spaghetti, then sleep like a baby?*

I grin at her mention of my love of horror films, all films actually, but everyone must have a few hobbies to keep them sane. The difference is I know those are all fake. *Aside from the fact serial killers really do exist, it's quite different sitting in a room with several hundred vampires consuming human blood dishes like we're at a State dinner.*

Dria nods and sits next to me, running a hand over my back in a soothing gesture. *If it makes you feel any better, I*

think they used some cow and goat blood for the soup to set it off from the other dishes.
If you all can drink animal blood, why don't you? I never understood that.
It doesn't have the same nutritional value and doesn't taste as good. She stops caressing my back when she hears voices approach the alcove next to us. *Compare it with eating bugs everyday rather than following the food pyramid. Some things you were meant to have on a daily basis, and others, like crickets, will only suffice when you are extremely desperate.*

The rustle of clothes and the rasp of a lowering zipper reach us through the wall and in a moment the sounds of new passion greet our sensitive ears. As far as distractions from the dinner goes, it's a nice one—I absentmindedly listen to the creaking of furniture as the chaise next door gets a good pounding.

What was your impression of Coraline and Lucas earlier? Dria asks, seemingly oblivious to the noises of randy coupling drifting through the wall.

She didn't seem to know about your mind manipulation in January, but she still hates your guts and suspects you of something. A low moan from a woman with whispers of "please, please…" have me picturing the last hour we spent on the airplane before landing yesterday. I shift in my seat, trying to push out the naked images of making love to my wife that the primal sounds induce.

Dria pats her hair, checking to make sure the pins are tight in her upsweep. *Lucas has always had an axe to grind with me. I wasn't surprised he ran off to find Cora the moment he could.*

Who was that striking Mediterranean-looking woman with the long dark hair and strong nose who called the two away?

113

She calls herself Persephone. I can't imagine she was born with that name. She's one of the Ancients.

The fucking next door takes on a higher new level. When it's apparent the woman is close to climaxing, I rise from the chaise. I pace to the curtains in two strides and turn back. "Unless you want me bending you over this chaise, we need to leave."

My wife smiles and joins me at the curtain. *Tempting offer, but I can wait 'til we're alone in our own room. Can you?*

The woman's orgasm shatters the last of my control. I grab my wife and kiss her deeply as the waves of the woman's crest sounds a few feet away. "Yes, my pet," comes a husky whispered voice in the neighboring alcove. "Now, come for me again while I feed."

I break off our kiss, all too aware of the danger around us in the Seat of Darkness and yank our curtain open. This is not the time to lose myself in my wife's body. Heading quickly across the foyer, I hear the woman's next release while her vampire lover pushes her into the abyss of pleasure.

The lights and sounds of the gambling room are loud enough to drown out the frantic fornicating. My cock is tucked tight against my body and its growing thickness will soon be noticeable if I don't clear my head of the enticing noises. Dria catches up to me, the grinning minx, and slips her hand around the crook of my bent elbow.

"You ran out of there like the hounds of hell were on your heels." A hint of laughter sounds in her tone.

"What can I say? I'm a guy and the sound of people going at it and enjoying themselves flips all my switches."

The room you chose may not be a good one if you're becoming aroused.

Rafe

I look at the gaming tables filled with vampires holding cards and tossing dice and wonder what she means. I've been to a few of these big soirees in the past, but they didn't offer gambling.

What could be the big deal? They're betting with cash chips, right? I can handle that.

Not always, my dear. Stay on your toes. I'm not a fan of what goes on when my kind decides to gamble.

We stroll past craps tables and come to a thick gathering of male and female vampires around a slim counter. A gorgeous young blond woman stands on a raised dais behind it. She's dressed in a short, pagan-inspired robe with fall leaves woven through a complex braided hairstyle. A lighted sign states her blood type as AB negative, her age, and her sexual orientation as bi. The sheer fabric of her robe hugs her tiny breasts and her dark, aroused nipples stand erect underneath, begging to be sucked.

"Modified black jack," a young vampire shuffling a deck of cards states. He's behind the table facing the crowd, while chips are tossed into a pile from the waiting vamps. "Highest hand from two cards, without going over twenty-one, wins her for the night. Tie for best cards settled with a second hand." He motions an arm to the woman on display. "She hasn't fed a vampire in a month. She's aroused and ready to go."

To emphasize his words, the young woman slips a hand between her legs, drawing up the short robe as she fingers her swollen nether lips.

"Come, my dear," Dria says while the eager vampires step up to receive two cards from the deck. "You won't be able to handle the rest."

"What? Why? They aren't going to hurt her are they?"

A throaty laugh spills from my semi-immortal wife. "No, darling. But the winner is going to feed from her in front of the ones who lost... and sometimes they wind up doing more than feeding."

I've been to Tribunal parties where public sex happened on stages, and lots of semi-private pairings, like we heard in the alcove—and a few rare gatherings that had a BDSM feel to them. But I've never been to one that gambled with sex.

"Fascinating," I say as the whoop from the winner reaches my ears. We head to another table with the name "The Best Bite" broadcast on a lighted sign. Female names and times show on an electronic scoreboard, and stacks of chips on a red felt betting table cover other names spread across the width.

A tuxedoed male vampire with long blond hair tied in a ponytail steps forward and says to the gentleman taking bets, "Put me down for a thousand on Gerald, I bet he can make Veronica come for over two minutes." The man's bet is taken, and he turns, catching a glimpse of us.

"Alexandria! You're not entering the challenge are you?" He smiles and quickly kisses my wife square on the mouth, like I'm not standing next to her. Arrogant prick. "If you are I'm changing my bet. You always were quite talented in making it last well past the others."

"Hello, Daniel. Good to see you. You do remember my husband, Rafe?"

Daniel looks to me and a brief flash of recognition crosses his features. "Oh yes, how could any of us forget the big strapping German who caught your eye and turned you monogamous?" He offers me a hand and a genuine smile to show he's teasing. "No harm, old man. We had our fun decades before you were born."

I ignore the slow burn in my gut, not willing to rise to the bait. I know well my wife's sexual appetites before we were together; after all, she didn't turn into this sensual creature who feeds off of lust after meeting me. But, I also know none of the dalliances in the last few centuries touched her heart.... or she would have kept one of them.

"Really? She never mentioned you." I smile with all my teeth, to show I did mean the sting. Nothing deflates a guy's ego as much as finding out he's so unmemorable in a woman's life she doesn't even mention him to her husband.

Play nice, honey. You know I don't remember the encounters because they meant nothing to me... literally. Just a means to an end.

Oh, I do know. That's why it's so fun to rub it in.

"Don't mind him, Daniel," Dria says with warmth I know she's not feeling. "We're both tired from the flight. Arrived late last night."

He turns from me and shines a charming smile at my wife. "Are you staying in the city? I'd love to get together after this for a... chat. Assuming your husband lets you out alone?" A glint of something more lingers in his eye, and I hold back the urge to punch the fucker in the face. As if any human mate would be able to tell their vampire spouse what to do. Jackass is trying to piss me off.

"We're staying on the premises." Dria's eyes travel away from Daniel, dismissing his unspoken offer as if it was never implied. "I'm sure if you're around we'll meet up."

A slight grimace passes over Daniel's Nordic features, but he quickly hides it. The betting behind him heats up, and he turns his attention to the action. Dria tugs my hand and we walk down the line of bidding vampires, passing a display of women wearing ball gowns and standing on raised platforms.

"No skimpy clothes at this one?" I ask. "No nubile young woman feeling herself up to get their interest flowing? Seems rather staid compared to the last offering."

Dria smiles her famous enigmatic grin, indicating she's either amused, pissed off, or not really paying attention.

"The contestant must bring her to orgasm with just their bite and is not allowed to touch her genitals for added stimulation. The longest orgasm wins."

My mind travels back to the tantric bite we shared when Dria turned Paul on the icy path in Alaska. "Huh." That orgasm she gave me was a full body release lasting minutes on end, and she never touched my cock. I'm not really sure of the exact duration because I wasn't timing it. "I bet you did well at this game."

She looks at me sideways, the corner of her mouth curving in a smirk. "I always won." My half-stiff cock threatens to turn into full arousal at the memory of that cold night. Yeah, it sucked Paul had to be turned, but damn, that was an interesting bite.

We stroll to a craps table as the bidding continues behind us. "Maybe we could go back and watch that one when the game begins?"

Dria turns to me and pulls my head down to hers. She kisses me hard, pouring her passion for me into the exchange, in front of all the attending vampires. *The evening is still early, my love. Can you hold back for a little longer, or must I satisfy you now because you're too riled up?*

I break off our kiss and turn to the craps table. *I'm not some schoolboy who has no discipline... But, to be honest, I am affected by all the sex swirling around us.*

She smiles and steps up the table, preparing to bet. *You're not expected to be immune to it. If the vampires rouse the sexual appetites of all the humans, their own subsequent feedings will be more exciting and passion filled. The entire event is calculated to bring maximum pleasure for everyone attending.*

Yeah, I figured as much when we attended the live sex show a few years back. *You and I barely made it to a deserted room in time.* I smile at the memory while signaling to a chip girl circulating through the crowd. Peeling off ten one hundreds from my money clip, I hand them to the young woman dressed like a woodland fairy and collect chips for my wife.

Dria turns to me with one gloved hand raised to receive the chips. *Yes, but we weren't trying to discover who knows about my manipulator capabilities back then.* She faces the table and leans over the side to place her bet, her movements pulling the satin fabric of her dress tight across her ass in the process.

More than one man eyes my wife's backside before I step forward and nestle myself behind her. She straightens and looks over her shoulder at me. "Want to blow on the dice before I toss them?"

I lean and pucker my lips, blowing softly on the cubes laid in her gloved palm, staring intently into my lover's green eyes while I do so. Aroused heat sparks her gaze, threatening to overwhelm her motives for only a moment before she stifles her growing urges with ease.

I check out the other occupants surrounding the table and see mostly vampire men. I can't help but notice the event seems like an undead sausage party, regarding the ratio of male to female vampires. Why has this escaped my attention before?

Dria tosses the die while I mentally ask, *How many female vampires are there?*

The cubes roll to a stop at the end of the table. A two and a five show face up. The group cheers and Dria is handed the dice again while bets are placed. *I don't have an exact number for you, but I'd say as a norm there are two to three times as many males who survive past fledgling status than females.*

Why?

Most of the women are killed by other women, proving we're far more power hungry than the males.

I place my hands on her hips when she offers the dice again for me to blow. Cora pushes her way through the gathering and looks at the two of us with a snarl of hatred on her face. "How about we make the stakes more interesting on this hand?" No telling what that nasty bitch has in mind. "Or can you not throw dice well under pressure, Alexandria the Great?"

The excited tension surrounding the gambling table pauses as attention shifts to Coraline. I have no doubt the oldest bloodsuckers know exactly who my wife was when an enforcer, but I still don't understand why it bothers Coraline so much. A man of Asian descent with long black hair responds to her question, "What did you have in mind?"

Cora glances around the table, her gaze lingering on the human companions standing behind the betting vampires. "Why not a blood bet? Highest winner on a losing roll gets to taste the dice thrower's date?"

All eyes swivel to me and I suddenly feel like a bachelor auctioned as an escort at a charity event. I never would have thought this many male vampires preferred men, but they're looking at me like they might want a piece of me. Then again, she did say blood, not sex. I resist the self-preserving urge to shrink from a group of hungry predators and hold my ground, gripping my wife's hips more firmly to convey my displeasure at the suggestion.

I never needed to worry. Anger leaks from Dria and pushes out to encompass the entire table in one fell swoop of power. A buzzing tingle coats my skin, feeling like the blood rushing through a limb that fell asleep. The energy shuts down almost as quick as it occurred, but those standing near us cannot doubt its origins.

Rafe

A few gasps sound as Cora's smile grows larger at Dria's slip. Bitch orchestrated the whole thing.

My wife's voice comes in a rough whisper, expressing great control, "I do not share what is mine." She crushes the dice in her hand and sprinkles the dust on the felt. A dark-skinned vampire of Arabic descent standing near Coraline studies Dria with a calculated eye.

My wife pushes from the edge of table and stalks off to collect herself. Cora watches her leave then shifts her attention back to me. Gaming has stopped while the others absorb what they felt and what just happened. Cora's eyes narrow on me. "I wonder what makes you so special?"

"It's called love." I reply before turning away. "You should try it sometime."

Chapter Twelve
Asa

Jerry settles onto the couch in Vivian and Rafe's small office. The gray light of early evening shines through the window as I flick on a desk lamp. Grabbing an armchair, I drag it to the resident electrician's side. I take a seat and stare into the old engineer's hazel eyes, mentally preparing myself that this man I admire could actually be our shooter.

Pushing out my will, I lay a mind compulsion in my words. "You will answer all of my questions truthfully."

He nods and sits forward, running a hand through his gray hair and messing it up. "Let's get this over already. I've got plans with Margery later. Assuming she's not patching up more guests, that is."

"Did you shoot any wolves yesterday or today?"

"No."

"Do you know of anyone employed here who hates Jon's wolf-dogs enough to go after them?"

A snort comes from Jerry as he looks away and then back to me. "No one would harm those dogs after what they did to protect the children when Ivan was loose last fall."

Good point. I wondered at the validity of that question when Jon presented it. "Does anyone besides you have silver bullets?"

He shrugs and settles back on the couch. "Not that I know of. Only Margery and you bloodsuckers know I have them and make my own."

Jerry is one of the few on the resort who doesn't donate blood and knows what we are. I have no idea why Vivian allows it, but I'm sure she has her reasons. Seems odd that he'd tell the aging doctor about his silver bullets. "Why does the doctor know?"

"Because I love her, you fool." He grumps and gets to his feet, looming over me in his indignation. "A man shouldn't keep secrets from the woman he loves."

Knowing my vamp whammy is still in place whether I stare at him or not, I continue my questions. "Have you seen any new faces recently on the property?"

"No." He paces to the door.

"Where did you go on leave?"

Jerry spins back around, a spark of anger lighting his face. "I went to Fairbanks. Are we almost through here?"

I rise from the chair and walk to the older man. I stare into his hazel eyes and say, "You will forget this conversation and think we discussed an upcoming change to the generators."

"Fine." Not missing a beat, he opens the door then turns back at me. "Get me those plans for approval before you order anything, got it?"

I smile and nod my head. "Yes, sir. You have my word."

He storms through the kitchen, passing Romeo and Elsa seated with Jon at a round table. The back door slams on his way out, and the three alphas look to me. "He wasn't involved. Doesn't know of anyone who could be doing the shooting, and no one else has silver ammo—as far as he knows."

Before questioning Jerry, Romeo came in with another male Were from his pack. Each man carried the bleeding form of an injured werewolf in his arms. The patients are now downstairs receiving medical attention from Dr. Cook. Jerry's plans with the doctor will have to wait a little while, but damned if I was going to be the one to tell him.

Jon's shoulders ease from hearing the shooter wasn't Jerry, but tension still pinches his face and rolls off him in waves. A wail of despair comes from the direction of the basement.

"Has Kotsana been properly confined?" Romeo asks.

"He's been drugged and placed in a vampire safe room down below. Should hold him."

Elsa's delicate features and short pixie haircut look out of place on the sad alpha. "Jon, does anyone hate you enough to be doing this?"

Jon sits up a bit and looks to his former leader. "What makes you so sure it's because of me? The lot of you could have led an enemy here from Manitoba."

Romeo shakes his head. "It's too thought out, boy. Can't you see that? Scouting and setting traps takes more than a few hours. Whoever is doing this was here first."

I pull up a chair and sip bloodcoffee in a travel mug, not willing to let myself lose control of my cravings with this many injured bodies occupying the inn. "So, you're both suggesting this hunter, or hunters, was here before your plane arrived yesterday, right?" They both nod. "Who knew of your plans to come up here?"

The couple's faces cloud over. "Pretty much everyone in our entire pack," Elsa answers. Jon swears under his breath.

I set my mug down on the table. "And exactly how big is your pack?"

Romeo says, "Fifty. But they are spread out over the province. And no, they don't all get along."

"Are some married outside of the pack? Like to non-Weres?" Jon asks.

"Yes, one or two are even mated to vampires."

I wonder if those vampires get addicted to their mates' potent werewolf blood. But then again, Vivian never has with Jon's, so maybe it's not an immediate addiction with every pairing. "You can rule out the vampires, too much sunlight up here with no place to hide. It's not like there's a hotel near by."

Jon stares off with a speculative expression. "We do have all those empty cabins."

Romeo dismisses it with a wave of his hand. "We'd have smelled any vampires near the cabins."

Jon runs a hand over his face, for a moment looking much older than his normal mid-twenties appearance. "Essentially all of your pack's human mates could know as well?"

A little sound of distress comes from Elsa. "And not all of them have relatives who like werewolves."

Jon stands up and crosses to the fridge for a bottled water. "Weren't the mates sworn to silence?" He whirls back, anger evident on his face. "How could you let this many people be aware we exist?"

Romeo stands, his own frustration spilling out when he stands nose to nose with Jon. "Lots of people know about our species. We've been living amongst humans for millennia. You can't blame my wolves—"

"Calm down, you two. And sit!" Elsa barks out. The two men jump at her sharp tone and take a step away from one another. Romeo leans against a counter, deliberately not sitting, and Jon stands near the fridge. If it weren't so dangerous having two alphas ready to throw down in a cramped kitchen, I'd have laughed at how they both refused to obey the request. But the truth is, we need them working together right now.

"Do you think lots of people know about werewolves, vampires, magic, and all this supernatural crap?" I ask, completely unaware of what the answer might be.

Romeo answers, while Jon stares out the window. "There are always a few who have known." He shrugs. "How many exactly? I'm not sure. Thankfully, they sound crazy if they tell anyone, so we've gone undiscovered for the most part."

I take a sip from my travel mug and place it on the table. "Isn't it also possible then that someone who knows of our existence might not accept us?"

"You mean those who've tried to eradicate us in the past?" Elsa asks. "Like supernatural hunters?"

I nod. "Makes sense. Hell, if I found out there was a pack of werewolves vacationing in the woods of my old home town I'd probably have been out there with a rifle."

"He's right." Jon says, letting out a deep sigh. "Ignorance breeds hatred and fear of the unknown. Not acceptance and tolerance."

The phone attached to the kitchen wall rings, and I scramble to answer it, wondering why whoever it is didn't call one of our cells. "Yeah?"

One of the airplane mechanic's frantic voices comes over the line. "All of the planes have been vandalized."

"Calm down. Tell me what happened." The wolves with their sharp hearing sit up and listen to both sides of the conversation.

"Someone who knows planes systematically removed the starters and shredded all the electrical wiring to the panels."

My mind whirs, searching for possible ways we could still escape. "How long will it take to fix?"

Asa

"Days, and that's if I can find everything I need in storage."

"Get on it. Keep us posted."

The call ends and I look to the wolves one by one around the kitchen. "I'm sure none of our people did this. I would have heard a hint in the probing I did in their minds last night."

"It's time we face what we don't want to admit," Jon says, coming back to the table and lowering into a seat. "We've got supernatural hunters gunning for werewolves—and they aren't going about it half assed."

"These aren't just guys with guns," Elsa adds. "They're armed with silver and are systematically eliminating any chance we have of going for help."

"What about the roads?" Romeo asks. "Can't we drive away?"

Jon runs a hand over his hair, mussing it up. "No. This time of year the roads are un-navigable. Only one leads to Coldfoot and it's almost as dangerous right now as in a snowstorm. The planes were the only way out."

"And they knew that," I say. "Which means they arrived here by air, as well."

"Rather than discuss how they got here," Elsa says, "we need to make sure our people are safe. Let's pull everyone to the inn and regroup. Brainstorming together may help determine who is hunting us and why, but we still need to figure a way out of this mess."

I finally dig out my cell phone, remembering the mechanic didn't call that number first. The screen is blank, showing no reception. "Crap."

"What is it now?" Jon asks.

"My cell is out. That's why the guy called on the resort number—landlines are buried underground."

"What does that mean?" Romeo pushes off the counter and pulls his own cell phone from his pocket. "Why are our cells out?"

"It means whoever is after us has sabotaged our satellite dishes as well," I answer. "We're not going to have any Internet access. The regular phones could be next."

Jon shakes his head. "The phone wires might be underground, but if the hunters cut them at the pole that leads into Coldfoot we'll only be able to reach local business extensions to the main buildings and services on the resort."

"We need to call all the cabins while we still can," I say, reaching for the phone.

"Get the wolves based here at the inn." He moves down the hall, heading toward the office with the multiline phone. "I'll start calling the apartments and confining staff inside their homes."

"Do you really think they'll shoot the employees?"

"I'm not willing to find out. Anyone who helps us could be a target."

Chapter Thirteen

Drew

*I*t's well past two a.m. and my latest call to Jon has gone to voicemail, just like the one to Asa did a half hour ago. If things are going well there the wolves may still be out running the property. The spring melt conjures images of really filthy wolves shaking all over our pristine inn. Ugh. If the damn beasts didn't taste so good, I wouldn't see the need to keep the species around.

Rafe informed me of Pat's close call in the woods before he and Viv left for Buenos Aires. I'm sure the young Were is fine; wolves heal almost as fast as we do. I wonder if the Alaskan crew has figured out which employee may have been hunting sooner than the season allows.

I pace back and forth in our suite, debating on calling Rafe since I haven't heard from them recently, either. They should have landed hours ago and, while I would normally wait until I'd heard from Jon or Asa, a nagging apprehension trickles through my connection to Vivian.

Calling her direct could rile her up and piss her off more, one thing I'm loath to do—or it might settle the discomfort niggling in the back of my brain. I snatch up my cell, grateful Chelly went downstairs to watch a movie with Tommy and

Bob, giving me privacy to call. She really does have a good head on her shoulders, that one.

Decision made, I dial Rafe's number, knowing he's the more even keeled of the two. Managing a volatile master is nothing new in a seethe, no matter where you are. They don't become the masters of a seethe because they're pushovers.

After a few rings, the calm tones of the human radiate across the line. "Yes, Drew?" The sound of tango music grows fainter as if he's distancing himself from the source of the music.

"I hadn't heard from you and wanted to check in." I continue my pacing, unsure where the nervousness is originating.

"We landed a while ago and are currently holding our own at the event."

"Is Vivian okay? I think I'm getting a lot of hazy impressions coming through our connection. Like she's anxious."

"You 'think'?" he asks, puzzlement in his tone. "Wouldn't you be sure of your connection with her by now?"

I shake my head, trying to piece together what I mean. "I know I sound a bit like Paul right now—unsure and slightly out of sorts. But I've never felt such agitation through the link before. That's why I'm not sure if it's coming from her or not."

Rafe sighs, and I hear a door shut, muting the music. "It's a safe bet the agitation is coming from her, and that she just hasn't been shielding as well as she normally does. There are a lot of people here who dislike my wife."

"Any leads on who could be working with Coraline?"

Rafe is silent a moment, perhaps checking to make sure he's not overheard or weighing how much he should tell me, I'm not sure. "One named Lucas has motive to hate her, plus some guy named Jonah – possibly for the same reason. And three or four others who hide their hate and dislike rather poorly, but I don't know their names. They are avoiding us and watching from the sidelines."

I've never understood the grudges some of these older vamps hold onto. The hardest part in vampire politics is in not knowing whom you've slighted enough to make them want to bury a stake in your back when you aren't looking.

"That seems like an awful lot in so little time—you've been there only four hours, right?"

Rafe barks out a short laugh. "My lovely wife has had more than four centuries to make enemies of these bastards —even I don't know all her exploits."

I stop my pacing and slump into one of the club chairs in the sitting area. "What do you plan to do?"

A heavy sigh comes over the line. "Nothing tonight, as far as I can tell. I'm not sure how many of these guests will remain past morning. A few may stay for entreaties to the Tribunal."

Vivian briefed us that some seethe masters come to these events to play "court", similar to Europeans with the reigning monarchy centuries ago. Hobnobbing and mingling with peers to gain something for their family, arrange for a seethe transfer of a lower vampire, angle a marriage match among powerful undead, or for something as simple as securing a business loan from the Tribunal.

"Do you know when you'll be back?"

"We're still not sure, but the animosity swirling around is making this much harder than I thought to narrow the suspect pool."

"Getting Coraline *alone* might be what you really need," I say, hinting that Vivian could use her mind powers to force the information out of the blond vamp.

"We've discussed that, too. But she may have some protective magic around her like before—and triggering it so close to where the wielder might be is a big mistake."

"So effectively Vivian is flying blind? And you two are winging it?"

An edge creeps into Rafe's voice, "My wife and I have other strengths to get a job done, Drew."

"Right. I'm sure." I backpedal as best I can, realizing I'm close to insubordination and thankfully not messing up this call with Vivian right now.

"Have you connected with Asa or Jon yet?" Rafe asks, clearly willing to change the topic as well.

"No, both calls went to their voicemail."

A grunt sounds at the end of the line. "Give them an hour, and if you don't hear from them, call Cy."

"Sir?"

"Jon and Asa are both responsible. It's not normal for neither to pick up the phone, and Asa's training would ensure he'd call back asap, if he could."

A cold coils through my hand and I grip the phone tighter as I sit up straight. "Do you think something happened to them?"

"I'm not sure of anything, but we have protocols in place for a reason. If you don't hear from them, assume the worst and call in backup."

"Cy is pretty far away."

"He's less than twelve hours by plane, we're much further, and Vivian trusts him. That's the best we've got."

The realization this is not some getaway love-tryst with Chelly hits me hard. Tension tightens in my gut, and for the first time since we left Alaska I'm experiencing real worries. I'm next in line for making decisions with Jon unreachable and so far away. With less than six months in the seethe, I can't begin to guess the exact path my master might take in an emergency."

"Do you really think something might be happening up there?"

"Like I said, I have no idea. Vivian will take no chances when it comes to her vampire servant's safety."

"Yes, sir." I stand and turn to the balcony, gazing out at the sparkling lights of the tiny port town on the distant shore. "I'll call Cy when it hits two hours, okay?"

"Make it an hour. Asa is awake and there is no excuse for him, he's too good."

I glance at my watch and realize ten minutes will be an hour since I first called him. The music in the background grows, indicating Rafe has opened a door toward the noise and is perhaps about to end the call. "Rafe, wait!"

"Yes?"

"When should I check in with you again?"

"As soon as you hear from the boys on the resort. And if you don't, we check in every twelve hours. I don't trust this pack of bloodsucking fiends as far as I can throw them."

"Yes, sir."

We end the call and I run a nervous hand through my rumpled hair. The agitation doesn't end, and in my selfish mind, one thing stands above all others: I've not bound Chelly to me. She's not protected from other vampires.

I don't truly think we're in danger here in the couple's safe house on their remote island, but with the Seat of Darkness only a few hours away.... It's never good to let loved ones travel close to that danger without every protection you can provide.

Have I been a fool to drag out our union? Should I just follow her urging and get it over with? My gut clenches at the thought of rushing her seduction and our relationship. If I wanted a *slam bam thank you ma'am* encounter, I wouldn't have chosen Chelly. I hope for her to be my next wife, and that kind of intention deserves more than how you'd treat a quick blood snack.

On the other hand, not sharing my blood leaves her vulnerable. Other vampires smell she's a donor by my taint on her, and yet, without my blood scent coursing through her veins, marking her, she has no protection and retains the status of simply a willing donor among a pack of predators.

A knock on our suite door brings me around, and the beautiful blond head of my love pokes past the door. "Can I come in now? The movie was boring. I heard no voices in here and assumed you'd finished."

I nod and she enters, dressed in a snug long sleeved t-shirt and yoga pants, showing off her ample curves and robust good health. My eyes linger over the cleavage on display in the deep vee of her shirt and then trail down to the full breadth of her hips. No stick-like women for me. I prefer mine to look like real women—not pre-pubescent children. She's simply gorgeous, and I can't wait another moment to mark her as mine.

I hold out a hand to her. She notices the heat in my gaze and a slow seductive smile spreads across her lips. "Have you been thinking about me recently? You're eyes don't look too innocent."

My eagerness edges close to hysteria. I fear I'm going to fumble through this like some untried youth. I take a deep breath, and meet her halfway across the room. Wrapping my arms around her, I lean her back and nibble on her throat. "Do you know how much I want you, Chelly?"

"Oh, my. Keep kissing my neck like that and you can have anything you want."

I trail a hot path down her exposed skin, stopping before I'm tempted to nuzzle the fabric aside and explore the

Drew

creamy mounds of her full breasts. "I want to make you mine," I whisper against her throat.

She straightens. "Now, we're talking." Her hands tug her shirt up half way. "I can't say I've minded the wait, but damn, I'm more than ready."

I still her hands and stare into her dark blue eyes. "I want to share blood with you, Chelly. I want you to give blood only to me, to no other vampire. I want them to scent me in you... running through your veins."

My motives are pure, even if my timing is spurred by anxiety. Chelly stares at me. I see moisture pooling in her eyes. "I'd like that, Drew. Are you sure?"

I kiss her mouth. "More sure than anything I've ever done."

"Will it hurt?"

I smile, with my fangs fully descended, expressing my desire in my eyes and in the natural reaction from a vampire about to feed. "Not at all, my dear." I sit on the edge of the bed and pull her to straddle my lap.

A nervous giggle escapes my lover. "Drew, I think I'm falling in love with you." She ducks her head slightly and looks at me through eyelashes. "Does that sound silly when we haven't even made love yet?"

My cock surges to life in the confines of my trousers, which she can easily sense through the thin material of her yoga pants. Heat boils from her core as she rubs herself back and forth against my hardening length.

"It's not silly at all." I place my hands on both sides of her face to tilt her eyes up to look at me full on. "Without love, it's not making love, is it?"

She gives her head a soft shake and leans in to kiss me. My tongue slices on one sharp canine, allowing blood to trickle into my mouth. Chelly's lips press to mine and then her tongue tangles with my own. Blood eases gently into her.

The cut I inflicted quickly heals, but enough has gone into my lover to mark her as mine and keep her safe from other vampires.

To willingly try and feed off of someone's servant is asking for a fight. Dueling to the death among our kind is rare and purposeful slights will only escalate if a fight was the intention all along.

We kiss breathlessly, me murmuring heated endearments while Chelly grinds over my cock. The clock on the wall chimes once, reminding me it's half past two and well beyond the one-hour mark from when I should have heard from Asa. Reality crashes in and my body physically hurts to stop what we so deliciously started with a simple kiss.

I ease away, taking a shuddering breath. Resting my forehead against hers, I run a hand down her back to soothe our raging bodies. "I'm sorry. I have to make one more phone call. It's important or I wouldn't bother. Can we pick up in five minutes?"

Chelly swings a leg off my lap and rises, a mischievous twinkle in her eye. "I'm going to go run a bath in that big tub built for two. If you don't come in and join me soon, I may just have to finish off myself without you." She pulls her tight shirt off and slowly glides hands up to cup her bra-covered breasts. She thumbs her nipples poking through the lacey covering. "And it will be your loss, trust me."

She sashays away and shuts the bathroom door behind her. The water starts running and my girlfriend hums a happy little tune. She's "falling in love." Hell, I've fallen already and can hardly wait to tell her—saving it for the second I finally thrust deep inside her.

I grab my cell and dial Asa and then Jon again in quick succession. Still no answer. I bite the bullet and place a call to Cy. I don't think anything bad is going on in Alaska, but

Drew

damned if I can't follow a few simple instructions from one of my bosses, either.

Chapter Fourteen

Jonathan

The mid-size conference room in the basement, the one that magically transformed into a forest under Vivian's illusion in January, doesn't seem large enough to hold all the high-tempered Weres. As I scan from one enraged face to the next, I'm sure of it. The room is stifling, and I tamp down the urge to scream *shut the fuck up*.

Romeo and Elsa sit together at one end of the table and the rest of their pack is squeezes around, some seated, others standing. Asa takes a position behind me, unobtrusively holding up the wall in one corner. Eric and Pat flank me in chairs at the table.

Damn, what a struggle getting all the wolves changed back to human form with the scent of blood riding the air—then cleaned up, and fed—but we did it.

Unfortunately, two more guests suffered flesh wounds before returning to the inn. Gunfire can be heard for several miles, but not everyone may be in earshot when the resort is fifteen square miles in its entirety. No one scented anything but wild game and hunter's musk used to mimic the native animals.

Jonathan

Two males resting in the next room said they never heard a shot, so silencers must have been used. The doctor cleaned their shallow flesh wounds and treated the injuries like silver infections, just to be safe. Dr. Cook left afterward to rest in one of the upstairs rooms normally reserved for guests. Considering the two new patients, we need her here more than at the employee apartments a few miles away.

One glance at Romeo and Elsa tells me the couple feels as I do—like it's a struggle to maintain a steady veneer among the heated voices and fear. I take a deep breath preparing for what I've dreaded doing for the last five minutes: taking control. Right now, more than ever, I wish that smart-mouthed redhead were here, so I could smugly sit back and silently second guess her instead of being in the line of fire.

Whoever relishes a leadership spot in hard times has clearly never had to do it. No matter what choice you make, everyone has to help for the plan to come together, and credit is freely shared. But even the smallest error or miscalculation could send the best ideas crashing, and make no mistake—the leader will get all the blame.

I stand, pushing away from the table, drawing Eric and Pat's attention, along with everyone else's. My voice booms across the confined space, carrying the full weight of my alpha strength in it. "The time to blame who could have lead these hunters to us is past." I look around the table, meeting each wolf in the eye, a brief challenge in my gaze.

"Let's discuss what we have and move forward on what to do. We have water and food stores to last us for weeks. The electric to the inn is secure—but we have no standard outside communication. The planes will take days to fix and the roads are impossible to traverse, even in a jeep, for the next few weeks."

Naomi sits to my left, between Eric and Elsa, with Katrina and Ruby standing behind her. They women have been wolves for a while and aren't likely to panic, but yesterday and today have put a strain on even the calmest of natures. Spike sits next to Pat and stares at the center of the table, unwilling to meet my gaze. "An unknown number of supernatural hunters are out there trying to kill werewolves."

Ruby glares at one of the married women standing behind Spike and opens her luscious red lips to spew her adulterous accusations, again. I raise my hand to cut her off.

"How they got here and how they know about us isn't the problem." I stare down the pretty Latina woman. "Let it go, Ruby." She looks away, angry but silent. "What we plan on doing about these hunters and how to solve this current mess is."

I sincerely doubt a scorned lover would track down someone to settle a score by killing them and their werewolf brethren. I'm thinking more like a family member who was bitten or killed by a rogue wolf, but pointing that out to Ruby is liable to set off the hotheaded woman.

Asa clears his throat, reminding me to share what he found in the tunnels. Vivian had some late-model satellite phones in one of the old bunker type rooms. "We do have some good news. Asa uncovered four satellite phones and they're charging now. They should be operable in an hour or so—but it begs the question, who should we call? Who could get here in time to help us?" I glance at Asa, and not for the first time in my life, I've wish the Were society were more ordered and had some type of governing body like the vamps —or at least a hotline, for crying out loud. Not something like the vampires' creepy Tribunal, but anything would be good.

"Romeo, you and I talked about this long ago. Werewolves have lived like the wild, wild, west for centuries. Now, it could be the end of us if supernatural hunters—who

Jonathan

are well organized and have technology behind them—decide to go after us. I know this isn't the time to debate on how to fix it, but this current situation highlights what I've always said—we need a way to connect. There is always safety in numbers."

Across the room Romeo nods and takes Elsa's hand. He has two wounded wolves and a fatality in less than twenty-four hours. That's a lot for any alpha sworn to protect his pack to take.

I sit and feel the tension level in the room go down little by little. "So the main question is—do we catch them and find out what is going on or kill them?" The energy surges again as a cacophony of heated voices rises around the table.

We debate the situation for over an hour and decide to break for the night, agreeing to talk again in the morning. The wives of the injured males hustle out to be with their spouses in the nearby basement rooms. The rest of the pack trails upstairs to sleep in the guestrooms on the upper levels. Eric and Pat ask to go back to their cabin via the tunnels, but Asa doesn't think it's a good idea to have any of us split up. I agree, now is not the time to have those two where I can't see them.

Asa leads the pair to his two-room basement suite, ribbing them by saying he has a blanket they can curl up with on the floor. They could take a room upstairs too, but I think they're a bit unhinged by the day's events and don't care either way. Asa's on watch tonight and I decide to escape into the owners' apartment.

Several times today I've reached hard for Vivian in my mind, only to feel a slight tinge of awareness that quickly snuffs out. If we don't get a call out via one of the satellite phones soon, Rafe will activate one of the back-up protocols.

How could the simple suggestion of a summer of big-game hunting go wrong so fast? Paranormal hunters on my first time in charge—could I have worse fucking luck? An exhausted sigh leaves me as I trudge up the stairs, secretly looking forward to wrapping myself up in Vivian's favorite blanket and sleeping on their couch. Maybe I'll turn on one of Rafe's boring science shows, so I can pretend to argue with him about what a pompous jerk the English narrator is.

My inner musings come to a screeching halt when I sense someone in the couple's kitchen. More than likely one of Romeo's pack has hung back to chat. After the grueling shout fest downstairs, I really don't think I can handle any small talk.

The soft clearing of a throat draws my eye to a lean figure standing by the sink. Long, glossy mahogany hair frames a heart-shaped face. Two light brown eyes, like warm caramel toffee, stare back at me. A hesitant look crosses the delicate features of the unknown woman, and my gut reaction is shock.

My nose tells me this creature is Spike, but the trim athletic body and high, firm breasts scream woman. She's dressed in the same clothes Spike wore downstairs, but they hang loose on her smaller frame. Is this some kind of sick joke? Could he have a twin sister? Yeah, sure—and she dresses in big clothes to look like him?

Adrenaline courses through my system as I stride forward and grab the intruder by the upper arms. "Who the fuck—no wait—*what* the fuck are you?"

"Chill, Jon. I'm not going to hurt you."

Considering it's me who has her biceps in a death grip, it seems like an odd thing for her to say. I give her a little shake, my anger getting the best of me. "What the hell is going on?"

Instead of breaking free of my hold, she steps closer and lays her hands on my chest. She's tall, almost five eight, and close to my eye level. "It's me, Jon. Spike. I'm a shifter, not a

Jonathan

werewolf. Spike is just a shape I wear to stay safe. Other werewolves tend to ignore guys more than a pretty woman in their midst."

She tilts her head, like she's leaning in to kiss me and for a moment our breath mingles in the air between us. Then I smell the sweet scent of the mints Spike offered me after dinner.

I let go of her arms like I've been scalded and take a step back. "Whoa. Whoa. Just one damn minute here." I run a hand through my hair and pace the length of the kitchen, turning back in three strides to face the man/woman *thing*. "I don't understand. Are you telling me you're not a guy or you're not a werewolf?"

Her unique scent makes more sense, but surely, I couldn't have been the only one who's noticed it.

The woman looks at me with a sad little smile on her face, and drops her glance to the floor. "Both. I'm a shifter. I can take on any form I choose. I run with werewolves because it's safer than being alone."

I stop dead in the middle of the floor, my hip leaning against a chair in the kitchen and stare at the creature before me. "How can I tell that you're actually a woman and not a guy shifting to be a woman?"

She looks up at me, the pain in her eyes unmistakable. "And if that were true—what would it mean? That being with me would make a guy gay?"

I can't deny the attraction I've felt for her since the instant we met. Understanding she's a shifter certainly explains the cross pheromones and the desire bubbling below the surface whenever Spike was nearby.

"Attraction at a gut level isn't hinged on a person's gender, you jackass," she says with a stiffening of her spine. "Sometimes it just *is* and you don't need to question it to death." She whips away and storms out of the kitchen, heading into the living room toward the hall that leads to the entrance into the inn.

"No, wait!" I hurry after her. When I grab her arm, she turns to face me. "Please, don't go. You're right. I am acting like a jackass."

Her shoulders relax and I let go of her arm, trailing my hand down to rest in hers. "You have to admit that your announcement would throw anyone for a loop. Right?"

She nods and looks away, but not before I catch the sheen of moisture building in her eyes.

I tug her toward to the couch in the unlit living room, still unsure of where I want this to go but unable to deny I'm intrigued to learn more. "Can I ask you a few questions? You're the only shifter I've ever met."

"And likely the only one." We settle on the couch with a seat cushion between us.

"Really, why?"

"I'm the last in my line. My folks died when I was a teenager and my brother was killed a year later." Sadness crosses her face. I can only imagine the pain she's had to deal with having no one to turn to, not even a pack. No wonder she thought posing with a bunch of werewolves would be safer.

"I'm sorry," I say, feeling like my words are totally inadequate and I must sound like an idiot to even offer them.

She raises her eyes to mine and I see her earnestness and acceptance over the old pain. "You didn't kill them, it wasn't your fault."

"How did they die?"

"My folks died in a car crash." She looks off at the wall, no bitterness in her tone. "So simple, right? Turns out decapitation by a tractor trailer gets you no matter how supernatural you might be."

Jonathan

My heart seizes in my chest at the thought of losing both parents in such a way. Sure, it happens, but it never seems to happen to anyone you know. Of course, getting attacked by a werewolf on the way back to your dorm isn't normal either. We all suffer hardships in our lives—many take us from our families. Some tragedies appear more permanent and immediate than others.

"And your brother?" I reach for her hand across the cushion. I can't believe I'm sitting here having a heart-to-heart with someone I thought was a dude an hour ago. A dude who chomped at my ass after I came. Holy crap. That puts an entirely new awkward spin on things.

"He was killed in a robbery. Shot by the store owner. Can't say my brother made the best choices in life, but at sixteen, he tried his best to support us on the streets of Los Angeles."

Damn, she's sitting here telling me how her family died and I'm thinking about Naomi saying Spike went down on her once... or was it twice? This line of thought is not helping me be a kind and sensitive guy.

"Life sucks." Holy shit, did I just reduce her pain to some stupid platitude you read on a t-shirt? Panic flares in my chest as my eyes widen over my choice of words. "Um... I mean..."

She squeezes my hand. "It's okay, Jon. It happened over a decade ago, and I wasn't telling you to get sympathy." Her brow waggles. "Unless, of course, sympathy will get you out of your pants. Then I'm cool with using it."

Whoa. She wants to get me out of my pants? Wonder if she plans on going down on me like she did the hot Naomi. Mayday! Mayday! These thoughts are totally going to get me screwed. And not literally, either, which would be more fun.

"Umm..." I stutter. Yeah, that's suave. Idiot.

She laughs, tilting her head back and releasing a deep belly laugh. "Oh man, you should see your face. Yes, *dude*. I like you. And I would like to get you out of your pants. But, I'm okay if you don't feel the same."

A warmth spills through me, leaving me speechless. Thoughts of Vivian don't cloud my mind. Images of seducing her haven't plagued me in weeks. I no longer want to challenge Rafe when he comes out of their bedroom reeking of making love to her.

To say I'm in a unique place wouldn't even begin to cover it. I didn't feel this pull with Naomi, nor the last time Diane made me a love charm. Yeah, we went at it like fools for a few hours, but honestly that was more of a physical release than any type of emotional connection.

"I feel something, Sp— hey, what is your real name?"

She smiles and settles back on the couch, dropping her head back and snuggling into the deep cushion. "Spike was what I nick-named boy's 'parts' when I was growing up. Think about it...those jutting spikes of flesh. I couldn't resist."

She's positively adorable with those long eyelashes batting at me... what did she just say? Spikes of flesh? I smile in return. "Yeah, that makes sense. Guy's dicks are like spikes."

She busts out laughing. Crap, did I say that stupid shit out loud? Man, you'd think I'd never been with a girl before. Then again, after I left Romeo's pack at the age of twenty-one and hooked up with Vivian six months later, I really hadn't had a chance to just relax around someone in a normal situation in a long time.

I mirror her pose and hunker down into the soft confines of the couch, happy for this stolen moment of shared intimacy, even if I am sounding like an ass at times. "Hey, back on track. So, what is your name?"

Jonathan

She leans over, sliding onto the middle cushion to broach the distance between us. "My name is Candy."

"Mmmm?" I'm lost in her eyes, staring into the caramel depths. I wonder if she tastes like candy, too.

"Why don't you find out?" She presses her lips softly to mine.

I don't have time to contemplate that I must have muttered my ramblings out loud before heat races through my veins and lights a fire deep in my gut. Her soft lips mold to mine. After a few slow heartbeats, her tiny, pointed tongue pokes between my lips, diving into my mouth with abandon.

With a low moan I open and cup her head in my hands, pulling her across the couch to spill onto my lap. The spicy, sweet taste of the peppermint she ate floods my senses and fills my brain with clarity. I find that I really don't care if she is a he. Or if he is a she.

As my cock starts to grow in my pants and my mind is curiously free of all distractions, there is one thing am I certain of—this is a puzzle I'm going to enjoy solving.

Chapter Fifteen

Paul

"**What's a guy to do** hours before dawn and his friends are all in bed?" It's a rhetorical question, obviously. I don't think the pots and pans are going to start answering me now after ten years of talking to them when I'm alone.

I get out the fixins for a huge cauldron of one of my famous soups. I like to simmer the concoction for hours, then chill it over night in the fridge, and let it cook again the next day. Or in this case, swap the days and nights, and I'll be reheating when I wake late this afternoon.

I've been attempting to stay up past sunrise each day, little by little. The lull of a vampire's sleep pulls hard at my consciousness within an hour after sunrise, but with the weak sunlight this time of year I'm usually able to stay huddled awake in a semi-aware state longer—if I'm in total darkness.

A couple of hours past sunrise and I see a hint of gray sunlight peeking around a bend, my limbs weaken with every breath. I have no idea how Vivian does it. She could stay up around the clock and barely have a hair out of place. By noon I look like a stumbling drunk who needs to have his stomach pumped after a night of serious binge drinking.

Asa

Chopping vegetables while pre-made beef stock simmers with beans reminds me of home. Our whole family loves my soups. Thinking of them has me glancing at the kitchen clock. Bunny likes to call me before bed, even when I'm locked in the basement of the resort, and sometimes I get lucky and she's feeling frisky for a little phone sex.

The petite woman has a larger than life personality and accepted my changed state in stride. She has a level head and knew if I could control my blood urges, this alteration in my existence would be the best chance our children could get to know their father.

Almost dying last fall has brought our family closer, even though the kids don't understand what happened. We told them I started a new diet to explain the weight loss, and that I took a double day shift so Mom could do her share in the home schooling program with the other mothers on the resort. They seem content with those answers, for now. When they get older, who knows? We'll cross that bridge when we get to it.

I grab the small remote off the counter and click on some music from the docking station across the room. My collection is an eclectic mix, and soon the notes from one of Coldplay's older albums fill the room. The rhythm of chopping and dumping veggies in the pot soothes my mind and soul, reminding me once again why I love to cook. The smell of the spices, the chemistry of combining the ingredients in the right steps to create a unique meal... aside from my family, cooking is the one thing that truly makes me feel whole.

One song ends and another begins. The loose notes of the background guitar accentuate the drawn out male voice and draw me willingly into the music. My body sways side to side while I pick spices, stirring memories of Bunny and me cooking together at home with our children sleeping nearby.

I miss her by my side, lip-syncing with a wooden spoon... and whacking me on the ass with it every now and then to get a rise from me.

A sultry voice breaks into my musing. "You look sexy when you move your hips like that."

I whip around to find one of the delectable twins leaning against the archway between the kitchen and game wing. I don't know which one she is, and I can't help but wonder what she's doing here at this hour. She's either up very late or very early. Long dark hair spills over one shoulder, and a smile that could either be sleepy or calculated, curves her full lips. She's bundled up in a thick, gold robe and one bare leg peeks through the open fabric, long and lean and ending with a fuzzy high-heeled slipper.

"W-What are you doing up so late?" I ask.

She shrugs and approaches the stove. "Couldn't sleep, so I thought I'd see who was up." She grabs a clean spoon and tastes the broth. "Hmmm... yum." She licks the metal and locks eyes with me. "You're more experienced than you look, no?"

Desire coils in my gut, and I fight with every fiber in my being to not lean forward and sniff the air near her. She looks like she'd enjoy it and who knows where it could lead... My fangs itch, and I practically jump two feet away, closer to the sink. "Yes," I squeak. "I've been cooking professionally for almost two decades."

One slim, sexy eyebrow rises as she skims me over from head to toe. She lowers the spoon to the counter and steps toward me. "Really? You don't look a day over twenty-five."

I thought all the staff here knew what we were, but now, I'm not so sure. My gaze jumps around the kitchen, looking for a distraction to put more distance between the two of us. My eyes land on the carafe of bloodcoffee and I lunge to the pot. I fumble with my empty mug and pour the reddish brown liquid.

"Gee, thanks. Good diet and exercise, you know."

Her eyes widen slightly, as if knowing and challenging my statement. If she does know, why is she here with me right now? Does she want to provoke me to bite her? None of the ladies at the inn act like this around me and I'm at a loss on how to handle myself.

I take a long drink from my mug, hoping to quell the tide of desire coursing through me. I don't think Bunny or Vivian would be happy if they knew what was filling my mind. God, why the hell did I stare at her ass before? Did she see me? Did I somehow ask for this tonight? I'm not even sure which one she is.

"So, it's Carmella, right?"

She shakes her head and steps closer. "No, I'm Mina."

I nod and look away. My mind scampers for a safe topic of conversation, hoping she'll soon get bored and wander off. "Er... umm... how do you like the island?"

She laughs softly, a feminine tinkle of sound that draws my eye back to her, as I'm sure she intended. "Shouldn't I be asking you? After all, you're the guest."

The dark haired beauty reaches for my mug and pulls it from my hand. She sets it on the counter without looking and steps nearer, almost brushing her tight tits against my chest.

"I'm married," I blurt out and step back. My heart pounds in my chest, something it's rarely done the past few months. I swing my eyes to the other side of the kitchen island. My fangs fully descended and my traitorous cock hardens behind my fly.

She laughs again. "I don't see your wife here."

Shit! Where are the others? Surely I can't be the only one awake? A frantic, trapped panic squeezes my heart, making me feel like I'm going to puke. I bet vomiting up a bunch of blood and coffee all over her robe would be the trick to turn her off.

How do the others stare into someone's eyes and control them? Vivian hasn't taught me how to do it yet, and I have to admit, I've been scared to try it on my own. Could I mess her up if I do it wrong? Could I hurt her somehow?

I turn back and stare her deep in the eyes. Doing my best to channel Obi Wan, I use my closest *these are not the droids you're looking for* voice and say, "You don't want me. I'm not your type."

My direct stare doesn't seem to carry any weight and she steps closer, running a hand up my chest. "Oh? You seem exactly like my type."

Fuck. That didn't work. Wonder if there is some trick to it. The others make it look so easy. Then again, it's not something they often do in front of me so maybe I need to play closer attention. Or ask how they do it. I bet that would help.

Her hand trails up and cups the back of my neck. The warmth of her palm slides over my exposed skin, her fingers tangling in my hair. "Cool, composed, and powerful," she whispers.

She leans in, angling her mouth to kiss me, and I jerk back. This kind of thing never happened when I was an overweight cook—how the hell do I get out of this?

My phone rings, using the nuclear alarm ringtone I favor. I don't get many calls and the alert is loud enough to wake me from a deep sleep if needed. Mina jumps back, startled by the blaring noise. I smile, relief draining the tension from body.

"That's my wife. Got to run." I bolt like a yellow chicken from the kitchen, scurrying through the dining room and foyer as fast as I can. I press the talk button before the third atomic meltdown warning sounds. "Hey, honey. Boy, am I glad to hear from you."

"Hi, sweetie. I'm using our satellite phone. If you need me, use this number."

I race up the stairs to the safety of my quiet suite, glad the soup is on low, and I don't need to go back down there for a while. "Why? Did you get a late season storm that took out the phone lines or cell towers?"

"No, something worse."

Bunny fills me in on all she knows, which turns out to be quite a bit. Apparently, Asa told her more than the other employees because of her relation to me, and he trusts she'll keep her mouth shut.

"They think the shooters are werewolf hunters?" I ask. "That sounds paranoid—like something out of a *Supernatural* episode."

"I know. I thought the same thing at first, too. But they seemed pretty certain after the second wave of shootings earlier tonight."

I pace back and forth in my room, unable to sit and relax like we normally do when talking. "I don't like the sound of this, hon. Can you get away with the kids? Go someplace safer than our cabin?"

"Asa said he'd come here in an hour and take us to the apartments. He's going to use the private route."

That's our way of mentioning the underground tunnels. I only know of them because of my inclusion in the seethe. For safety purposes Bunny was briefed but compelled to never speak of the passageways to anyone who didn't already know of them. Wouldn't be good to have her shoot me if I emerged from a closet in the middle of the night. "What about the children?"

"He's going to 'tell' them we traveled by road when we arrive at the apartments."

I nod, realizing there is no other way; a five and seven year old can't be expected to keep such a secret. The crushing weight of helplessness pushes against me. "I don't like this, Bunny. I'm not the most experienced fighter, but I'd feel better by your side than stuck here knowing my family is in danger."

A heavy sigh reaches me, and I know my strong wife is feeling the added pressure. "Me too, dear."

"These hunters are probably human, right?"

"That's what they're thinking. Why?"

"Arm yourself with everything we've got. If they're human then they'll be easy enough to kill with a bullet if they come after you."

"One step ahead of you, Paul. According to Asa, employees have been directed to arm themselves and told to shoot anyone they don't know coming within sight of the apartment building. They're taking no chances on our safety, but still... none of *us* are the targets, you know?"

I continue my pacing, glad there's a carpet to muffle my frantic steps. "Maybe we should fly back. I'll talk to Drew and see what he says."

"Why wouldn't you talk to Vivain and Rafe direct?"

"They went to Buenos Aires to feel out what's going on with the Ancients."

Her voice pitches higher. "And they left you alone on the island?"

"Well, we've got the staff here and the rest of the crew from Alaska as well."

"Uh, huh," she sounds skeptical. "What staff?"

Heat rises to my cheeks. I'm glad she's not here to sniff out my recent issue in the kitchen. "The caretaker's family. Husband, wife, daughter, two aunts. That's it."

"That sounds like an awful lot of women." Compared to our mostly male dominated state of Alaska, she's right.

"One is married, one is their kid and the others are two unattractive spinsters. No need to worry." The lie trips harmlessly off my lips.

"Why would I worry when I know where you sleep during the day?" She laughs to take off the sting of the unspoken threat she'd follow through in a heartbeat. "After all, you're coming home. I'll be waiting here when you do. Being semi-dead hasn't changed our vows, and I know you'd never forget it."

I swallow before forcing a little humor I'm not feeling into my response, "Yes, dear."

A knock sounds at my door, causing my heart to freeze. Who the hell could that be? If it's one of the twins come to try and seduce me, I'm screwed. I'll have to keep the door locked. Damn! I don't think I locked it when I came in. Before I rush to the door and fumble like a fool I should see who's there. I hold the phone away from my mouth, "Who is it?"

"It's me, Drew," comes the muted reply through the thick wood.

Fear loosens its grip, and I reply in a level voice, "Come on in." I turn my attention back to Bunny. "Hon, I need to tell Drew everything you told me about the shootings. Can I call you in a few minutes?"

"Sure, lover boy."

We end the call as Drew strides into my suite smelling like fruity bubble bath soap. "I just talked with Jon. Was that Bunny?"

"Yeah, she told me about the lines being out and used the emergency satellite phone we keep at the cabin."

Drew crosses the room and lowers himself into one of the club chairs near the balcony doors. "Man, things sure got out of hand there quick."

Pent up energy and fear pushes through my body, sending me pacing the floor, again. "Should we fly back? Should we call Vivian to ask what she wants us to do?"

Drew shakes his head and stares out into the charcoal darkness beyond the windows. "I spoke to Rafe a few hours ago, and they're tied up with the inner politics of the event guests. I'll inform him of what's going on at our next check in. I followed protocol when I couldn't get through to the inn a few hours ago, and called Cy."

"He's that guy in New York?" From what I was told, Cy is one of Vivian's vampire offspring. She turned him several decades ago and set him loose relatively quickly. He had good control or some such shit.

"Yeah. He was on a business trip in Washington state. He should be at the resort in a few more hours. Cali, his werewolf wife, is manning their club while he's gone."

I think of my wife and children and wonder if one vampire will make a difference. "Is he bringing back up?"

"I don't know. I'm assuming he's following whatever he agreed to with Vivian ahead of time." He rubs a hand over his face. For the first time, uncertainty in the situation cracks his calm façade.

Now is as good a time as any to tell him what I've been thinking regarding the twins. "Drew?"

"Yeah?"

"Mina came on to me tonight." I shrug my shoulders and try for nonchalance, like a sexy girl hitting on me every day is normal. "I tried to mesmerize her to get her to back off, but it didn't work.

"Forcing your will on someone doesn't come easy. You need to practice at it. Was that your first try?"

I nod. I don't think I need to tell him the time I "asked" Bunny for head one night. She laughed and told me *"if you want it, you had better give it first."*

Asa

"The ladies hit on Chelly and me last night," he says with some speculation in his eye. "I wondered if something's going on. Neither Bob or Tommy reported any luck with them, despite their numerous attempts."

"So, they could be hitting on us because we're vampires?" I ask.

"Maybe. Although they seemed more interested in Chelly than me, so I'm not sure."

"It's odd though, right?"

He nods and stretches. "Certainly bears monitoring. How did you go about trying to influence Mina's thoughts?"

"I stared into her eyes and tried to force some will into my words. I felt a little stupid at the time—maybe I did it wrong?"

"Conceptually, you got it right. I placed compulsion on all three women the other night, so it should have worked... unless..."

"Unless what?"

"Unless you did it wrong or they were already under compulsion from someone more powerful than you."

"Could Vivian have put a vamp whammy on them when she arrived?"

Drew gazes out the window at the gradually lightening sky. It's still quite dark, with less than ninety minutes until the sun rises. "If she did, I wouldn't have been able to break it. And why would she want the ladies to be friendly to you when she promised Bunny she'd watch out for you?" He shakes his head. "Makes no sense. I'm thinking you did it wrong."

Anxiety presses through me, stirring up my gut and souring the recent blood I've consumed. "I'm worried about my family in Alaska."

Drew turns to face me, concern in his eyes. "I know, man, but there's nothing we can do about it from here. We're too far away. We can't desert our master and fly back on a whim."

I nod, knowing he's right.

"We need to have faith in the seethe members left behind. Asa is loyal to a fault. He'd take a bullet for your family without a second thought."

I try to smile through a blurry haze in my eyes, "Yeah, that bald bastard has an honest soul. He was a perfect match for serving our country."

"That's right. You need to keep that in mind. He'll do whatever it takes to keep your family safe, even above every other employee, without being told."

I recall the way he's played with my kids, and the shine my seven-year-old daughter has taken to him. She calls him *Uncle Asa* and he never bats an eye.

"Maybe they should stay in the tunnels for a few days?" I ask. "There are lots of unused bunker rooms down there." Hope makes my voice a little high. Drew is the highest-ranking vampire we have after Vivian. If he says no I know the ex-soldier won't consider breaking the decision.

"I think if you're worried, then hiding them below ground is the safest solution." A sigh escapes me at his answer. "But do you want your kids cooped up down there for a long time?"

"I want them alive. They'll get over being bored." I reach for the phone while Drew moves toward the door. "Thanks, man."

Pain tightens his features and I have a brief moment to wonder if he's lost more than his wife Angie. He nods to me and leaves. I'm beginning to realize a long life may not be all it's cracked up to be. Sure, I may last for decades, even centuries, longer than I should. But from what I've seen that doesn't come without a lot of drawbacks, too.

Asa

Losing those you love, experiencing the pain of their death over and over with a sharper memory than when you were human, facing life without them... a shiver runs through me as my wife answers the phone. I don't want to face those hardships. I'm not ready. But then again, when is anyone ready for true death?

Chapter Sixteen
Asa

The eerie calm of the tunnels surrounds me as I descend the first few rungs of the escape ladder in Bunny and Paul's bedroom closet. Bunny went first and I handed their bags down to her. The children followed, both sleepy but excited by the adventure of something new. Like every child without a care in the world, they have no idea of the danger they're in. And with careful planning they might never know about what's going on the surface for the next few days.

I closed up the house and secured the doorways before heading down. The wooden floor of the closet was lowered into place and with one last spin, I tightened the hatch leading to the secret exit. Locked up tight.

They'll be safe.

I finish shimming down the metal rungs of the ladder and land on the concrete floor next to the waiting family. These kids remind me of my younger cousins years ago. I vividly recall how much those two loved exploring new places. A smile forms as I try to match my expression to the excitement I see on their faces. "Who's ready to see the cool underground bunker room?"

Asa

Two high-pitched voices screech their enthusiasm, and their small bodies look like they will barely be able to contain themselves another moment. "Me!" they yell in unison.

I grab their bags and start down the tunnel toward the inn. The trio follows me through the many twists and turns for about fifteen minutes, with the occasional calling out of words and phrases from the children to hear their voices echo in the tight space.

Eager to join in the fun, I call out "Hi ho, hi ho, it's off to work we go...." The three accompany me, one verse off, until it sounds like a squadron of Disney dwarves fills the dimly lit space. Thanks to the singing, their spirits are high and they seem unaware of the possible danger that drove them underground to begin with. Good, I'd rather not have to field difficult questions like that myself—let their mom deal with it.

I round one last bend and stop at a steel door, which lies about fifty yards from the north wing basement entrance. Behind the cold metal are two interconnecting rooms, the smaller one having the only functioning sink and toilet combination this close to the inn.

I reach in to flick on the overhead steel-caged bulb. The light illuminates the couch and TV that were in my bedroom. The small makeshift kitchen holds the borrowed fridge and microwave from the conference room, and a folding card table with chairs from a supply room on the main floor of the inn.

The kids burst through the opening and run squealing with delight around the center of the room. Bunny follows and puts her bag on the folding table. She looks around in awe, shocked at the clean appearance of the drab concrete room. "Wow, Asa. You really outdid yourself. I was expecting dusty Army cots in a 60s bomb shelter."

I shrug, not willing to admit the hours it took to clear out all the old munitions and supplies. It was a simple task and I was glad to do it for them. "Sorry—don't want to disappoint you—but cots are in the next room. They are newer and have clean mattresses."

The kids race into the smaller room and start to screech in excitement, "Mom! Mom! You have to see what's in here!"

She stops briefly near the coffee table, glancing at the PG movies I borrowed from Rafe's collection, and the Wii remotes and games. "These plus the books and school work they packed should keep them busy."

Bunny walks into the next room and stops dead. I'm right behind her and stay in the doorway to not crowd the family in the tight confines. Bed sheets from the upstairs guest rooms line the walls like closed curtains. Gathers of fabric, where I used the masonry gun to nail them to the concrete ceiling, drape to the wall, creating a tent-like feel to the room.

Cots line three walls, head and feet almost touching in the cramped space. The open door rests against the remaining wall with a naked sink protruding a few inches past it. Beyond the porcelain, sheets hang diagonally across the corner. Paul's son races to inspect what lies behind the fabric.

"Mommy," the five-year-old boy says with wonder, "there's a potty in here!"

His older sister ignores him, rushing to claim the cot she wants and tossing her backpack on top. "I love it, Uncle Asa! It's better than camping. No woods or stinky outhouse to pee in!"

Bunny turns to me, a look of astonishment on her face. She opens her arms and walks to me with moisture in her eyes. On tiptoes, she wraps herself around my neck and hugs me.

Asa

Unsure what to do, I close my arms loosely around her and hug her back gently. "Thank you," she rasps through a tear-ravaged voice. "You really went above and beyond."

Her grip loosens and she steps back. She pushes her dirty blond hair off her face and dries an eye. I let go and look away, not sure what to say in the face of her gratitude. I shrug, glad to see the three are happy with the results. Vivian won't be too pleased with the ruined sheets, but I'll replace those before they get back.

"I'd offer to cook you a meal in thanks," she says while looking over her shoulder at the squabbling children, "but we both know that won't work. And I'd offer you your preferred meal, if I didn't think Paul would be pissed." She smiles on the last comment when turning back, letting me know she's joking, but the sentiment is there.

A sharp squeeze around my heart surprises me. Absolute horror fills me for a second at the idea of biting her. Years of military training allow my face to remain expressionless so she's not aware of my thoughts. "It was no trouble. I'm glad to be of help."

I'd never want the physical pain of my bite to hurt someone I consider a friend. I look at the three a moment longer and then turn back to the main room, readying myself to leave. The agony of never having a family of my own overwhelms me. I hope Paul knows how lucky he is to have what will be denied to so many of us—forever.

Slipping the comfortable, stoic mask I always wear into place, I angle toward the steel door, remembering the map at the last minute.

"Asa?" I turn to Bunny while fumbling in my pocket for the paper. "How long do you think we'll be down here?"

"I'm not sure. Probably only a few days. I'll let you know." I unfold the map and pass the hand-drawn image to her. "This is a diagram for the remaining one hundred yards to the door leading to the north wing. Only come to the basement if there is an emergency."

She accepts the drawing and examines it. "This map isn't complete. Where is the rest of it?"

"Vivian won't allow maps of the tunnels. I did this partial so you'd get a general feel of where you were."

She nods. "Okay, but staying inside these small rooms might prove difficult after two days or so."

"Yeah, I know. But we might be using the tunnels and it really won't be safe for the kids to be wandering. It's very easy to get lost." I smile. "Trust me." I point to the hardwired phone on the wall. "This still works with local extensions on the property. Call us if you need anything."

Bunny rests her small hand on my arm. "Really, Asa, I can't thank you enough. Paul will be touched when he hears all you've done for us."

I shrug again, realizing I'm doing that a lot right now, and feel really stupid. "You're welcome. It was my pleasure to do it for the kids. It's a difficult situation, and I know Paul would do the same for me."

Bunny looks around the neat improvised room and shakes her head. "You obviously don't know Paul as well as I do. Manual labor was never his thing." She smiles to lessen the sharp implication of her words. "I love him to death," she breaks off, laughing at her own pun. "More like, I love him after death. But he's not the handiest guy on the planet."

I start once again for the door. "Oh, and your satellite phone won't work down here. You'll have to come to the main level and use it near an uncovered window."

She sighs and settles onto the couch. "Yeah, I figured it might be something like that. Thanks for letting me know."

I nod my goodbye and close the door, hearing her and the kids calling out their thanks and goodnights. It's almost

Asa

five a.m. I wonder if she'll be able to get them back to sleep tonight or if the little buggers will be up for the day.

Within a few minutes I'm in the command center. Eric kept watch while I readied the rooms and brought the small family underground. He's stretched out, his feet up on the desk, alert and scanning the monitors. Good. Considering he napped only briefly before relieving me, I'm impressed he's awake.

"Any news?" I ask, expecting nothing.

He turns to look at me, and yawns. "As a matter of fact, yes."

I raise an eyebrow and wait for him to elaborate.

"Call came through from the airstrip. They got a radio signal from a small plane asking to land."

"Really? The radio works? When did the call come in?"

"About five minutes ago. Yeah, something about radio waves not needing a cell tower but a direct radio frequency. It works as long as we have power."

"Could we reach Coldfoot with it?"

"Not sure. Might be too far away. But I think it would only work if someone was listening." Eric gets to his feet and stretches. "Don't you want to know who's about to land?"

"I know who it is—Cy."

"He's the one married to Aunt Cali, right?"

"Yeah. I stayed with them for a couple of years after I got back to the States. They run that club up in Manhattan."

"Yeah, I remember, now. When you were so close and yet still never visited us in West Milford." His grimace quickly drops to show he's joking. "I still haven't talked to Aunt Cali since I changed. Funny how everyone always called her crazy when she talked about *other species* living among us. Turns out she wasn't, huh?"

I nod. "Kind of ironic that she hooks up with a dead guy so soon after she was infected by a werewolf. He's not bad, though. An information and computers expert. He runs all Vivian's background checks and digs up dirt on people."

"Isn't he the one that gave you all the false info on Emiko three months ago?"

"Not his fault. Someone planted it. The fake cover was pretty in depth and took some time to build. He's more careful, now."

Eric shifts his attention to the monitoring. "Really? Gee, that instills confidence. Hey, look at this." He points on the screen where lights on the wings' tips flash in the dark sky over the resort's airport. "Something's wrong. He's coming in fast and his wings aren't even."

We watch the image together, waiting to see if he'll make it in safely or crash trying. The small four-seater plane comes into view as it's about to touch the ground. The wheels touch briefly before bouncing on the tarmac, careening the plane into the air off the runway. Eric toggles the cameras to the next angle, ensuring we miss none of the action.

The wings totter up and down, and the nose keeps dipping. It takes some fighting on the pilot's part but the aircraft touches down. The landing gear rips off from the impact and the plane thunders through the darkness, leaving a trail of sparks before skidding to a stop in the tundra beyond the airfield's landing lights.

A figure emerges from the mangled hull, and in a blink it's gone. The camera has trouble picking up what we could discern easily—a man racing toward the hangar.

"Holy shit!" Eric whips around. "Did you see that?"

"Yeah." My brows draw together in worry. "That shouldn't have happened. He's been flying for years."

"Maybe something happened to his plane."

"Where's Jon?" I ask, worried there may have indeed been something *very* wrong with Cy's aircraft.

"He's sleeping. He said to give him 'til *at least* six."

Asa

My watch reads quarter past five now, and darkness lasts until almost seven this morning. The phone on the desk rings and Eric jumps at the sudden sound. "Man I'm jittery. That landing was intense."

I grab the phone and hear my Aunt's undead husband on the other end. "I made it. But just barely."

"We were watching from here," I say. "What happened?"

"Someone fired several rounds when I circled to land. I was pretty high up, so I'm guessing it was a long-range rifle. Took out a lot of my electrical systems and fluids started pouring out at an alarming rate. I'm lucky it didn't go up in flames on the skid."

"I don't recommend you leave the building the conventional way. They could be watching the exits and vehicles."

"What do you suggest?"

I weigh the options in my mind and realize Vivian and Rafe must trust Cy or they wouldn't have used him as a backup plan if things went south and they hadn't heard from us. Then again, they were probably counting on him coming with help and not being alone on the West Coast for a business trip at the time they made the arrangements. "Give me about twenty minutes, and I'll be there from underground."

"Underground passageways?" he barks out with a touch of disbelief in his tone. "This I've got to see."

Chapter Seventeen
Vivian

It's hours past dawn when Rafe and I enter our suite. The undead partying and verbal backstabbing continued for hours into the morning. Most of us older ones can stay up around the clock, if we want to. All we need is a blood pick me up, and we're good to go.

Usually, our spouses and dates can't keep up the pace and need to call an end to the gathering or they'll drop where they stand. Rafe is no exception, and I knew if we didn't break when we did, there'd be no fun in our suite.

Rafe's warm hands glide down my back. A loving glow envelops me as I step over the threshold into the beautiful room. The Tribunal never skimps on décor—the rich antiques and expensive blue and yellow silks and brocades of the suite don't disappoint.

"Are we safe here?" Rafe asks.

I look around, wondering if the Tribunal's vow of no harm to guests will be enough to protect us. "As much as we can be. I doubt Coraline would make a move less than twelve hours after we show up." The creep of apprehension climbs my spine. "But, we can lock the thick doors, lower the steel blinds, and re-evaluate in a day."

Rafe checks the door while I flip the window switch that will darken the room when we rest. "If it appears that Coraline, or anyone else, is circling too close, we can leave and stay somewhere else in the city."

Rafe takes off his jacket and drapes it over the back of a nearby chair. "Would some random hotel in the city be any better?"

I shrug, still unsure exactly what we're getting into and worried for the first time in years. "I'd like to think it would make us more difficult to find during the day."

"You feel like rehashing all the people who gave you the stink eye tonight?" Rafe asks.

A sigh escapes as I step out of my heels, thankful to give my feet a break after all our dancing. "No, not really. They'll still be there when we wake." My gown fits snug over my hips —the only way this number will come off is with the release of the zipper. I reach behind for the clasp, but my lover's eager hand beats me to it.

"Here, let me."

As my husband lowers it one slow inch at a time, I strip off the long gloves and toss them on a nearby chair.

"You love dragging it out, don't you?" I murmur over my shoulder.

"Every day feels like Christmas when the present is this nicely wrapped." Once the zipper stops, his warm palm slips in to cup my ass. "I've been aching to do this all night."

Recalling his hot hand on my thighs when he sliced the material before our tango, I'll admit, I've ached for it, too. The dress slinks down, and I catch the edge before revealing my bare breasts.

Rafe smoothes one last caress over my bare buttock before withdrawing his hand. "I've got it, darling."

He steps closer, nestling his growing, pant-covered cock against my ass and wraps his arms around, taking the top edge of my dress in one hand. With the other, he skims beneath the purple silk and caresses my breast. He weighs it in his hand then uses a thumb and forefinger to tease and pull the taut nipple.

Jolts of pleasure spike from the tortured peak to my pussy, drawing a soft moan from my lips. "You've certainly 'got' something there, mister. Care to continue?"

Warm lips trail soft kisses down the side of my neck and I lean my head to the right to give my husband better access. Every few kisses he nibbles on the skin, exciting me further with his teeth. "You know I love it when you bite."

"Precisely, my dear. I'm no fool. I thought a little boost between us might be a good idea, too. Considering the company we're keeping."

His teeth latch onto my shoulder muscle, bringing an exquisite pinch of pain to focus my attention on every hard tooth digging into my flesh. Oh... and then there's the slippery wet tongue soothing the spot afterward... "What was that, dear? You lost me for a moment there."

"I'm thinking..." he bites down again. "... I should take blood from you while we're in this nest of vipers."

"Yes, good point."

He drops his hold on my dress and the material puddles at my feet. Two warm palms grasp and fondle my breasts, pulling the engorged tips while he bites firmly on the skin between my ear and my shoulder.

"Need some help?" I ask when he clamps down once more, harder this time, bringing the pleasure and pain to a near orgasmic level. He murmurs his approval against my skin, and I reach up with one sharp nail to help.

Rafe pulls his hot sucking mouth away for a moment while I pierce my skin right over the thick pulsing vein in my neck. Warm blood cascades out of the new wound and my lover's mouth latches over the small hole, lapping at my flesh and drinking deep.

One hand leaves my chest and travels down my body in a long sinuous path. My God, when he drinks from me it feels like every inch of my skin is alive.

His fingers coil in the soft mat of hair atop of my mound before plunging deep between the wet folds to find the hard nub of my clit, already swollen with desire. I reach behind to stroke his shaft through his trousers and snake the other hand to cradle his head against my neck. "Bite me again, baby."

His finger teases my hard button as he bites the healing wound, pressing it open for more hot liquid to flow into his mouth. He moans against my flesh, taking in my stronger vampire blood. From experience I know what I've got in store for me. Whenever he drinks from me it works like Viagra, fueling him through the night to relentlessly do me over and over until we're both begging for mercy.

A tightness coils in my pelvic muscles, the innuendos and suggestions from the evening push me to a fast peak. "More, take more," I whisper as my crest sends me up and away. The small cut over my artery heals as he clamps down, catapulting me that last little bit into oblivion.

My hips buck forward, spasms rippling across my frame. A tantalizing pain centers on my nipple when he pinches and pulls at the height of my release. "Yes!"

I slump against his well-muscled body, relaxing in the afterglow of orgasm—content to enjoy the rush for a moment. This is only the beginning of our fun and to drag out his satisfaction too long would be cruel and unusual punishment.

Rafe licks my neck with the tip of his tongue, igniting senses on the freshly healed skin. "That was divine, my dear," he says in a soft voice, rough with desire.

A low chuckle escapes as I turn, naked, in his arms. "Isn't that my line? I'm the one you brought to a glorious peak... and all while you're fully clothed. Aren't you just the over-achiever?"

He unwraps my arms from where they coiled around his neck. "Well, then... I think it's time we got more equal in the clothing department." He strips out of his expensive tux, diamond buttons popping and flying in his haste. His lightly haired chest and defined body never fail to draw a deep passion from me, no matter how recently I came. I want to not only possess him, but own his very desire. Wrap him up in my essence until nothing exists, but the two of us.

A simmering heat burns deep in Rafe's gaze. A fire I see only after he's fed from me and has gladiator strength at his beck and call. "I will make you scream tonight, Dria." His cock juts out as he stalks closer to me, driving me against the huge four-poster bed in the middle of the suite. "I will make you remember why you choose me as your mate and not any of those other men we saw tonight."

Ahh... so he's feeling a little possessive of me, is he? That's fine with me. A slightly jealous lover can also be an extremely passionate one. "Will you now?" I can't resist baiting him. Truth be told, I like when he's a little rough. The back of my knees hit the bed and I lay back, staring into the eyes of my lover the entire time.

He looms over me. His proud cock bobbing in all its glory, slick with pre-come and pulsing with his heartbeat. The engorged head begs for a delicate tongue to lick it, and I rise onto my elbows to comply.

"Oh no, you don't." Work roughened hands push me down then slide lower to spread my thighs. "That first one was just a warm up. Wait and see what I have planned for you."

Before I can protest, he kneels between my knees and dips his head to my swollen nether lips. Two thumbs spread my folds and a wet, pointed tongue strokes the sides of my aroused clit. Warm breath replaces the pressure as he blows on the sensitive skin, bowing my body off the bed in response. "That's it, liebling. You like that, don't you?" He blows on my aroused flesh again, sending me racing toward another release. I'm close to coming—and when he changes tactics, I know he senses it, too.

Two thick fingers plunge into my wet depths, stretching the entrance and sending a flood of sensations coursing through me. My hips circle of their own accord, seeking the pressure I need to go over the edge once more. "You know what I like better than finger fucking this tight little pussy of yours?"

My head thrashes back and forth on the bed, unsure if he wants an answer or he's teasing me. Without waiting for a reply, he amps the tempo on his plunging fingers and latches his mouth over my clit. He sucks the swollen flesh between his lips then tickles it with his tongue. The pressure building in my middle shoots through my body in shuddering waves as my second crest washes over me. My back arches and his free hand grabs my hip, pinning me while he rides my peak higher and longer with his clever tongue and thick fingers.

Rafe slows his pumping and then gradually slips his hand down my thigh, allowing my sensitized flesh a minor respite. He smiles at me, his grin both self-satisfied and hot as hell. "Come on, baby, you must know what I like better…"

What? He wants a coherent answer while I'm still experiencing the glorious aftereffects of my latest orgasm? My eyes drift lower in hazy contentment. Good God, he's a great lover.

Strong hands slip under me, one at my ass and one at my back, shifting me further up on the bed so Rafe can join me on the mattress. He gently tilts me onto my side and grabs a pillow, placing it near my knees. He slides my top leg up, cocking it at the knee to rest on the pillow, while climbing over me to straddle my bottom thigh.

His heavy cock nudges my wet slit, seeking entrance. "I like fucking your pussy with my cock the best..." A low chuckle sounds in his throat when he looks down at my lazy, soft expression. "But I need to wake you up a bit and get you back in the game, my dear."

A loud resounding clap echoes through the room as my husband smacks the flat of his hand across my ass. The jolt of his flesh on mine sends a thrill of adrenaline through my blood and my eyes fly open in surprise. "Hey! I was comfy... enjoying some expert lovin' from my husband. Can't fault a girl for that."

"Of course not, and if I wanted an unresisting body that'd be fine." The large head of his cock dips into me, slowly retreating and advancing to coat his length with my multiple releases. "But I don't. I want you wild and crazy for me, Dria. Just me." One hand presses my top thigh further up, opening my legs more to his hungry gaze. "Your pussy is so pretty... dark pink and full... practically begging to have my cock buried inside."

His slow press and withdrawal have served their purpose of getting me aroused again. Within minutes I'm wiggling as best I can from this position, trying to squirm his cock in deeper. "Put it in, Rafe. Stop your damn teasing."

His hips slide closer, driving his girth half way. Rafe's hand snaps back and the sharp crack of flesh on flesh resounds through the room again. The stinging burn of the smack melts away in a soothing circular rub from the guilty hand. "Settle down there, Dria. No sassing me." His grin is pure evil as a moistened thumb circles the tight rosebud of my ass. "I'll be the one who says when the teasing is over."

The short strokes of his dick drive me crazy and I circle my hips again, encouraging him to play with the tight pucker. I know ass play will push him over the edge and have him forcing that meaty cock into me, in no time. His thumb edges inside, spiraling needles of pleasure join with the push and pull sensation of his prick inside me.

Little by little, he eases in back and forth until his length is completely coated with my juices. The entry of his glide is slick, and he pushes deeper on each thrust, matching his thumb in my ass on every plunge. Unable to contain myself, I slide a hand down my stomach to find the swollen folds of flesh pressed against the pillow. The previous attention from my lover has ensured my body is ready for more. The blood-engorged outer lips are open, eager for my touch. The hard bud doesn't need direct stimulation, so I scissor two fingers to the right and left, stroking back and forth through my own wetness.

Grunts and moans from Rafe pepper the air as he works my tiny pucker, picking up the rhythm of his battering hips. My fingers rub a frantic tempo as I race to catch up to my husband's growing pleasure. His twisted facial expression looks almost painful, but his intense feelings aren't reflective of agony... not by a long shot.

He tosses his head back and lets out a strangled cry, "Christ! You feel so good." Rafe draws his thumb from my ass and lowers both hands to the mattress, on either side of my waist. With added leverage, he pummels me with thrusts, driving in his cock deeper and with more urgency. "That's it, baby. Rub that little clit. Bring yourself off with me."

Sweat from his brow drips onto me. The scent of our lovemaking fills the air, forcing out any lingering aromas from the Seat of Darkness. His claiming of me tonight holds a stronger meaning. He wants to remind me of why we're together, but he needn't worry.

I didn't choose him for what his body does to mine, but for what his heart makes me feel. As he pushes into me, calling my name, I am reminded the he and I are truly one. My third release ripples over me, eclipsing the previous two with its intensity and length. Stars blind my eyes, my fingers working back and forth in my slick folds. The inner shield I hold so tightly about me cracks, and for a brief moment, my love and power are equal in the brightness they exude, cascading into the room like an electric burst, raising the hair on my lover's arms.

Tiny shudders wrack my body while I spiral down from the pinnacle. I gather in my power and lock it tight, unconcerned with the slip. I'm sure I won't be the only old vampire on the premises tonight getting it so good their control slips.

Rafe places a light kiss on my shoulder and brushes his stubbled chin back and forth in a soft gesture, tingling my skin with the rasp of the short hairs. "Whew," he whispers, "that was a big one."

I stretch lazily as he slides behind me, pulling my ass to snuggle against his hips. In a moment his cock stirs and begins to harden again. "Ready for number four?"

I circle my hips, content to lie here for a bit. "What do you have in mind?"

My lover places small kisses up and down my neck, similar to how we started the session. "Did you pack that little bag of anal plugs? I'm thinking it's time to work this tight ass of yours and give it a good stroking tonight." He bites down on my neck, pulling my vampiric lust to the surface with the hint of pain.

"You want to work in that thick prick?" The heady thought fills me once again with desire.

Vivian

Rafe rolls my shoulder back and leans over me. "I want to love you all night... any way you'll let me."

A soft smile curls my mouth as I reach up and touch his cheek with one hand. "Feeling high from my blood, aren't you?"

His bright blue eyes take on a manic gleam, like he didn't just fill me with his seed two minutes ago. "Oh yes, that's part of it."

I laugh, full and deep. The sound bubbles up and erases every care I have in the world. God, how I love this man and needed this connection tonight. I reach to pull him toward me in a kiss, but he has other ideas.

Rafe grabs both my wrists and pins them over my head. "I told you earlier—before we stop for the night I'm going to have you screaming my name." He lowers his lips to mine, slipping his tongue inside to taunt and entice. He uses just enough pressure in his kiss to show me he's got plenty of energy to keep going for hours. I can hardly wait.

The hot bath water has longed since cooled, so I decide to rise and take a short nap next to Rafe. There's nothing quite like a soothing soak in a bubble bath with a good book when you're too keyed up to sleep. Sure, the hours of carnal pleasure dulled the edge, but when my husband drifted off, the anxiety I first felt upon arriving returned. What is that trickle of unease I feel whenever I'm at rest?

I grab a fluffy white towel and begin to dry myself.

Could the apprehension be a trick of the mind from dodging the vicious Coraline and her lackeys all evening or is it something more? My blood starts to boil, when I think of the incident at the craps table. The audacity of the woman to think I'd wager with my husband. If we weren't surrounded by hundreds of vampires I might have been tempted to challenge the bitch, once and for all, and put an end to her jealous meddling.

I could take her in a fair fight. But who says the conniving wench would fight fair? I smirk at the vision of blowing up her head. Then again, who said I'd fight fair, either? Although, yes, I could explode her brain without exerting too much energy, but to do so would be stupid and point a big ole arrow right at the person who hates her the most—me.

Could Lucas be working with her? And what about Jonah, the lover to the second pedophilic Ancient I killed over four centuries ago? Then there was the suave Asian guy showing too much interest at the craps table. Come to think of it, I haven't seen my old lover Daniel for years, could he be here for different purpose, too?

I sigh while hanging the towel. There really are too many people here who could suspect my unique traits.

My fellow ex-enforcers think I hunted alone on the difficult cases out of my own arrogance. Reality was I trusted my secrets with no one. I've never met another manipulator and have often wondered—are they in hiding or do none exist? After slipping on a pair of shortie cotton pajamas, I go through my skin care routine and prepare for sleep.

Due to the recent blood I had from Jon before we left Alaska and my topping off from Rafe an hour ago, I'm not exactly tired. But it certainly won't hurt to lie down and turn my mind off for a little while, too. I rinse and dry my hands then turn to wander back into the adjoining suite. A rush of anxiety hits me, freezing me in my tracks.

What the hell? I felt this when I left the limo earlier tonight, but it's stronger now. I'm not the anxious type, but all of a sudden my vision tunnels and my head feels light. Holy shit! Is that a spell?

Vivian

Before I have a chance to reason through the panic, a whoosh of air blows my hair forward. A hood shoves over my head, a cinch tightening it closed around my neck. Strong hands grab and pin my wrists behind my back. I jerk my arms forward while slamming my head back, hoping to bash my attacker. The harsh bite of silver stops my arms and the lash of my skull fails to land on a target.

Not to be easily taken down, I lash out with a leg, connecting with someone's midsection. An expulsion of air follows the blow and then something heavy crashes against my skull, pitching me to the cold tile.

"Bitch is quick. I'll give her that." The male voice sounds familiar, but muffled by the ringing in my head from the blow. Before I have a chance to launch myself in the direction it came from, a booted foot lands in my midsection, knocking me back to the floor.

A scuffle sounds in the next room, and for the first time in decades, my heart squeezes with real panic. How many attackers are there? Do they have Rafe subdued already?

I reach out with my mind to find I'm blocked. Well and truly blocked—the kind resulting from silver on my head. Whoever is here knows exactly what I am and what I'm capable of.

I try to slow my ragged breathing as I pick myself up from the floor, movements hindered by the silver bindings around my wrists.

"What do you want?" I ask in an even tone, keeping the rage out as best I can.

Cora's voice comes from the next room, where the smash of a lamp against the wall indicates the struggle with Rafe still thrives. "Come now, my dear. Surely you couldn't have thought you fooled us all?"

Hands grasp the hood on the side of my face as another set of hands latch onto my upper arms from behind. The hood is adjusted and Coraline's angry features appear through two eye slits in the silver-lined cloth covering. "There, that's better." She grins—her full hatred of me no longer hidden by the sheen of civility. "Wouldn't want you to miss the best part."

I'm dragged into the suite and my head is twisted to face the bed I shared with my spouse earlier. Three vampires struggle to restrain Rafe, only one I recognize—Lucas. He holds a huge knife to my husband's throat, a gleeful look on the bastard's face.

The vampire on Rafe's left looks like he lost one too many boxing matches before he was turned, his nose appears flattened and his features look rough and muted. The one on his right has stringy black hair and an almost pasty-golden hue to his skin, bespeaking of a distant Asian relative. I've never seen either one before, but they'll be dead the second I see them again.

Cora's voice grates in my ear. "You will tell us what we want to know about the other manipulators, Alexandria," she says in a singsong manner. "Or he'll be the first in a long line of deaths we lay at your feet."

Frantic to get to Rafe, I struggle against the vampire holding me. "I don't know what you're talking about."

Lucas draws the blade slowly across Rafe's flesh. A thin line of crimson runs down my lover's neck. "Try again, bitch," the vampire says, "or I'll cut your toy right through to the bone."

Rafe stares at me, our eyes lock through the slitted hood. "If you kill him, I'll tell you nothing," I say.

Held as a hostage doesn't sit well with Rafe, and he shakes his head once. I stand straighter, testing the hands holding me to see if I can break the grip when needed.

Once again, a blow to the head knocks me to my knees. Whatever they're hitting me with, it sure as hell hurts. Stars

Vivian

cloud my vision as I watch Rafe struggling with his captors again, desperation on his face when he sees what they hit me with. I try to look back over my shoulder, but the slits don't allow much of a view.

Coraline's heavy breathing punctuates the air, and I catch a glimpse of a thick wooden shaft with a fist-sized studded metal ball on the end. Bitch looks like she'd gladly bash my head in if I move. She raises her arm again, preparing to bring the mace crashing down.

Rafe lurches against the vampires restraining him, pulling an arm free. They scuffle for a moment and it looks like Rafe may overpower the one on his right. A low guttural growl of anger spills from my husband as he clenches the throat of the vampire. In a flash, the second man punches my husband across the jaw.

It takes all three of them to subdue him again and the tension in the room runs sky high. A bellow of frustration comes from Cora and she screams, spittle flying from her mouth in her rage. "He's not worth the trouble. Finish him!"

I whip around to see Lucas' arm slice across Rafe's neck, a fountain of blood shooting into the air. "Nooo...." rips from my throat as I lunge to my feet and barrel across the room with every ounce of strength I possess.

The heavy mace knocks me in the shoulder. A sickening crunch of bones precedes an acute shooting pain radiating out from my left side. The force of the blow propels me to the rug, where I struggle to rise. As I gain my feet, the two vampires holding my husband toss him to the wood floor where a large pool of red starts to spreads around him.

The blackness I keep so tightly leashed rages to the surface—the animal instinct to kill sprints to the forefront of my mind. I flex my arms and pull with all my might. The bonds weaken and my wrists move a few inches apart. I *will* get out, and I will rip them apart with my bare hands.

There's still time to save Rafe if I can close his wound and give him more of my blood.

"Hit her again!" screams the same muffled male voice from the bathroom. "She's stretching the silver!"

I reach my husband's side as the mace connects with my skull, a resounding crack echoes through the room. Pain explodes through my head and wetness runs down my face inside the hood. I fall to the floor next to Rafe, watching the room fade to black. *No!* I scream in my mind, battling to retain consciousness. As the darkness encroaches, I lose control of my limbs.

The final words from Lucas seem to come from miles away. "Take his body and throw it out back with the rest of the trash."

Jonathan

Chapter Eighteen

Jonathan

My eyes spring open in the darkened living room. The time on the tiny DVD player near the television reads not quite six a.m. Hmmm... after staying up late into the night talking to Candy, I can't imagine why I'd jolt awake after the drama of yesterday's shootings. God, what a mess we've got on our hands.

Despite the horrors we have waiting for us my mind feels curiously light. Something seems off... no, wait... different might be a better term for it. Like a burden I wasn't aware of has been lifted.

I lie still for a moment, getting my bearings and try not to disturb the young woman sleeping next to me on the couch. My eyes close and I sink into the cushion, reviewing what I did yesterday and what could make my mind feel like this. Concentrating on my connection with Vivian I realize it's not there—that's what seems off. She's not there for the first time in over seven years. Is it the physical distance between us or has she deliberately muted it more to give me space? She promised to not cut me off, so maybe it's the distance.

Should I call her with one of the charged satellite phones? We spoke yesterday, and it's not like we said we'd talk every day. I get the feeling she's pulling away for my own good, but I don't like it. I run a hand over my face, determined not to obsess over the ancient vampire—especially after discovering who Spike really is. Vivian has told me enough times that she and Rafe can handle everything without me, so I might as well take the hint.

The simple joy of last night's one kiss floods through me. I wanted the moment to go on and on almost as much as I wanted to press my advantage and try for more, but the timing was off. It would have been shitty to make a move on her when she'd earlier witnessed her packmate jerking me off.

Last night, here in the dark, I opened to the shifter like I haven't with anyone in years. I told her about how I came to be Vivian's servant and she shared her tumultuous late teen years living on her own, which lead to masquerading as a man to stay safe.

We've both been through the ringer and talking to her felt like one of those moments with someone when you first connect and realize you have a lot in common. It was kind of freeing, actually.

I glance over at the stunning young woman. A lock of soft hair is brushed behind an ear while she sleeps on the pillow next to my hip. Her delicate heart-shaped face and cute button nose look even more sensual when she sleeps. Damn, I've got it bad.

Long after midnight, she stretched out on the sofa cushions and I stayed propped up on the connecting chaise. I'd wanted to scoot over and hold her in my arms but didn't because the raw feelings and desires scared me. That and the whole "grows a dick" thing still had me feeling a little off my game.

Jonathan

I'm dying to ask her about the sexual encounter with Naomi, but had a feeling if I brought it up she'd want to talk about the moment in the woods she witnessed... and reminding her of my indiscretion didn't seem prudent.

A small smile lights my face at the thought of Candy's wolf's teeth snapping at my ass yesterday. She was interested in me for a good long while and I had no idea. I still can't believe I thought I was gay. Fucking pheromones.

She said she understood my loyalty to the vampire and didn't have an issue with it. Could that be true? My heart swells at the mere thought of having someone for myself, outside of the loving couple... a true mate of my own. Would she consider moving here and join my growing pack?

Geez Louise. Listen to me. I sound like a chick. I shake my head at the desperate thoughts. Placing more importance on the evening than I have any right to. Best thing would be to wait and see how things develop. Maybe if I suggest she stay for a few weeks this summer that might be more of a safer approach.

I slide off the couch to kneel on the floor next to her. The mysterious shifter lies on her side, an arm curled under a throw pillow. Her breathing sounds low and steady, like in a deep sleep. My gaze travels to the dip of her waist, noticeable even through her bulky men's clothes. Before I can stop myself, I reach out and place a palm on her jeans-covered hip. It's not creepy to touch her without her knowledge if I don't actually molest her, right?

Warmth spreads through me as I softly mold my hand over her feminine curve. She feels slender and athletic. I've always admired a woman who stays in shape. Okay, I'm being creepy now. I need to stop before I do anything else and seriously regret it.

I pull away the offending hand and glance back at her slumbering face. Her eyes are wide open and she's staring at me with a thoughtful look. Crap! Tell me I did not just get caught doing something that falls precariously close to illegal.

"Er... umm... I..." I say, frozen in my guilt.

Candy lifts her head and leans forward. "Shh...." She softly places her lips on mine and gives me a tender kiss. I press closer, deepening the contact, and cup my errant hand around the back of her head. In a moment that's over far too soon for my taste, she pulls back and flashes a sly smile. "Do you normally feel-up sleeping women on your bosses' couch?"

No longer ashamed of my actions, I grow bolder and push the envelope even further. "Are you sure that was feeling you up?"

Her eyebrows lift. "Maybe it wasn't." The confident young woman leans back and stretches, reaching her arms past the pillow, pushing up her breasts to strain against the shirt buttons. When she glances to see if I'll take the bait there's a clear invitation on her face. I could be dead wrong, but in the dim light from the kitchen it looks like she wants me to go further.

The devil inside, aka the raging boner painfully shoving into my thigh, encourages me to take the leap. Not wanting to appear like some callous youth groping her at the first opportunity, I lean in near her neck, where the top two buttons of her shirt lay open. Taking a deep breath, I fill my senses with her unique spicy musk.

The aroma clearly in not male or female, but somewhere in between. While in this form she definitely smells more like a chick—at least, that's what I tell myself as I trail soft kisses down the exposed flesh and slowly edge my lips under the loose fabric.

She feels silky under my touch. When I gently suck her skin into my mouth, her breath hitches and her heart

Jonathan

thumps faster. Before I have a chance to decide how far to go, she pulls her arms back down and opens a few more buttons.

"It's not 'feeling' if you don't use your hands, now is it?" She spreads her shirt wide, revealing two hard nipples sitting atop beautiful breasts. My breath catches in my throat as the slit of my cock weeps in my pants. Those tits look pretty enough to fuck.

Never one to disappoint a lady, I gently cup her sexy offering, determined to make sure if I feel her up, I do it properly. When I lower to taste one dusky peak, she arches to press herself deeper into my touch.

I pull the tightened flesh between my lips and tease the ridged peak with my tongue. A low moan comes from the languid shifter, encouraging me to continue. My warm palms squeeze her flesh and press the two globes together, creating a channel I'd love to slide my prick through. I flick my tongue over one nipple then reach for the other one, closing my hot mouth over the aroused areola and loving it like I did the first.

Her voice rushes out on a husky sigh, "Now that's more like it, Jon."

I chuckle inside, my humor radiating like a low grumble that vibrates against her skin. By the shift of her hips on the couch, she likes the added sensation.

I pause in my ministrations to clear my lust-soaked brain. What am I doing? How far do I want to take this?

The sexually frustrated man within wants to rush headlong into whatever Candy might be offering, but the calm inner alpha who Vivian left in charge raises his unwelcome head and reminds me quite pointedly of my responsibilities.

Supernatural hunters. A dead werewolf. Several injured Weres. The arrival of Cy due to sabotaged communications.

A heavy sigh issues as I pull away from the tempting display and draw the young woman's shirt together.

Her eyes hold a question, a slight tinge of uncertainty coloring the depths. "Is something wrong?"

I shake my head. "Not in the way you think." I kiss her one last time, lingering over her luscious lips, leaving no doubt that I do indeed want her.

"We're in the middle of a situation here, you know that. As much as I might like to push it all aside and spend hours exploring every inch of your body, I can't. Another of Vivian's vampires was scheduled to land before dawn and I left instructions for them to wake me," I glance at the clock, "in ten minutes."

Candy sighs and nods her head. She reaches to button her shirt and I brush her hands aside and complete the task myself, taking my time and running my fingers over her skin while I'm at it.

"How do you want to play this?" she asks.

There's wariness in her expression. I wonder how many times she's revealed her true self to someone she's interested in and they've rebuffed her. It can't have been an easy game she played when she chose to disguise herself as a man.

I smile, eager to take the pain from her eyes and try to inject a little humor in the situation. "What—are you assuming I'm worried about people thinking I'm chasing a guy? Don't I look confident enough to you that I can pull it off?" I sit back on my heels and strike a body builder pose with my upper body. "Surely they will quake at my manliness and keep their thoughts to themselves."

Candy laughs softly and sits up, swinging her feet off the couch to rest on the floor next to my knees. "You'd do that for me?"

I think back on the hours we spent talking in the dark last night. She knows about my dedication to Vivian and

Jonathan

didn't berate me my choice or try to convince me to leave the vampire—which is way more than the last few woman I'd been with ever did. Diana's thinly veiled jealously leaps to mind. I found it surprising she was able to keep it in check whenever she was around Vivian. Good thing she doesn't work in the main building. Lori from Romeo's pack was more vocal in her opinions on my choice.

"Yeah, I would." I tilt my head to the side while I examine Candy. "But I think this is your choice. You've presented yourself as a guy in Romeo's pack. It should be you who decides who *you* want to be as we move forward." I clear my throat before speaking my next thoughts, unsure of myself but not wanting to mislead her. "Although, when we're alone, I'd prefer you to be yourself... you know... as a woman...."

She laughs loud, and takes my hand. "Are you sure about that?" She winks to soften her implication. "I could have sworn I saw you checking out Spike's ass a little too closely, once or twice."

Heat burns my face at my remembered confusion. God, I thought I was going crazy. I think I had almost convinced myself I might be bi. For a fleeting moment I picture the slim and athletic Candy naked, a woman in every sense of the word, except for an erect cock jutting out from her hips. The image doesn't repulse me like I thought it would.

If I'm perfectly honest with myself, I have to acknowledge the past times I've tried to seduce Rafe with my werewolf pheromones. Granted, the purpose was to get into Vivian's bed, but the truth is there, nonetheless. "I won't deny I'm curious about your form-altering... er... ah... abilities. But I have no idea how far or fast I'd be ready for changes."

She nods. "That's fair enough." Candy glances to the dark living room windows. "I have no problem revealing my true self to Romeo's pack..." Her voice trails off. She looks back at me with a touch of worry on her face. "But the ladies might not be too happy when I do."

It's my turn to laugh. The sound spills into the air like I haven't laughed in ages. Tears gather in the corners of my eyes, "Oh man, how many of them did you go down on?" Picturing this attractive woman on her knees between the thighs of any of those gorgeous Weres gets the blood flowing to my cock again.

She shrugs, unsure of herself. "I was lonely and they were willing. We both enjoyed ourselves. I never took it beyond oral sex."

"You think that matters? If they consider themselves straight they might really be pissed."

She looks me right in the eye. "We had a president who said it wasn't sex. We'll just have to see, won't we?"

Her strength is admirable. She's willing to face the unknown by revealing herself to her pack to spare my image of being with a man. I tug her hand and draw her closer to me, placing my free hand behind her head to pull her lips to mine. The kiss is over quickly, but it has the desired effect for both of us—we're ready to face the outcome to see what could be between us.

"I think you're amazing," I say.

"And I think you're freakin' hot," she says with a smile. "Want to do that muscle pose for me again, big guy?"

I get to my feet and pull the brown-haired beauty with me. "Let's get some coffee going first. Then, I'll show you my moves."

Her infectious smile warms me as we head into the kitchen. I never expected this moment and I want to cherish it for as long as I can.

Chapter Nineteen

Rafe

"Should we let him live?" A man's voice cuts through my haze of pain... it sounds like Lucas.

"He could prove useful down the line," Cora answers.

"I don't like it," Lucas says. "I'd rather we kill the troublesome bastard now and be done with it."

"Patience, my dear, patience." A snort sounds nearby. "Look at his body. He could prove an entertaining distraction while we torture his wife."

The boxer briefs I slipped on before sleeping are the only thing between me and the bare floor. Coldness seeps into my flesh, reminding me, despite my discomfort, that I am well and truly alive. If I hadn't had so much of Dria's blood earlier my neck wouldn't have been able to heal before I bled out. My low moan when they moved my prone body from our suite gave away my status. They bundled me deeper underground in the Seat of Darkness, to depths I'd never traveled with my wife on our many visits.

The air smells stale and old, as if the room was left empty for a long time. Weak light shines from an overhead bulb, the exposed wire indicating it was added after the stone walls were originally built.

I can't feel Dria in my head, due to the silver hood they placed on her, but I have no doubt she's still alive—especially after hearing that bitch's last comment. Dria's way too valuable for them to kill. If they try and use her abilities they will find out what Mikov discovered centuries ago—no one can control a true manipulator against their will. At least, not for long.

A chill runs down my spine when I recall Dria killed her second husband to escape her first seethe's clutches. The situation was different, though, and I don't think the same fate applies for me. The pair in front of me will likely be my undoing rather than my wife.

"Come now, Rafe," Coraline's sickly sweet tone cuts the air. "We know you're awake. Quite surprising how you healed from that fatal wound. A lesser man wouldn't have succeeded."

A male voice speaks before I stir from my position on the floor. "Or he could have just had her blood. It would speed the healing."

"Good point, Justin. The real trick is—does she know he had enough or does she think he's dead?"

I raise my head to examine the occupants of the room. Lucas stands next to the blond, curly-haired bitch, both dressed in all black, as befitting their stealthy attack. A tall, lanky man lounges against the wall. His body language appears nonchalant, but his keen gaze rests on me, curiosity burning in its depths.

"If her screaming and thrashing were any indication," Lucas says, "I doubt it. She looked like a rabid dog in need of putting down."

Justin's face tightens with distaste, and he looks away. I wonder who he is, how he got dragged into this mess. His skin tone is too vibrant and tan to be a vampire, unless he was changed very recently. And if he was a new fledgling I doubt he'd be trusted enough to be with this group here.

Feigning a weakness I don't feel, I slowly pull myself into a seated position, my back to the stone wall. Cora tracks my every move, her eyes glittering with intensity. "Have you wondered how you were both caught so easily?"

Justin glances at me on her comment, his expression pinched. Is that guilt on his stoic face? I have a pretty good idea he must have been involved in them getting the jump on us. I grunt a non-committal sound, hoping Cora will reveal more in her desire to lord her superiority over me.

"There are secret passages in the aboveground Tribunal buildings. Perhaps they were built centuries ago for the inhabitants to roam freely and avoid the sun." She lifts a shoulder. "Or maybe they were hidden servant corridors. I'm not sure." The blond vampire stalks forward, leans down to haul me to my feet and throws me into a nearby chair. "Either way, they let us into your suite."

Her explanation doesn't cover why neither of us sensed them enter our quarters, nor is Dria easily taken by surprise. Lucas claps a hand on Justin's shoulder. "Add the skill of a wizard to the mix and Dria never had a chance."

I glance at the tall, brown-haired man. Why would an experienced wizard with enough power to trick a vampire Dria's age, if even for a moment, get into a fight like this? His hair brushes his collar and lays lank against his forehead. He's dressed in black jeans, clunky black boots, and a black button down that has seen better days.

Justin straightens under my scrutiny and shifts his weight to his other foot, avoiding my gaze. Money or blackmail is my best guess. Which means he could be reasoned with, if I get him alone.

Out of nowhere, Cora's hand sails through the dimly lit cell and lands hard against my left cheek. My heads whips to the side, a slow trickle of blood runs down my chin. I look up at her perky blond visage, for the first time feeling true hate running through my blood. I will make this bitch pay for what she's planning. The question will be in the timing.

"That's better, Rafe. I see my love tap has brought some spark back into you."

Justin's discomfort gets the better of him and he leaves the cell, closing the door behind him. Cora and Lucas share a look and Lucas shrugs. She bends down and brings her eyes close to my own. In a moment I feel her force of will probing against my mental shields, seeking entrance.

She's either trying to see what I know by directly invading my mind or is about to place compulsion on me to answer her questions. The training Dria and I have done over the decades holds and I don't feel the other woman's insidious presence invading my mind.

"We're going to ask you questions about your wife and you are going to answer all you know." Her mental strength feels immense and I probably wouldn't have been able to keep her out if I hadn't had Dria's blood last night.

"Okay," I play along, unsure if she knows she's not in control. A lie can't hurt and I can try and string them along while revealing very little.

Cora's features smooth out and a hint of relief flashes in her eyes before being quickly hidden. "Good." She paces to the far end of the room and back, eagerness vibrating in her movements.

"Is Alexandria a manipulator?"

"Yes," I answer immediately. They already know it so confirming it can't do her any more harm this late in the game.

Rafe

A smile forms on the delicate face of the vampire who hates my wife beyond reason. "I always knew she must have had an edge when she hunted."

Professional jealousy can't have been her only motive, even she couldn't be that vain and petty. It's got to be something else. I'll be damned if I tell her Dria can't mind control a vampire she's never met and that her kills as an enforcer were legitimate ones based on skill. It would only piss her off more.

"Do you know of others with her abilities?"

"No." That one didn't require any lying, either. If there are any vampires with her precise skill level I've certainly never met them.

Cora stalks over and trails her gaze up and down the exposed flesh of my body. Interest glints in her eyes. I worry she might take things farther than I'm willing to fake. In what looks like a quick decision she straddles my lap. Her dark jeans rub across my thighs as she settles her weight onto me. I'm not tied to the chair, but if I make any move to hurl her off me, it would be quite apparent her compulsion didn't work.

I have to wait her out.

Besides my underwear, I'm still wearing the metal watch that never leaves me. They didn't think to remove it, and that small slip could be their undoing. There's a thin razor wire coiled inside the housing behind the watch face. Using it will be tricky and risking it now with two of them in the cell would be plain foolhardy. Best to wait for an opportunity to present itself.

A cool hand grips under my chin, the vampire's long nails digging painfully into the skin below my jaw. She tilts my head to the side and leans in to lick the blood off my chin. The rasp of her tongue against my stubble brings a fresh rush of goose bumps to my arms. What would have

195

been an intimacy gladly shared with my wife has become a gross, manhandled version with Cora, reducing me to the status of food and nothing else.

"Come now, Cora." Lucas says. "This is no time to play."

A low rumble of pleasure comes from the bloodsucking bitch as she leans back from her task. "On the contrary. Haven't you ever wondered what makes him so special to attract Dria?"

My eyes dart to Lucas, grateful to see disgust in his expression. Cora twists around to her cohort. "What? If they're over twenty and heavily muscled you're not interested?"

Lucas sniffs and pulls himself up straight. "To each their own, Cora. And besides, I'm not hungry."

Cora returns her attention to me and runs her hands slowly over the defined planes of my chest. "Oh, but Lucas..." She leans closer and trails her pointed tongue down my neck. Her breath fans my deltoid as her mouth hesitates over my shoulder. "It isn't always about feeding..." She nips my flesh, making me involuntarily shift in my seat.

She takes my discomfort for interest and bites harder, stopping shy of puncturing my skin. "I think he might enjoy some alone time with me—wouldn't you, Rafe?" She presses her will out with her question, revealing her desires to me with that simple push of compulsion.

"Not in here," I say casually, hoping to steer her toward taking me someplace else within the underground lair. I need to get my bearings and figure a way out. "And certainly not with an audience." I run a hand down her back, just one, to convince her my words are spoken from the heart, not with guile.

She smiles, a self-satisfied expression, showing she got the reaction she'd hoped for. She climbs off my lap and can't resist looking down, eager to see if she stirred a response in my body. I can't fake an erection, so I look docilely ahead of me and let her think the compulsion is still in effect.

The next hit comes as a complete surprise, ringing my ears and flushing my face with anger. The backhanded blow was delivered with a closed fist that time, aiming for more pain. "I like to do my own sort of tenderizing to my meal ahead of time, dearie." The grin twisting her face looks cruel, triggering a flicker of doubt across my mind. If she plans to beat me before attempting to feed there is only so much cooperation I'll be able to fake before self-preservation kicks in.

The last memory of Dria being pummeled with the mace enters my mind, and I steel myself for the next punch. Cora's color runs high, and I have a feeling she may be one of the old ones who feeds off pain or fear, as well. A cold quiet washes through me as brace for her fist. I can put up with anything, for as long as it takes, to save my wife from a situation worse than death. And I have no doubt that whatever they are planning, it is much worse than dying a vampire's true death.

Lucas approaches, pushing the sleeve of his right arm back. "Now, this is the kind of interrogation I prefer. Let me have a shot at him and then we'll continue the questions."

The two of them kept up their tag team beating for an hour before growing bored with my repetitive answers. There wasn't much I could say about the existence of other manipulators or their plans when I honestly didn't have any information to give them. The two of them so thoroughly believe there is some kind of conspiracy going on among manipulators that I fear what they have in store for Dria.

When I sagged my head forward in a not entirely feigned display of exhaustion, they left. I have no doubt they will be back.

Clearly, without some knowledge on my end to impart, I have become a very useless hostage at the moment. They won't reveal my presence to Dria until they deem her belief of my death is no longer useful to them. Holding back and taking the two vampires' abuse was harder than I anticipated. It would have been easier if I were tied up. Sitting here pretending to be helpless burned in my gut, but I knew if I revealed I wasn't controlled by Cora's vamp whammy I'd be in deep shit.

I drag myself to the bare cot in the corner and drop onto the stained fabric. The cold radiates off the wall and I debate on pushing the cot a few inches away just so I don't have to feel the chill coming off the stones. I'll wait a few minutes and let the cuts and swelling on my face go down first.

After the mental control exerted to not defend myself against two very powerful vampires at once, I need a moment to lie here and do nothing. A glance at my watch reveals it's almost three in the afternoon. Drew and Paul will be rising from their restorative sleep soon. Assuming the older of the two, Drew, would have waited up for my call this morning, they should be worried at not hearing from either of us.

If Drew follows procedure he and Paul will be on their way here once the sun goes down. Worry swells within me. The two won't have any idea of what they're walking into and I doubt their presence will be very helpful. It's times like this I think these fail-safe procedures aren't so freakin fail-safe.

A wizard working with Coraline? Could he be the one who crafted the charmed brooch she wore to Alaska this past January? Diana seemed sure it was the work of an experienced witch and I haven't heard of wizards stooping to such "parlor tricks", as they call them.

He looked competent and sure of himself, at least until the two vampires resorted to violence. What the hell did he think getting involved with a bunch of power hungry vampires would be like? A freakin' walk in the park? If I read his expression right, he could be a compassionate link I might be able to exploit further.

A sound in the corridor breaks into my musings. The heavy steel door swings open, and I roll over to see who is next to interrogate me. The lanky form of the wizard stands in the doorway, the brighter light from the hall casting his face in deep shadows.

With the flick of wrist, he tosses a wrapped bundle into the room. "Here. The stones make this place pretty cold." Without another word he leaves, drawing the door shut and locking me once more inside.

I wait until his footsteps retreat down the hall before getting up to investigate. I unwrap the long sleeves of a familiar shirt, to see a pair of jeans, a t-shirt, socks, a pair of shoes, some protein bars and a bottle of water. Justin brought my clothes from our suite. He didn't have to. He could have let me sit here in the cold.

As I get dressed, my mind races. Who is he, and why does he care? I sit on the cot and tear into the food and water, all too aware another captor could take them away if they so desired. The nutrition will not only help my body heal, it will keep me strong when I make a break for it.

Whoever that guy is, maybe I won't kill him when I get loose. Perhaps he doesn't deserve to die like the others. Unless, of course, that is exactly what I'm supposed to think.

Chapter Twenty
Asa

It's mid-morning, close to ten a.m. The wolves are awake, clustered once again down in the basement around the small conference table. A few of the Weres suggested meeting upstairs, but there's too much exposed glass for my comfort —and not just because of the sunlight. We'd all make excellent targets for a sniper if we presented them such an easy opportunity.

The hurricane shutters installed throughout the resort are in the guest rooms primarily, not in all the major living areas. The metal was intended to protect guests from sun in their rooms, not make the hotel virtually unsusceptible to siege from an enemy.

Cy has proven to be an interesting addition to the mix. His slick, charismatic personality easily smoothed the raised hackles of the nervous werewolves. Reassuring them that he and I would be helpful during this difficult time. Although, all Romeo and Elsa had to hear was he was an offspring of Vivian and they settled right down.

The shocked conversation and angry accusations surrounding Spike's revelation to be a woman were far more distracting to the group, and probably helped keep the focus off Cy more than anything else. The expressions flashing across Jon's face the past couple of hours, especially when a few of the ex-cheerleader Weres started yelling, were classic. Apparently Candy had some fun with quite a few of the ladies in the pack, much to Jon, Eric, and Pat's amusement.

Eric leans over and whispers to me while shouts of "Hell, no!" once again rip from the fiery Naomi. "I think the funniest thing is most of the ladies 'Spike' played around with turned Pat down flat. But damn, at least he was a real guy."

I don't think the situation is quite as funny as the two of them do. If anything, it should indicate how crappy he came across in his attempts—and maybe hit home the fact that his pick-up skills need some major work. I clear my throat and whisper back, "Or, you two could recognize that a woman knows how to come on to another woman better than you two nobs do."

Candy looks my way and smiles. I freeze for a moment, unaware she was listening to our conversation. That'll teach me not to try and say anything in a room full of dogs. I nod back and drop my eyes to the table, searching for a pen to give me something to do. I never spoke to her while in her 'Spike' form and haven't much since she came out as a woman, either.

Her long reddish-brown hair spills past her shoulders in a sheet of silky, wavy fibers. She has a heart-shaped face with a dimple in her left cheek and the most interesting shade of light brown eyes I've ever seen. Her slim form is hidden by the big, baggie clothes she wore as a man, and I can't get a read on if she has any curves or not. Based on the glare I just got from Jon, I'm guessing I should stop studying her outright.

It's a fascinating ability she has to shift to any form desired. I'd love to ask her about it sometime. Jon reaches across the distance between their two hands on the table and squeezes hers reassuringly. My eyebrows creep up my forehead at his display. I wonder how this new development is going to fly when Vivian returns.

Cy leans against a wall in the corner behind Jon. Every now and then he looks like he's about to burst out laughing. He quickly brings his coffee mug up to his face and hides behind it until he can smooth his face back out. Too bad our Aunt Cali wasn't with him in Seattle. It would've been nice for her and Eric to hook up again after all these years. Then again, this dangerous situation isn't exactly ideal for catching up.

Romeo has finally had enough of the bickering women and stands up. "Alight, if you're all done bitching for the moment..."

Pat snickers and earns some nasty glares from the women.

The Alpha continues, "Maybe we can get down to business and form some search teams to go out and find the hunters."

A few Weres raise their hands to indicate they'd like to volunteer. Jon frowns, "You all still have no idea which one of you could have led the hunters here." He looks around the assembled faces, checking for signs of guilt. "No one let it slip where they were going?" He shakes his head and locks gazes with the alpha pair across the table.

"Why focus on this now, Jon?" Elsa asks. "What difference can it make on how they found us?"

Jon stands, matching Romeo and the tension in the room increases. "It might not be hugely important *right now*. But it may help when we catch them." At the blank looks on the pack's faces he continues. "Could it be a scorned

Asa

lover?" He cuts his eyes to the wife of one of the Were's who was shot. "Or a relative who went off the deep end when they discovered someone's new affliction?"

His gaze goes back to the Alphas. "A neighboring pack who wants to seize control of your territory?" A negative reply leaps from Romeo's lips before Jon can even get the rest of his sentence out. Jon raises a hand to cut off the older man's further protestations. "Okay. How about another route—how many people do you all work with day in and day out who could have guessed your secret? Have you all been able to hide it as well as you think?"

Elsa looks around the room, taking in the expressions of uncertainty on the faces of their pack. "How can we possibly know the answer? And what good will come of knowing it? No matter what, we need to protect the pack first."

"Look, I know we talked about a lot of this earlier—but it matters. I'm bringing it up again because those are real people out there," Jon says in a quiet, controlled voice. "Before we all head out there to track them we need to keep the possibilities firmly in our mind. These might not be some cold-blooded killers, but a jealous lover, grieving family member.... Who knows?"

Nods from the assembled wolves leave me wanting to shake my head and scream. Jon can pretty it up all he wants, but the buggers loose on the resort took the first shot and have killed a woman. They aren't here out of some misguided angst, they're here to destroy. The sooner this group gets that through their furry heads the better off they'll be.

I glance over at Cy in the corner, his whipcord lean body and wide chest not moving as he contemplates the agitated wolves around him. He meets my eye and nods. Perhaps he's thinking the same thing I am. We'll have to wait 'til the wolves file out to converse.

Jon organizes small parties numbering three and the wolves head up into the daylight. They're going outside as humans on the off chance the hunters might not shoot if they think the person could be entirely human. Smart ploy and for their sakes, I hope it works. Cy and I are stuck down here until dark, unable to do more than monitor the cameras in the command center.

After the boisterous group leaves the basement I reach for the carafe of bloodcoffee. "Want some more?" I ask my old master.

"Sure," he answers while holding out his cup. He takes a seat two chairs from me and sips his drink.

The combined coffee and nutritional jolt helps my fatigue, but I'm running on fumes and will need to take a nap if I'm going to be any help to Jon later.

Cy takes a sip of his drink and stares at me. I feel his heavy gaze weighing on me as I shift in my chair, uncomfortable under his scrutiny. I've known him for two years and can't help but wonder at the intensity he's aiming toward me.

"I'm going to bed soon," I say. "You'll be in the room down the hall I showed you. Kotsana, the one whose wife was killed, has been moved upstairs for now, drugged and sleeping."

Cy nods, his stare not flinching. "What can you tell me about Vivian?"

My brow furrows in confusion and I feel the beginnings of an ache behind my eyes. That's odd. I've never had a headache since becoming a vampire. "What's that now? You're asking about Vivian?"

"Yes. What have you learned about your new master since coming here last fall?" I feel a push against my mind and recognize a force trying to work its way in. "We haven't had the chance for a nice heart-to-heart over the phone—have we?"

Before I work out completely what I'm doing I draw my Smith and Wesson 500, loaded with silver, and aim it at Cy's skull. "Dude—are you fucking with my head?"

Cy's eye glitters with an edge for a moment and then the pressure inside my brain dissipates. "It was just a question, Asa."

"Why are you asking me about Vivian?"

The older vampire settles back in his chair, acting like nothing just happened and I'm not holding a gun on him. "No reason. Relax."

"Relax? Are you fucking kidding me? I felt you trying to get into my mind!"

"And how would you know what that feels like?" He leans forward, eagerness on his face. "Has it happened before? Has Vivian done it to you?"

Answering him might reveal more than I'd like. I know Vivian has been inside my head more than once—the last time being when I shot Joanna. I've worked my ass off to build mental barriers since then to ensure I'll have some type of warning if she ever attempts it again. But her touch was much lighter, I'm sure of it. Actually, I wasn't even aware she did it until she told me later. Hindsight made me think I recognized a light sensation, although I could have easily been wrong.

The fear that gripped me, knowing she could get in my brain anytime she wanted and play marbles with my mind, freaked me out for days. I realized then why manipulators were deemed too powerful to live. Hell, the forest illusion she cast in this conference room was a cheap magic trick compared to the violation of physically altering a man's mind at will.

A cold shudder races down my back at the thought that perhaps Cy has a little of the same gift as Vivian. Maybe he doesn't know what she truly is. Could he be trying to dig up information from me because he's just as clueless as Paul is regarding his powers?

"Dude, you *ever* try to get in my head a gain I'll blow your head off." I flip the safety back on the gun and ease it down to my side. "Are we clear?"

Cy's cold, black gaze watches the gun with fascination. "Crystal clear."

No longer comfortable with the man I thought I knew, I leave, taking the bloodcoffee with me. I venture to my underground bedroom and lock the door, well aware Cy could break it down and come in when I'm sleeping.

Should I call Aunt Cali? I'd need to venture upstairs near a window to get any reception. Would she be honest with me and tell me what Cy is capable of? Does she know? Why is he asking me questions about Vivian, and does it mean I can't trust the slick bastard?

The pull of sleep rides me hard as the sun climbs in the sky. Making a snap decision, I gather an old sleeping bag and my satellite phone. Eric and Pat will be manning the command center while I sleep and all three of the seethe's wolves have my number—not that I'll know immediately if they do call, but having it with me gives me a small sense of reassurance.

I walk down the corridor and through a wood door, into the unfinished portion of the basement. After a few yards, I turn down the section under the north wing of the inn and keep going 'til I reach the hidden submarine-like door that leads into one branch of the tunnels. Each of the three wings of the hotel has an escape door, and all have a coded lock on them—all with different numbers. Codes I didn't give Cy when we came through one earlier today from the hangar.

Asa

The whoosh of the metal door closing behind me releases some of the tightness in my chest. I can't believe that sonovabitch tried to get into my head. No way I can turn my back and drift off to a vulnerable sleep not knowing his motives.

I go into the first room, flicking on the caged bulb overhead as I enter. The dim dish-water light won't bother me when I lay down to succumb to the call of rest, but I'll sure feel a lot better knowing there's a steel door protecting me.

Chapter Twenty-one

Drew

I **bolt up from** restorative sleep, the concern I had when lying down to rest still front and center in my mind. Grabbing the phone next my bed, I confirm Rafe didn't call when I was out for the count.

"Chelly?" I call into the softly lit room.

"Over here, hon." She lounges in the balcony off our room, her voice carrying through the open door. In a moment she peeks her head in. "You're up early today."

I rub a hand roughly over my face. "I know. I'm worried something happened to Vivian and Rafe. Neither of them called you by chance, did they?"

Chelly comes fully into the room, her face reflective of the concern in my voice. "No, I'm sorry. They didn't." She settles on the bed next to me and runs a hand softly up and down my stiff back. "What does it mean that you haven't heard from them?"

"It means we need to get the hell to Buenos Aires as fast as we can."

Chelly's breath catches in her throat. "You think it's that serious?"

Drew

I turn to my girlfriend, the woman who drives me physically bonkers beyond all reason, and take her trembling hand into my own. "I do. I need you to be strong, not falling apart on me, okay?"

Her spine stiffens and her trembling stops. "You're right, Drew. I'm not a wimp. What can I do to help?"

"Pack your clothes while I wake Paul. I'm not taking you to the Tribunal with us, but I'm sure as hell not leaving you here either."

She nods and heads to the closet for our bags. I leave her to pack and proceed to Paul's room for the difficult task of waking a slumbering vampire.

It took a good thirty minutes until Paul was awake enough to move around the room and dress. I took a perverse pleasure in slapping him into consciousness. Reminded me of the days the lads and I used to overindulge in spirits back in London. The day after a long night was quite similar to trying to revive the undead, like I did with Paul. The young men who were less ragged and arose first, used to smack the rest of us into wakefulness with unabashed glee.

Ahh... what I wouldn't give to be back in that carefree time instead of this current predicament. All we worried about then was the sum we gambled the night before when deep in our cups.

"Jesus, Drew." Paul rotates his jaw with one hand. "Did you have to hit me so freakin' hard?"

I suppress a grin, sure it will gain me no favor from the young fledgling. "When the polite taps didn't work, I had to apply more force."

"Uh, huh. Yeah. So you say."

I place a hand on his shoulder and deliver a well-meaning shove in the direction of the closet. "Come on, pack your stuff. We need to get in the air as quick as possible."

"We don't have a seaplane here anymore, do we? Didn't a pilot take it back after he dropped off our luggage?"

"Yes, you're right. We're going to take a boat back to Puerto Santa Cruz and rent a plane to fly to Buenos Aires."

He yanks his bag off the top shelf and stomps back to the bed. Maybe I hit him a little harder than I should have. Oh well, he'll get over it. "I called ahead to Vivian's hangar and the rental is being prepared now."

There's a knock at the door and Tommy and Bob let themselves in. "Hey, are you two going somewhere and didn't tell us?" Tommy asks. The dirty-blond hair of the fit Aussie falls over one eye, concern visible on his face.

Damn. I wasn't counting on taking the entire entourage, but if Chelly is going with us I'm not sure leaving them behind is a good idea. "You're coming, too," I say, making a split decision. "Pack up and be ready in ten minutes."

The two leave and I turn back to Paul. He's fiddling with the contents of his bag, a look of consternation on his face like there's a question weighing on him. "We've got bagged blood, Drew. Why would we need to bring them?"

A trickle of unease slides down my spine. "I don't want to split us up. It might not be what Vivian would do, but I'm going on instinct here."

In a surprise show of support, Paul claps me on the shoulder. "You're doing fine. I trust you, man." His face twists into a grimace. "As long as you're not the bastard waking me up every day."

A half smile forms on my face as I turn to leave, eager to check on Chelly and keep us moving. Out in the hall one of the twins is walking toward our suite. I raise my voice to draw her eye to me. "Can I help you?"

Drew

She pauses with her small fist poised to knock on our door and turns toward me. A warm, welcoming smile spreads across her lovely oval face. Her dark brown eyes twinkle in the soft light of the hall. "Drew, just the man I was hoping to see."

I raise my eyebrow at her statement. I'm not sure which twin she is, but they both seemed more interested in Chelly than me the last time we tangled. "Yes?"

"My father called. The boats are being repaired. You won't be able to use them until we get parts flown in. They're due by the end of the week."

"Boats? How many do you have on the island?"

"Three."

"And all three are out of service at once?"

"Yes," she replies, without a hint of guile in her voice.

Something doesn't feel right. I press my will forward, staring deep into the young woman's eyes. "What is wrong with the boats?"

Her eyes widen slightly, indicating she's under my influence and will answer truthfully. "I don't know. I don't know anything about boats."

The answer doesn't help me figure out what's going on, but at least I know she's not bald face lying to me. I pull my will back and nod, dismissing the young woman. "Thanks...?" I trail off, unsure which woman I'm addressing.

"Carmella."

"Yes. Thanks, Carmella. We'll head down to the dock and see what Dalton says about the repair work."

The South American beauty shrugs a shoulder, uncaring one way or the other and walks back down the hall the way she came. I move to open our door only to have Chelly beat me to it. "All packed," she says with a smile, love shining brightly in her eyes to anyone who bothered to look. "I did yours, too."

Warmth seeps through me at her thoughtfulness. Relief relaxes my shoulders, releasing tension I didn't know I was holding. One way or another we'll get to the bottom of this and have our time together. And when we are alone next, I don't plan on waiting to show this luscious creature exactly what I want to do with her.

I step forward and take her round cheeks in my hands. Leaning in, I place my lips on hers in a light kiss of gratitude. "Thank you."

Within twenty minutes the five of us are walking to the dock, the modified golf carts parked at the bottom of the sloping hill. The wind whips our light coats against our body and sends Chelly's longer hair flying into the breeze like a flapping flag. The smell of the ocean overpowers the weaker aromas of the tiny island, oddly uplifting with the water's cleansing scent despite the wet weight of it in the wind.

The sun has started its descent, weak light slanting across the gravel road, casting long ragged shadows behind us. Paul and I have every inch of skin covered to avoid exposure, including scarves around our ears and faces. To the observer we might appear to be covering up from the chill, even though the fall temps here are nothing compared to what we're used to in Alaska.

"How long will the boat ride be?" Bob asks.

The clock at the house read a quarter after six when we left. Which means we'll be flying in full dark by the time we get to the hangar and take off. "A little over an hour."

"I hate boats," he continues. "They make me sick."

Tommy snorts. "Considering you finished a huge bag of Cheetos a little bit ago, that can't be good. I won't be sitting near you on the boat."

The good-natured ribbing keeps up all the way to the dock, where a stoic Dalton greets us. The dark-haired man stands stiff, his face lined in worry. "I'm sorry, sir," he says to me, "the boats are inoperable. Didn't my sister-in-law reach you?"

I motion the others into the boathouse so I can talk to the caretaker alone. "Yes," I begin, pressing my will forward with the word, snaking deep into his consciousness. "She did pass on the information. Can you tell me what happened to the boats?"

He opens his mouth to respond and hesitates. There! I sense a presence in his mind. Another vampire has been in here, and by the subtlety implemented, I'd guess they weren't expecting their actions to be discovered.

"The motors won't turn over on two of them. And the third won't hold oil." The caretaker meets my eye, appearing to believe ever word he says. "My engine knowledge is not the best. We're waiting for a boat mechanic to come from shore with parts."

In a flash of insight, I snag a vague memory floating in Dalton's mind of him sabotaging the boats. The image is buried so deeply, he's not even aware he did it. Which can only mean someone else directed in his actions. Without being cognizant of it, the handsome caretaker has recently become a vampire pawn, probably in a plot against the family he's served for two decades.

I delicately look for a trace of mental contamination that may lead me to the culprit, but whoever dallied in his brain was very delicate, not disturbing too much or planting overtly traitorous actions in Dalton's mind.

It will take more skill than I possess to dig through these fine threads and uncover the truth. I pull back my will and smile reassuringly at the man. "I know my way around an engine. Let me try my hand."

His face pinches, but he nods and steps aside. I enter the boathouse to see Bob already tinkering in the engine compartment of one of the boats. A glance over my shoulder reveals Dalton walking toward the home he shares with Flavia. Could he be up to something else?

I shake my head, wondering if I'm doing the right thing, or if there could be a more elaborate trap in store for us. A cleared throat brings my attention back to our group. The others sit on their luggage, eager to begin this new segment of our journey. Chelly sends me an encouraging smile and I nod my reassurance. I grab a toolbox near a support beam then leap onto the boat deck.

I'm surprised another vampire has compromised the caretaker—but, more so that Vivian didn't check all of the island's inhabitants when we arrived for possible corruption. Sloppy. That's what that is.

I ruminate over her actions while clicking on a flashlight to aid Bob in his exploration. She respects the humans loyal to her beyond what is safe, and now it's come around to bite her in the ass. Could Dalton be implanted with silent orders extending past keeping us on the island? Have the others been affected and that's why the ladies have been overly familiar too soon?

I crouch down and angle the beam of light deeper into the engine compartment. "What do you think, Bob?"

He scratches his head, pushing thin flyaway hair into disarray. "The starter is disconnected, and a few other wires have been pulled away from their connections." He reaches a hand into the toolbox and grabs a wrench. "Give me ten minutes and we'll try the engine. If it still doesn't turn over, I'll dig deeper for another cause."

I pat the stout man on his shoulder in thanks and stand. "This one might work out," I call to the others in the boathouse. "With any luck, we'll be out of here soon."

Drew

After a rough, fast-paced trip over choppy water—punctuated by Bob repeatedly hurling his stomach contents over the side—we arrive in port. I manned the small boat as if the hounds of hell could swim and were pursuing us. No matter how hard I tried, I couldn't shake the unease and anxiety filling my gut, pushing me to go faster.

I checked my cell phone often, and unlike our compatriots in Alaska who called after we sent in Cy as back up, I never heard from Rafe. True fear for them began to set in after the boat engine turned over. I joined Vivian's seethe for a reason—I don't want to lead. Never have.

Some people might consider such a trait as a weakness, but I don't. Knowing your own strengths and weaknesses takes a lot of soul searching and honesty—something not everyone will take the time to explore. Doing so might reveal things they'd rather leave undiscovered. Plausible deniability.

Everyone likes to play armchair quarterback from the safety of their homes via instant replay, but making an instant decision when the stakes are much higher than a simple game can be paralyzing. Are you making the right choice? Will a mistake cost the lives of the people around you? Have they put their faith in you to make the best decision when even you aren't so sure of the correct path?

I smooth my facial features, keeping my expression free of any inner turmoil—in the same way an experienced vampire can become still and not reveal their presence to those around them. A useful skill to develop when living among a species that thrives on back stabbing, politics, and intrigue—which many of my past seethes have.

A hired car takes us to the small inland airport and Vivian's private hangar. The flight plan was filed on our behalf ahead of time—after I do a last minute check we should be ready for takeoff. I motion the others inside and race through the safety list.

I climb the rented aircraft's stairs and pull them closed behind me. Everyone settles into seats and gets themselves comfortable. I glance to the front of the small dual-propeller plane and call out, "Paul, come sit with me."

He stows his bag and joins me in the cockpit. "What do you need?"

I nod to the seat next to me as I place the communication headset over my ears. "I want you to join me so you can get a feel for the way things work. Sort of an introduction to flight. Also, I want to talk to you about some things."

I wait until we're airborne and cruising at a good altitude to talk about what's really on my mind. "Can you feel Vivian in the back of your mind?"

Paul looks away from the many lights of the dash to glance in my direction. "What do you mean?"

"Sometimes, I've been able to detect her moods and feelings if I concentrate hard enough." I roll my shoulders, trying to shake the apprehension I felt when talking to Rafe on the phone then stare out the windshield into the dark sky. "But when I woke up today that slight presence was gone."

"What do you think it means?" Paul asks, concern coloring his voice.

"I'm not sure. That's why I wanted to check with you."

I see Paul's shoulders rise and drop in his reflection on the windshield. "I'm not too aware of what's going on in my head regarding all this vampire mind linkage stuff yet. Usually she's just there without my knowing how it happened." An audible sigh comes over the headset. "I'm not much help am I?"

"Don't worry about it, Paul. You're still learning to sort everything out. It'll come to you in time."

Drew

He snorts. "Oh yeah, after decades and decades of feeling like a dork... gee, what a great thing to look forward to."

"Better than being dead, isn't it?" I shoot back, annoyed at his attitude.

Paul sobers and looks down at the control panel. "Touché."

This opening sounds like what I need to ask about something else that's been weighing on my mind for months. "Hey, speaking of almost being dead—we certainly got lucky back in that hangar with Emiko, didn't we?"

Paul freezes. "Oh man, you're not kidding. I still don't know how she didn't see me as I was sneaking up on her."

"Really, Paul?" My tone slightly incredulous. "It never occurred to you *how* you could have done it?"

His voice comes across the speakers a little louder than before, "What the hell are you implying, Drew?"

I sigh and wonder what possessed me to bring this up now, like there aren't enough things on our plate, already? Best to get my suspicions out in the open and know what possibilities we're dealing with when we walk into the Seat of Darkness. "What were your exact thoughts when you were approaching her that night? Do you recall?"

Paul stares into the darkness, lost in memories. A long minute of silence passes over the headset, and I begin to wonder if I should prompt him to answer.

"I wished," the chef says in a soft tone. "Does that make sense?" He looks at our dual reflection in the glass and locks eyes with me. "I can't think of any other way to put it. I wished really hard to not make a sound, to be quiet as a mouse, so she wouldn't sense me."

I nod and glance down at the instruments to make sure we're still on track with our flight path. "I think you cast your first physical illusion that night, Paul. Pushed your will out into a wishful thought that became an illusion."

"Really?" his voice squeaks out, disbelief clear in his high-pitched whine. "How is that possible? Can *you* cast illusions?"

"No," I answer. "But Vivian's not my maker, either."

Paul folds his arms across his chest and sinks back into his seat, no longer interested in flying the plane. "I don't understand. Shouldn't I have been able to mind-control Mina in the kitchen, then? I thought I couldn't even do that right so I must be the vampire equivalent of a mental weakling."

Might as well come clean about everything I've learned and suspect. "That wasn't your fault, Paul. I think the caretakers and their family members had a visit from one of the Inner Circle's lackeys. I tried to discover who, but the vampire was subtle and skilled." Disappointment in my own mental abilities weighs on me. Sure, I might be able to control a group, but I can't wield the gift like a scalpel. "I feared going too deep and damaging their minds by trying to find out more."

"So you think I couldn't place a compulsion on Mina because she was already under the influence of someone stronger?" He shifts in his chair, looking uncomfortable by the direction the conversation has taken.

"Yes. That fits with what I've experienced in the past." I think back to my own learning curve when I was Paul's age. I wasn't in a safe environment like Vivian has set up for her seethe in Alaska. He's luckier than a lot of other fledglings, in more ways than one.

"Let me get this straight, you think I have the power to cast an illusion to momentarily deceive a fellow vampire, but not enough mojo to slip into a human's mind? Doesn't quite jive."

Drew

Content the autopilot can handle the plane for a while in safety, I swivel my chair to face the younger vampire. "Well, for starters, Emiko and I weren't under orders from a more powerful vampire—and secondly, they aren't the same thing. Think of a physical illusion like a magic trick. You with me?"

"Yeah, I suppose so."

"The best comparison I can make to vampire mind manipulation would be to line up a person who can do sleight of hand next to someone with extra sensory perception."

"ESP? Come on, people can really do that? Read minds, move stuff, see the future?"

I laugh. "Do you hear yourself, Paul? You're a vampire who cast an illusion of invisibility over himself to kill *another* vampire, and your boss talks to you in your skull anytime she wants—oh, *and* she forcibly entered Cora's mind in front of witnesses to change the woman's memories. Yet, you think ESP might not be real?"

His shoulders slump. "Okay, good point." The true implications of our conversation seep in, and he straightens in his chair. "Holy shit. That means I might inherit other parts of Vivian's traits as well? Down the line, like?"

"I'm afraid so."

He pales and his eyes go wide. "I could be hunted and killed by my own species for being a manipulator? That's not right."

"Think about it, Paul." I soften my tone to show I'm not against him, just trying to play both sides. "If someone could control *anything* the most powerful of us can do, wouldn't that make him or her too dangerous to keep alive? Absolute power corrupts absolutely."

"I thought you liked Vivian." Paul's voice rises with a note of hysteria in it. "I thought you were loyal to the seethe!"

219

I reach across the cockpit, and lay a hand on his arm. "Calm down, Paul. I *am* loyal to the seethe. I was trying to play devil's advocate. Manipulators have been hunted for centuries. Wiping them out seemed to be the only way to prevent the ruling class from rising again."

"Ruling class, what the hell are you talking about?"

"There are legends about manipulators who governed all vampires for a millennium."

"And what happened? How did it all change?"

I sink into my seat and let my head fall back, mentally exhausted and terrified of what awaits us when we land. "I don't know. Some say the rest of us had enough and killed those in charge, using silver hoods to incapacitate their powers. Other stories say a handful of corrupted leaders destroyed those with mirroring skills who opposed them." I shrug and turn my chair back to face the windshield. "Who the hell knows what really happened? The end result is the same—you were born into a line with a target on its back."

Jonathan

Chapter Twenty-two

Jonathan

Around noon, the fully-healed Pat, Eric, and I slipped through the underground tunnels to one of the empty family cabins. We're scanning the immediate area visible beyond the windows for signs of the hunters before we go exploring. I doubt the rifle-toting bastards will leave their secure positions covering the inn, just yet.

Earlier this morning, shots were fired at the doors when our organized groups of Weres attempted to leave the main building. A new plan had to be hastily thrown together. Not willing to go against Vivian's prime directive that the tunnels remain a secret, I told the others there's a hidden way onto the property only accessible by employees.

The pack grumbled quite a bit and Romeo looked frustrated enough to challenge me at one point, but the devastating loss of Deneishia, Kotsana's overwhelming grief, and the two healing Weres were enough to waylay him for a while.

"All clear in this direction," Eric says from behind the curtains near the living room window.

Pat's voice carries from the master suite. "Same here."

"Ditto for my end," I say after dropping the window blinds over the kitchen sink.

The three of us gather in the living room and start to disrobe. I stop before removing my pants, deciding to watch out for danger while the pups change. It can take them upward of a minute or more some days and they're vulnerable during the transition.

We already discussed what we plan to do—track and find the hunters' base camp. Once we determine how many we're up against, we can devise an effective strike. It's times like this, Asa's military background really comes in handy.

I watch the slow transformation of the young wolves and remember my own pain during that first year. It's not unbearable, but it's no walk in the park, either. Soon, the two are standing before me in wolf form, sides heaving from exertion. After one last survey with binoculars through the front curtains, I crack open the front door and remove my jeans before calling the change.

In a burst of energy, the air around me vibrates, and I'm forced to the floor. The muscles shift and flow in a speed too fast for the human eye to track. Fur rushes over my reshaped flesh. With a shake to settle my pelt into place, I glance over at my packmates. We wait a few minutes more until their breathing has returned to normal before venturing into the sparse woods surrounding the cabin.

As agreed, we angle through the brush, noses lowered, in a large circle around the main building of the resort. We already determined how far away the shooters would have to be to cover more than one exit and planned half a mile beyond that to ensure we'd be undetected while searching for scent trails.

The warm spell yesterday reached the low forties, creating mud that sucked at our paws, leaving the hunters a clear trail to find us when we hunted. Last night the

Jonathan

temperatures returned to normal and today's high will still leave the top soil frozen solid.

We would cover more ground if we split up, but I'm not risking Eric and Pat's lives with silver-loaded rifles in the vicinity. Pat rumbles a low growl. Eric and I slow our looping pace to see what caught his attention. A faint trace of artificial deer musk hangs on the low branches of a nearby bush.

We fan out and search deeper into the surrounding scrub to pick up the next mark in the scent trail. Eric yips, from the south, and Pat and I trot over to investigate. He's found a series of footprints set in the hardened mud, like uncovered dinosaur tracks frozen in stone. After five or six paces, the footprints disappear, hidden by the decaying, frozen vegetation covering the ground from last summer.

The general direction leads away from the main building, pointing deeper into the land bordering the park. While we don't technically have the right to patrol the protected lands, I am familiar with the terrain and lead the two young wolves into the thickening trees.

The hunter's musk, used to disguise a bow or rifle hunter in a deer stand, sends us on a twisting path. A wiff here, a stronger dash there. Part of me wonders if we could be walking into danger, and I slow our pace, watchful for hidden traps ready to spring. Brittle branches snag our fur as we weave through narrow gaps in the underbrush.

After a while we come to camouflage netting draped in a tent fashion between trees. Pat flanks right and Eric to the left, both on the lookout for signs of approach while I investigate the makeshift camp. There are no leavings from a fire, which is smart on their part. We would've been able to track them easier if they lit one.

Coils of rope, four shovels, and a few silver-coated steel traps lie piled near a long camo painted box. I can't lift the lid in my present furry state, but I can smell the gun oil and steel of the weapons the locker held. High-tech equipment lies further away the enclosure, near three rolled up sub-zero mummy sleeping bags. These men came armed with night scopes, infrared sights, GPS systems and several boxes of ready-made food pouches.

Are there only three men as the bags indicate, or are they sleeping in shifts? Even if there were more men, I'd think they'd want their own sleeping bag. I'll have to wait and discuss what I've found with Eric and Pat when we return. They may have found scent trails further from camp that will give us an exact number.

Nothing here leads me to think they plan on capturing a werewolf alive—ropes can't hold one of us, and I don't see anything large enough to hide a cage. A shiver raises the hackles across my shoulders. The shovels imply they plan to leave bodies here in the tundra. Too bad the bastards have no idea you can't dig deep enough to bury a body up here—not without a good fire going for days to thaw the permafrost.

What I don't see are ATVs of any kind to answer how they arrived here. I circle outside of the makeshift tent and nose around 'til I find what I'm looking for. Hastily bundled parachutes have been haphazardly shoved into a bunch of packs. Someone flew them here and would be radioed to pick them up, which means it will be much harder for us to kill these men and hide their presence.

I snuff loudly, trying to clear the musk smell out of my sensitive nose. Worry over this new development weighs on me and I'm not sure how we're going to get out of this scot-free.

In less than ten minutes I've found all there is to uncover—which also means there's no conveniently left-open diary or map that might betray the hunters' motives, either.

Jonathan

There are too many variables at play, too many reasons they could be here, and a very real risk that others know where they are and why.

I woof softly and the two young Weres pad through the brush toward me, not leaving a sign of their passing behind. Unwilling to risk encountering the hunters, we head due east before angling north, slowly making our way around the main building to the family cabins. No new scents mar the afternoon chill near the small house. We return undetected and change back to human form in the darkened living room.

I get dressed then rummage through the fridge while the pups struggle to complete their transformation. The contents of the fridge are sparse, mainly condiments, soda and a six pack of beer. I grab three Miller Lites and mosey to the loveseat.

I twist off the top and take a long pull. Bunny won't mind that we drink them, she's a pretty hospitable sort. I make a mental note to grab the rest and a bottle of wine to give to her when we pass her temporary location in the tunnels. There's no telling how long she'll be down there with the kids and I bet the alcohol will be welcome.

By the time I finish half the beer, both young men are dressed and panting on the couch. Even though they've been practicing, two changes in under two hours is very taxing. Eric's hand shakes as he reaches for a beer.

Pat flops to the floor in a dramatic fashion and groans. "Hand me my beer, dude. I don't think I can move."

I open one, passing the bottle to the grinning bastard. He raises his head to take a long swallow before dropping his skull back to the carpet with a *thunk*. "I'd tell you I love you, but I might disappoint you when I don't grow tits and sprout a pussy."

Eric spits some of his beer and glances my way with a shocked expression. I casually lean down and snag Pat's beer. He's too weak to put up much of a resistance. I put my thumb over the end and shake the bottle up and down vigorously before shoving it back in his hand. The carbonated liquid foams over the top and soaks the front of Pat's shirt.

The crooked-nose punk sputters, but doesn't move fast enough to avoid the worst of the mess. I settle back on the couch with a smile. "What were you saying, Pat?"

He eyes the remains of his beer and shakes his head. "Too soon to start with the bad jokes?"

My face hardens when I look down at my packmate. "Some things shouldn't be joked about. Especially when you don't know shit. Keep that in mind, puppy."

Pat lets it drop and drinks his beer in silence. I finish the remains of mine and relay what I discovered at the camp. When I'm done, their bottles stand empty, too. "Did you two find anything useful?"

"I can confirm their numbers," Eric says. "I found three unique piss spots."

I look to Pat, who's pulling his wet shirt away from his chest with a scowl on his face. "Pat?" I prompt.

"Huh?" He looks up. "Yeah. Three distinct scents."

"Alright," I grab their empties and stand, "let's talk over what we found with Romeo and Elsa."

"Not their whole pack?" Eric asks.

I shake my head and wander to the kitchen with the recyclables. "I'm getting tired of the drama in talking to their whole group. Since they are effectively grounded inside the inn 'til this mess is over, I figured their alpha's can deal with telling the others what they want them to know."

Jonathan

Remembering first to grab the booze for Bunny, I make my way to the master bedroom where the tunnel hatch is located.

"Should we try to flush them out?" Elsa asks.

We're gathered in Viv and Rafe's kitchen, seated around the wood table. Eric and Pat did a good job with covering the damaged window with plywood, so we're safe from pesky gunfire at the moment.

"Not a bad idea," I say. "How do you suggest it? Use one of us as bait?"

The pixie-like features of the female alpha screw up in a measure of distaste. "I don't want to suggest something that could get one of us killed."

Romeo nods and leans forward, placing his elbows on the table. "We could ask the vamps to give it a shot tonight when it gets dark. There are two of them now, right? It wouldn't be like we're sending one out alone."

"With any luck," Elsa adds, "the hunters won't be aware of their presence."

"Okay," I nod. "I'll talk it over with Asa and Cy when they wake. What stance are we going with here—kill or catch and question?"

Elsa and Romeo look to each other, and Romeo nods. "In light of the information regarding their transportation into the resort, and possible outside connections, we think catching them and finding out what they know is the safest course."

Tension I wasn't aware I'd been holding drains away at his answer. If they had answered differently, Romeo and I might have had our first physical fight, a confrontation I avoided eight years ago by leaving his pack, and one I still wasn't looking forward to now. The stocky man is built like a tank, even if he is a few inches shorter than me. I'm not saying I couldn't take him, but the wily bastard has been Manitoba's alpha for three decades for a reason—he's a tough and a scrappy fighter, proven to have the stamina to outlast his opponents, no matter their size.

"Good. The bloodsuckers will be up in a few hours." My stomach growls and I recall the food we have in the fridges for cooking outside in the grotto. We can't use the grills anymore, but we've still got stoves in here. "Who wants to eat?"

The couple smiles and moves through the apartment toward the resort's kitchen, with Eric and Pat right behind them. I shout I'll join them in a few minutes, and make my way into the couple's office to stand near an uncovered window. She and Rafe need to know what's going on, plus I haven't heard from them in a while.

I power up the gadget, hearing a warning blip indicating a waiting message. It's Paul, calling from a plane, telling me to call him back pronto. A sliver of worry skates across my back, bringing a chill of apprehension in its wake. I punch in his number while panicked thoughts bounce through my mind. Why and where are they flying to? What the hell has happened down there?

CHAPTER TWENTY-THREE

Paul

I end the call with Jon, turning off the speaker function when I hang up. Drew and I relayed all that's transpired, and after Jon calmed down he told us what's been going on up there. The gratitude I feel toward Asa overwhelms me. He took care of my family like he said he would. I might not always understand the bald muscle man, but as a seethe mate, I know I can count on him.

Drew handles the landing with ease and confidence, never betraying his conflicting thoughts whirling below the surface. If he hadn't told me he was on edge and concerned about making a wrong decision, I wouldn't have known. Makes me glad I'm not in his shoes, that's for sure.

The most stress I ever had to deal with as a chef was making sure the diner liked their meal. And since I came to work for the V V Inn that has never been a concern—most of the patrons prefer blood.

Chelly booked a large suite of rooms at a high-end hotel during the plane's descent. She made sure to get a fridge, so we can store all the bagged blood. Drew insisted we bring the entire supply, because we didn't know what shape Vivian might be in or what awaited us. Even though he doubts himself, I think he's making the best choices he could for all of us, so far.

It's close to midnight by the time we get checked in and hire a car to take us to the Tribunal's townhouse across the city. I asked if we were planning on walking up and knocking on their door and Drew suggested that might not be the smartest move. In hindsight, he was quite diplomatic. Rather stupid of me to think we'd just walk right up like nothing was wrong.

The only intel we have regarding the building is memories of the city block and property boundaries uncovered when we researched Emiko's possible guilt in January. My memory isn't the best—it wasn't like I was studying the maps thinking I'd be visiting anytime soon. Do we have enough to go on, or will this turn out to be a colossal mess?

Drew signals for the driver to pull over a few blocks from the address. We're both dressed in dark clothes, but one glance at the surrounding facades of the imposing architecture tells me we're way underdressed for the area. Thankfully, I doubt many homeowners will be out and about this late at night to raise the alarm. Then again, if these wealthy streets have a lot of patrolling police, we'll stand out like crooks in a heartbeat.

Drew pays the driver and the car disappears into the night. The air carries a damp chill and smells clean from a recent rain. The streets glisten with moisture and puddles, like fresh ink has been poured across the dark surface. The temperature feels much warmer here than on the island we left almost six hours ago.

"Are you okay, Paul?" Drew asks.

"Hmm?" I say, lost in my own thoughts.

"We need to pay attention. I'm not sure how far the Tribunal's land reaches in this area."

Paul

"Yeah, I hear you." I fill my lungs with the cool night air. "It still seems like we don't really have a plan."

A heavy sigh comes from Drew as he walks next to me along the sidewalk. "I thought the best bet would be to scope out the townhouse and see who comes and goes. See if we can find a way in undetected. Are you implying that's not good enough?"

"I'm not criticizing, man. I don't have a better idea, either." We step off the curb, crossing to the other side still two blocks from the address. In the middle of the narrow road, a tingle encases my whole body, like the mild after-effects of a limb that had its circulation cut off for a moment. Anxiety, quick and sharp, stabs me. Before I have a chance to figure out what I'm experiencing, the sensation is over. "Did you feel that, man?"

"Feel what?" Drew steps onto the curb on the other side of the street.

I shrug, not sure how to put it into words. "Was probably nothing. Felt a tingle over my body."

"Like déjà vu?" A late night wind whips by, dislodging the water on the overhanging tree branches to send a light sprinkle on our heads.

"Nah. That's always more mental for me than physical. Did you feel anything?"

Drew scans the neighborhood ahead of us. "No. Nothing. But that doesn't mean it wasn't there."

I laugh nervously, appalled when the sound comes out more like a high-pitched giggle. "Why would I feel something that you didn't?"

"Each of us has different strengths as vampires. Lots of abilities repeat among our kind, and a few are more rare. Your reaction could have been a form of intuition."

"Great," I say, my voice higher pitched than normal. "One more thing to figure out." We walk in silence a little longer until my curiosity rears its head. "How much further?"

Drew motions with his head. "Down this block and the main townhouse should be at the far end of the next block we come to."

Two shadows melt out of the night and step in front of us. I stop in my tracks, turn my head to address Drew and catch two more slip into place behind us. A faint wisp of death and blood clings to the men, indicating they're vampires. The light from the next streetlamp lies too far away to make out facial details, but they're all wearing dark clothes and black overcoats.

The larger of the two in front of us steps forward, radiating menace. He looks to be six foot five and must have been a weight lifter before he changed to have such a huge build. "Planning an unannounced visit to the Tribunal?" he says.

Somehow they knew we were here and must be advanced security. Well, there goes our crappy *sneak up and check things out all stealthy like* plan.

"We're here to speak with our master," Drew says. "She came here for the event last night."

"And who might that be?"

"Vivian Alexandria McAndrews."

The muscled man relaxes, his stiff posture gone in a blink. "You're part of Alexandria's seethe?" He extends a hand to Drew then me. "I'm George. Follow us back to the house."

Without another word, we're shepherded to an elegant four-story townhouse. The men surrounding us don't seem angry, but there's no doubt we're expected to do as told. I open my mouth to ask Drew a question, and he shakes his head once in the negative, not wanting to talk with these men in hearing distance.

Paul

George leads us up steep front steps and through the grandest foyer I've ever seen. The woven wall hangings vie with lit torches for my attention. Good God, burning torches? What century is this? Strangely, they don't smell smoky or of the fuel they must be using. I wonder what makes them burn. Magic?

The huge vampire turns to look back at us to make sure we're following. Like we have a choice? Under the bright light of the chandeliers, I get a better look at the massive wall of a man. He's got short black hair and a goatee on a face that looks like he's seen his share of fighting. The other three vampires in our escort break away in the foyer, leaving us alone with the silent George.

He leads us to a secluded room with no windows, located in the back of the dwelling. A plain wood table sits inside surrounded by four hard-backed chairs. The walls are bare of decoration. Compared to the opulence we saw on our way in, the set up reminds me a little too much of a nicely appointed interrogation room. A glance at Drew's narrowed eyes indicates he might be thinking the same thing.

The gigantic vampire motions us inside, a reassuring smile on his face. "Please, go inside. Someone will be here to speak with you shortly."

The thick wood door closes behind us, and a lock clicks into place.

Drew swears like a trucker before lowering himself onto a seat. "That didn't go as planned."

"What's the big deal? We're here aren't we? That George guy seemed pretty easy-going. We'll find out what's going on in a few minutes. Maybe Viv and Rafe's phones broke or something."

Drew hangs his head then peers up at me. "*Both* their phones? Did you not hear the door lock? The big security guys might be polite, but make no mistake—we're not here as guests."

I take the seat across from him, more comfortable than my partner in crime. I laugh. "How much you want to bet it's something simple, like they lost their phones and there's a 'do not disturb' sign on their bedroom door?"

Drew's face emanates a slow burn as he struggles for control. "Listen, you fool—" He breaks off when the door opens and two men slip inside, closing the door behind them.

One is tall, with a lanky runner's build and a broad chest. He looks to be in his late twenties and is dressed in head to toe black, his shirt looking a bit more faded than the rest. There's a smell coming off him that I can't quite place. I don't think he's an undead, that's for sure.

The other man appears more ageless with dark hair, wearing clothes befitting class and money. Dark dress pants, pressed with a sharp crease, and a dinner jacket over a starched white shirt. This chap is a vampire but other than that I couldn't say how old or powerful—the old ones know how to shield extremely well.

Drew bolts from his chair, pointing a finger at the scruffy guy in black jeans. "A wizard? It's never good when one of you is among us. What the hell is going on?"

Horror crosses my face. What is the matter with him? He's acting like they're out to kill us or something. The other vampire speaks, the smooth rolling tones of his voice pours into the room with a faint Spanish accent. "You'll find out soon enough, Mr. Lipshultz." And with that, he flips a button near the door and the floor opens beneath us.

The table and chairs cascade down a long, wide chute, with us tumbling along, too. Screams rip from my throat as I fall through the darkness. We crash to the cold stone below, the chairs and table splintering on the impact. Loud,

Paul

sickening crunches—not of furniture breaking—accompany my landing. Pain radiates out from every inch of my body, confirming the sounds were bones snapping.

An overwhelming reek of death permeates the air—like a mix of blood past its prime, stale air, and an undercurrent of unwashed vampire bodies. Ugh. I've never smelled anything quite so disgusting before.

I lie still in the darkness, waiting for the shock to recede. A low moan issues from my left. A door flies opens and I hear something being dragged out of the room.

The door shuts, and now the only noise breaking the silence is my own labored breathing. The full despair of the situation hits me as I lie here, waiting to heal. Someone came and took Drew. I'm all alone and completely unprepared for whatever happens next.

Or, as my lovely wife Bunny would tell me, "Honey, you're fucked."

Chapter Twenty-Four

Asa

I don't trust Cy and want to know why he tried to push into my head, but, I've shoved my fears and worries aside to listen to Jon. The werewolf relayed the discoveries of the day and shared the alpha's thoughts on a plan utilizing Cy and me.

We're sitting in the command center, the blank screens of the security monitors glowing slightly even with no picture displaying. To make matters worse, all of the cameras on the property, aside from the ones attached to the main building and the apartments, have been shot out.

We won't have any advanced warning of their movements as this siege progresses. Risking our guests' safety to leave the property has become much greater—we may be forced to let them access the tunnels just to get on a plane.

Energy coils inside me, causing me to open and close my fists in a sign of a nervous edge. I may not want to work with Cy, and part of me wants to beat him to a pulp, but the rational section of my brain knows such an attempt would be foolhardy and not solve the current dilemma.

Asa

As a soldier, I have to work above my personal dislike of a comrade. I have to trust he'll do his job even if I don't want him covering my back. Biggest problem with my logic is Cy is not military and ignoring the screams of protest in my mind make my head hurt. Best to shove my feelings into a tight corner and focus on what we can do in the here and now to protect the werewolves from further harm.

I look to my master's servant as he pulls up an aerial view of the property on an iPad. Jon points out the location of the hunters' base camp and explains how he wants us to try and interrogate these men using our mind control abilities.

"Three men to take down over a dozen werewolves?" Cy looks skeptical. "It doesn't sound like their original plan was smart odds when they thought it up."

Whether I like the bastard or not, he's made a good point. The equipment Jon described sounds more like armed militia or weekend warrior than government trained grunts. Why would you bring three against almost twenty wolves? I look at Jon and contemplate what enemies he could have made over the years. "Could they have come hunting for only one and found more when they arrived?"

Cy raises an eyebrow and looks at Jon. "Hmmm.... Who'd you piss off, boy?"

Jon's shock rolls off his body. "Me? What the fuck are you saying?" His voice takes on an angry edge. "I've spent the last seven years isolated in this frozen corner of the world." Realizing the unlikelihood of our implication, his anger leaves him as quick as it arrived. "You two are barking up the wrong tree." He smiles at the pun in his own phrase. "I didn't lead anyone here, nor does anyone hate me enough to come knocking—at least, not that I know of."

The cagey vampire from New York stands and stretches. "No matter. We'll find out when we question them, right?"

Jon nods and leads us down the hall toward the tunnel entrance in the north wing. I wave Cy forward, not eager to have him behind me sooner than he needs to be. I never had a chance to tell Jon about my run in with Cy, and despite my apprehension I must follow the path we've set tonight. Jon is still my superior in the seethe. Cy's arrival doesn't change that. The more I thought about it early this morning, they more I wondered why Cy tried what he did with me.

Could he be a manipulator, and suggested me for Alaska with the hopes I'd find out information on his maker for him? Holy shit, would Vivian have suspected me of such actions, and maybe that's why she went into my mind? I shake my head, appalled at the complexity in the inner secrets of seethes.

Vivian turned Cy loose after only a few months in her company, confident in his abilities that he wouldn't run rabid and kill people indiscriminately, putting the species at risk. But could he have developed vampire compulsion powers afterward and she was unaware of it? And if that's the case, how many of her earlier progeny could hold the same traits?

Jon keys in the security code, out of Cy's view, and opens the door to usher us in. "You've got your phone, Asa?"

I pat the device in my front pocket and the gun strapped to my thigh, too. "Yup."

"I'll stay upstairs near a window. Call me if you need my help."

I nod, sure I won't be calling and risking my master's servant even if I do run into trouble. I slipped on a Kevlar vest before putting my jacket on. Unless the hunters find a way to behead me, I'm pretty secure.

Cy and I move single file through the tunnel, silently passing the rooms holding the young family. I lead the way since he has no idea where we're going. We decided to use

Asa

Paul and Bunny's cabin again for its location and convenience. I take us on the long route, deliberately making the path harder for my old master to memorize.

"Quite a maze down here, isn't it?" Cy asks after passing through the sixth steel door.

"Yes, it is," I say, careful to hide my grin. With any luck he'll be thoroughly confused when we arrive at the couple's bedroom closet.

A chill works its way into my gut and takes hold. I could very well be in the middle of something much bigger than I bargained for. Unlike during my time living with Cy and Aunt Cali, I am well and truly bound in blood with Vivian. I re-pledged my loyalty to her in January after she revealed her true powers and I don't doubt the decision.

The information I've been able to dig up on her rare branch of vampire power has been extremely limited. I have a feeling Drew knows more, but he hasn't been forthcoming with me. Then again, it's not like I've asked him. I've been so happy since Eric and Pat arrived, I didn't want to rock the boat with digging deep in things best left unknown.

Vivian's abilities scare the shit out of me. My own meditation started to safeguard my mind. It could do nothing when facing her true power—but I had to try something. I never dreamed strengthening my own mental shields would be needed against my aunt's husband. After a dozen more turns we make it to the ladder leading into the cabin.

"Jesus. That was a hike," Cy breaks the silence when I stop and check my supplies once more. "This is it?"

I nod, still not willing to engage the bastard in conversation. In a few minutes, we're standing by the living room windows, using night scopes to check for signs of movement.

239

"Follow me to their encampment," I say. "If we don't find them we'll split up and search, making our way back to the inn separately. If there's gunfire, we meet back here and travel the tunnels to return undetected. Clear?"

Cy agrees, and we slip out into the darkness of the icy night. The temperature dropped back into the single digits when the sun set, reminding us that the short spring the tundra sees is still a ways off. The warmth of the cabin seems like a distant memory as the cold sears my throat and scorches a fiery path to my lungs.

We race through the black, dodging trees and passing soundlessly among the brush. Quickly, we arrive at the map location Jon showed us. The hunters' campsite appears empty with no sign of recent use. We split up, both of us searching the area for hunters or traps they may have left for the wolves.

Once my old master disappears from view, a heaviness I was unaware of slips from my shoulders. I must have been tenser in Cy's presence than I wanted to admit to myself. The silence of the woods cocoons me, bringing a measure of peace to my racing thoughts.

I breathe in and out slowly, trying to focus my thoughts and open up my mind's eye to the energies around me. No matter how much I might like to, I can't will the hunters to appear before me. After a while, I realize searching quietly through several square miles of woods reminds me of digging for a needle in a haystack. I begin to doubt our chances of finding them.

A thin line of darkness stands next to a slim tree trunk. I creep forward and discover a noose trap hidden along an old animal trail. Grabbing a dead branch from the ground, I trip the rope to trigger the trap and render it useless.

I uncover several more traps like this over the next few hours, including four steel bear traps. Looking high and low,

Asa

I search the narrow trees for signs the hunters may be lurking, rifle aimed toward the inn. Nothing. My time in Afghanistan, even in winter, wasn't an environment even remotely close to the Alaskan tundra, but I had really expected my training to give me an edge in finding them.

If that slick city vamp finds them before I do, it will burn my ass. I flex and tighten my hands again, hoping to drive some of the biting cold from my extremities. The temperature started to seep in over an hour ago, as it invariably will if you're not protected well enough from it. The thin coat I'm wearing was to ensure stealthy movements more than warmth, and now, I'm regretting it.

I tighten my path to the inn on every pass, but still see no signs of the actual hunters. The cleared property closest to the inn is landscaped way beyond what would thrive here in nature. The gardens look good, even in the dead of winter with their light-festooned statues, small bushes, and lots of lit mini-Christmas trees—there is certainly not a lack of things to hide behind as I work my way to an entrance.

Within the hour, I'm seated in the conference room, sipping from a piping hot travel mug filled with bloodcoffee. A small note of pride filled me upon hearing Cy withstood only half the time outdoors that I did. Unfortunately, he didn't locate the hunters either, so I wisely keep my boastful thoughts regarding his weakness to the cold to myself. The bastard never would have lasted long in January when they hunted Emiko.

"Jon," Cy says, "why haven't you connected mentally with Vivian to tell her what's going on?"

Jon waves him off. "Our link is weaker due to the distance. She told me it might happen."

Cy puts his mug down. "Nope, that's not right. You're her vampire servant, right?"

A wary look comes over Jon. "Yeah. What's your point?"

"That bond should stay strong permanently, unless the vampire weakens it on purpose."

"What are you saying? Vivian promised she'd never cut me out again." Jon's face freezes, realizing he may have revealed more than he'd wanted.

Cy laughs and looks at me. "He doesn't get it?"

I shrug.

"Get what?" Jon asks, anger coloring his tone.

"A werewolf getaway in Alaska. Lots of available females."

Jon looks confused. "What does that have to do with my link to Vivian? She wouldn't push me away if I needed her—and this little vacation idea has turned to shit fairly quickly."

"Wake up, man." Cy reaches for the carafe. "She couldn't have predicted the danger, but she was thinning the link on purpose."

"Why?"

I answer the Were, the light clicking on for me a lot sooner than it has for Jon. "So you could find a mate."

Jon freezes for a moment and then bolts from his chair, emotions flying across his face. Hope flares to life for an instant and then he closes his eyes and stills himself.

His eyes slit and stares right at Cy. "You said 'thinning the connection', right?" The vampire nods. "Well, what if the link is gone completely?"

The room goes silent as we all mentally weigh the implications his statement could mean. I lean forward and place my mug on the table. A heavy sigh rolls from my chest and I resist the urge to put my head in my hands. "Oh man, that can't be good."

Chapter Twenty-Five

Vivian

My wounds heal slower now that the demented pair has drained half my blood. I hope the fools drink it, then we'll see who laughs last. The ties a vampire has to their own blood is independent of manipulator traits. The silver hood will restrict me from mind controlling them—but, if they are stupid enough to swallow a taste while I'm still alive, I'll use my blood like a weapon, cutting them down from within.

A thin silver blade slices down my thigh, leaving a wake of fire in its passing. When the torture started, I laughed, the maniacal noise bouncing off the tiled room, echoing through the air like a crazed hyena.

The intense pain helped me block out the loss of my spouse, and I welcomed it with open arms. Now, hours later, every cut draws a scream from my throat, sounding to my ears like the ragged, deranged shrieks must be coming from someone else.

Agony pumps through my veins with every slow beat of my heart. The bastards stuck silver needles into my flesh and add another every time I give them an answer they're unhappy with. Again and again, they ask me questions I don't have any information about. All along, I thought Cora hated me for me, not for what I am and the unknown threat I represent to the vampire species.

How stupid I'd been. It was for something greater all along.

I drift for a moment, skating the boundary between consciousness and oblivion. When I skirt too close to the edge, and the burning pain recedes, the real dread begins. I rage against the offer of peace my body longs to give me, banging my foot hard on the table to keep myself awake.

I exist solely within the pain now, fearing the darkness in my soul, embracing the suffering like an old friend in order to delay my grief over Rafe's demise. I anticipate the death awaiting me, eager to grasp it to my breast while my sanity holds. I know my husband may be on the other side.... or in my next life. No matter what lurks in the great beyond, I have no doubt it has got to be better than this burning, never-ending torture.

Lucas' face, twisted with his hatred and disgust, looms over me, dripping spittle on my exposed flesh as he rages. "Tell us what you know of the other manipulators!"

I repeat what I've said every time. "Nothing." A note of pleading enters my tone. "Kill me." I close my eyes and turn my hooded head away. My mind keeps echoing, *I have no reason to live.*

The replay of Rafe's last moment tumbles over and over in my mind. The last look of rebellion on his face as he struggled against his captors. His blood shooting into the air... and then spreading in a large pool around his discarded body on the floor. The helpless denial torn from my lips as I crashed toward him, determined to save him even in those last seconds.

What a fool I've been, to think I could escape what every manipulator before me could not. My own helplessness washes over me, tears springing to my eyes and falling unseen beneath the silver hood.

Too strong to use, too dangerous to live, too valuable to kill.

What an idiot to think I should be allowed to love again. Did I not learn before? All those close to me used against me in the end. Their reward for loving me was death.

Death is all I am.

One more silver needle slides into the sensitive, exposed skin of my underarm. The burn spirals deep, my flesh trying its best to crawl away from the inflicted wound, while an answering wail rips from my lips.

After a minute, Cora's voice cuts through my screaming. "Let's try another train of questions." She stalks across the room to where I'm strapped, spread-eagled, with silver chains on a metal autopsy table. "What do you know of the Atlantians?"

Her words filter through my haze of agony, and I open my eyes, to gaze through the slitted hood at the woman responsible for taking away the only person in my life who helped me cling to sanity—to my remaining humanity. Her question makes no sense to my pain-rattled mind. "What?"

A spark of interest lights in her dark blue eyes. "Do you know of your ancestry? Your ties to the ancient race?"

I shake my head, grateful for a respite from the silver torture, but still have no idea what she's talking about.

"Who was your maker?" she hisses. I flinch as the flat of a silver blade is held against my stomach, burning my flesh before she pulls it away. "Your sire is not listed in the archives."

Unsure if I should answer, confused what the knowledge could lead to, I speak, hoping to learn from their interest. "Take out the needles and I'll tell you." A gleeful look of triumph crosses her face and she pockets her dagger. Cora yanks out the dozen needles, one by one.

"What are you doing?" Lucas barks from across the room.

She's doing exactly what I want. The extraction hurts as much as the insertion and the pain will keep me awake. Too much torture will shut me down, so I need to balance it. It's a dangerous game I'm playing. Dragging out my death to ensure I die with my sanity intact. Fire plumes bright as each needle slides out and I wrap the sensations around my mind, shielding myself from grief.

"Shut up, Lucas. We can put them back in when she stops cooperating."

My body starts to heal, albeit very slowly and not without problems. Every time I think the pain receptors must be dead, a new wash of agony shoots through the damaged flesh, proving me wrong.

"Tell me, Alexandria, or I'll let Lucas put the needles back in."

Bitch is enjoying this way too much. "Mikov was my maker," I say through gritted teeth.

"When were you turned?" Cora asks, leaning down to my ear.

The physical pain recedes, allowing the crushing loss of Rafe to rush in. A sob hitches in my chest and a small part of me wishes the needles were back inside so I could focus on the pain instead. The black depth inside my soul reaches up to smother the memory of my love, attempting to save me with the peaceful oblivion of the dark acts of my past.

Kill or be killed. Blood and more blood. Lust and sex.

The monster needs no emotions, just action. Slice, suck, drain to death... laughing all the while. A mindless beast, a pure killing machine... the dark beauty of my prior actions entices me to give up... to give in. No more pain, simply surrender to the black hole no amount of blood can ever fill.

No more love, no more loss.

Cora screams, "Tell me! When were you turned?"

I don't care if she knows, but now I need the pain of the silver to hold the devil inside me at bay. If I succumb and accept the darkness I will lose everything I value—I will lose my memories of Rafe and the love we shared. I will lose myself in the evil I will become. How much of the pain can I take? Will my mind shut down before they decide to kill me?

"Fuck off, bitch," I say, decision made.

Her face mottles with rage, and she stabs me, plunging the silver dagger into my shoulder, then withdrawing the blade in one quick strike. Fire sears through my blood, racing toward my heart, causing the organ to skip its slow steady beat.

"Cora!" Lucas yells, stopping the psycho vampire from sinking the knife again. "What difference can it make when she was turned?"

"I knew of Mikov." Cora replies, anger and speculation in her tone. "He died with his whole seethe in a farmhouse in England."

"So?"

"If his whole seethe died, why wasn't *she* with him?"

I wrap the pain of the recent wound around the tattered remains of my mind, pushing the black abyss away one more time. I'm ready to die, but I'll never be ready to lose what remains of my humanity ever again.

"Stay focused, Coraline. More important than where she was or when she was turned—can we use her power? Can she reveal more of their plans?" Lucas walks away, his steps across the tile floor sounding measured and precise in the sterile room. "Does she know about the others, or do we know more than she does?"

247

"She's too old not to know what's going on."

I don't know what the hell they're talking about, nor do I care. A conspiracy of manipulators? If I had the strength to laugh, I would. This whole witch-hunt against me was to find out what I knew about something I had no idea even existed. Fat chance they'll believe me now.

A familiar voice calls from a far end of the room. "From what we've uncovered, she's isolated herself from our kind most of her life. She could very well know nothing."

What the hell is he doing here? Has that smooth-talking bastard tricked me all these years? I shake my head slightly at my own foolishness. Ah... what difference does it make? I know nothing they need and with any luck I'll be dead soon and joining my husband.

Steps sound across the tile, bringing the traitor next to Cora. "Most helpful would be the names of all those she's turned over the years."

Cora's breath pulls in sharply. "You mean she could have produced more manipulators?"

A mad bubble of hysteria blossoms in my chest, only the muted burn of the stab wound keeping it locked inside. Me? Turn other manipulators? God, wouldn't that be a hoot? Paul's the only one I'd ever seen who exhibited illusionary skills in over four hundred years.

An unwelcome thought pushes to the forefront of my mind. *But then again, you never kept the others around very long, did you?*

An image of Paul flashes across my brain. What about Paul and his disappearing trick in the hangar with Emiko? A small spark penetrates my foggy desperation craving death. *Must not reveal Paul.* Whether his skills will develop into mine or not is still unknown, but there's no way I'm pointing these jackals his way if I can help it. At least if I die here he'll be protected.

Vivian

"You never know. She could have," he answers.

Considering I've forgotten almost as much of my life as I can recall, I'm not worried about revealing names to my tormentors. In my current mental state I can't even remember the last five I turned who lived past three months old—except for Cy. There was a stretch of time I changed one every decade or so, but that was centuries in the past. Surely, if any of them were alive I would have run into them by now.

Not unless they remained hidden, like you did.

Content I have enough fortitude to not throw my offspring to these wolves, I relax, embracing the last of the healing pain as the stab wound in my shoulder finally closes. The best I can hope for is a quick death or a pain filled existence until I do expire. Anything less would end me as I am. I need to stay alert, too. My mind won't hold onto the agony when I'm unconscious, leaving my subconscious vulnerable to attack to my monster within.

Can I provoke them into killing me? That would be far easier. If I let the emotional loss in, my vampiric self-preservation could overcome my weakened mental state and block out everything good I've ever done in my life.

Every kiss, every caress, every life I saved... all of it will be gone. When they kill me, I'll be like all those mindless rogues I hunted years ago—how will I be reunited with Rafe then?

My head drifts back against the cold metal of the table. Darkness seeps in around the edges and for once in the past few hours it's not the pull of madness but of oblivion. No! I can't let go yet!

The suave, smooth voice cuts across the void, sounding like it's coming from deep in a tunnel. "I think she's had enough for now, Cora. Let's start again in a few hours."

As consciousness slips from my grasp, the dark abyss rushes in to claim me.

Chapter Twenty-Six

Jonathan

I raced out of the basement meeting with Cy and Asa, unable to talk with the two bloodsuckers a minute longer. What's happened in Argentina? Why can't I feel Vivian in my mind? That stupid jealous bastard should have let me come. I would have protected her!

There are no planes that work. The roads to the south are still impassable. There is no one in Coldfoot whose safety I could risk to call in to fly me out. And even then, how would I get to her?

I've dialed her number over and over to no avail. She wouldn't willingly cut me off, would she? My frantic pacing has led me to the windowless dojo on the resort's main floor. A body bag for boxing hangs in one corner and I launch myself across the space, eager to take out my frustration on the inanimate object.

"You promised me!" I yell, hitting the canvas as hard as I can. The heavy piece of equipment is double chained, to the floor and ceiling, limiting its swing after each strike. Anger pours from me, fueling my actions, lending a vicious speed to my fists. I pummel the stiff fabric again and again, no

Jonathan

rhyme or reason to my blows, just straight punches with the strength of an angry werewolf behind them.

Where the hell are Paul and Drew? They called when they landed—but that was hours ago. Nothing since then. I hit the bag, both fists flying through the air, in every combination I can imagine. I start to sidestep around the bag, hitting it on the swing instead of waiting for it to settle. Maybe I should call Chelly? What good could she do? Calling her will only make her worry more than I bet she already is.

My face heats from exertion, and my throat scratches raw as I continue to yell and hit. A long scream rips from my lungs as I strike again and again, my knuckles leaving blood on the tan material. This should have never happened!

"No!" I pant out, voicing my anger to the room. "We do not end like this, you redheaded bitch!" Tears stream down my face, mingling with sweat. My hands lash out over and over until the pain in my fists registers.

I pitch forward, hugging the bag in both arms, sagging to let the chain hold my weight. After several minutes, my breathing slows and returns to normal. Acceptance enters my brain as the worst of the fear and anger dissolved during the mindless hitting.

She would not leave Rafe willingly. And if he were with her, one of them would call. If there is a way out of whatever is happening to her, I must have faith that she will find it. She promised me she would not cut me out of their lives again, and I need to take her words at face value. She's given me no reason not to trust her. Something is blocking our link and I have a feeling it's the one thing in the world that could make her break her word to me—a silver hood.

My pulse slows, and I come back to myself. My hands have already started to heal and the stinging wounds feel good. I flex my fingers, working the stiffness out of them while I straighten up. For the first time in the seven years

I've dedicated my life to her, she truly needs me, and I'm not there for her.

I roll my shoulders back and lean my head from side to side. No matter how hard it is to take, I have to face that I can't control the actions or choices of a half-millennia old vampire. *If* I were there, is a whole 'nother line of doubt I don't want to put myself through.

I leave the room and cross the hall into the gym. The window has long been repaired from when Vivian dove through the glass and ripped Vikram's head off. A small smile lights my face at the memory of that night. I was almost gone, and she brought me back from death's door. If anyone can get through being hooded in the Seat of Darkness, it's Vivian.

The peaceful warmth of the water calls out to me. I strip my sweaty clothes and drop them on the bench near the large shower. Rafe and Vivian bathed the blood off of me after the attack, or so they told me. I turn on the faucet and look back at the wooden bench. I don't recall much after she dug out that vampire fingernail in my side. Must have passed out from my injuries.

The hot water feels good after the pounding I gave my muscles. The anger needed to get out. I didn't hurt anyone else or break anything, so I'll count that as an alpha success on my part. I've always laughed at the concept of anger management classes. I think most of those unhappy bastards just need to freakin' exercise and beat up a punching bag once in a while. Let out that built up frustration and testosterone.

I lather myself and rinse off, standing under the spray of hot water, not ready to get out of the relaxing shower yet. A throat clears beyond the glass door. "Yeah?" I call out. "Be done in a minute."

Jonathan

I hear the rustle of clothing over the noise of the water and then the shower door opens. "Hey—" I whip around to complain and face the gloriously naked shifter, Candy. "Oh, wow. Hey."

A mischievous smile decorates her face, a dimple flashing at me through the steam. Her toned body is more than I could have ever bargained for—defined waist, fit legs, slim hips, and breasts just begging to be sucked. Blood surges to my crotch, and parts I have no control over start to stir. Damn, I pray she's here for what I hope.

"Would you like some company?" Her eyes travel my wet body, lingering briefly on my healing hands before dipping lower to my rising cock.

I smile, surprised I'm able to let go of the hurt and worry of earlier. It's still there—defused by my physical release on the punching bag and manageable—not so stifling now.

"What did you have in mind?" I ask, wanting to make sure I don't overstep myself. Hell, she could be a cock tease for all I know.

She takes the soapy scrubby from my hands and slowly runs it from her neck, between those gorgeous breasts then over her stomach. Her eyes are locked on mine the entire time. "I heard you in the other room."

I tense up, my face freezing. What is this, some kind of pity seduction?

"I wasn't spying on purpose. I was worried about you."

Does she think I'm some crying sensitive bastard now and I need a shoulder to lean on? "I'm okay now, thanks." I try to move past her, out of the shower, and she stops me with a hand to my chest.

"I know what she means to you, Jon. I admire your loyalty and dedication. She sounds like a woman worthy of it, and that's impressive—hard to find nowadays."

I look past her, unwilling to meet her penetrating gaze. "She's not from 'these days'. She's an alien figure from the past. One with a dangerous history and a lot of enemies. She's often cold and very powerful." What the hell am I doing? Trying to push her away? I look down at Candy, not sure what game she's playing, but ready to lay my cards on the table. "She's my general in the war of life. She does the jobs no one wants, and she'd do anything for the people she cares for."

"I know that, Jon. Your words and actions told me." Her arms twine around my neck and she presses her wet, soapy flesh to mine.

The range of emotions I've experienced in the past hour have left me raw and exposed. Maybe I'm not ready for some quick, meaningless poke in the shower. A sigh escapes me as my pain and desolation crash back. Hell. I tilt away from her embrace, unsure what the devil I want.

Candy's perky nipples rub against the tight skin of my chest while my erect cock nudges her stomach. "I don't want to replace her, you idiot," she says. "I want to be here to ease your pain and tell you I understand."

A snort of disbelief escapes me as my traitorous body screams to take what she's so freely offering. "You understand I love another woman?"

She reaches up and places her lips on mine, tender yet firm. Giving and taking, all at once. "You'd love her even if she were a man—that's what the vampire bond does to you." She rubs herself against me, the slip and slide of her skin on mine almost enough to bring me off right here. "I also know that bond isn't the same as being in love."

I grab her upper arms, not sure if I want to shove her away or pull her closer and bury myself in her up to the hilt. "Oh yeah? And what makes you so smart?"

Jonathan

"I knew someone once who explained it all to me." Her hands trace circles on my chest, gradually fanning lower while the hot water streams over us. "There's room in your heart for more than one love, Jon. Let me in. See if I'm a good fit."

And just like that the dam breaks. My will folds, my desires and secret wants barrel to the surface, urging me to claim this woman and make her my own. I press my lips to hers, almost crushing her softer flesh in my desperation to climb inside her.

The spark of my passion fuels her own and she meets me, lunge for lunge, battling my tongue for position. "Oh my God," I mumble when I come up for air. "You taste so freakin' good. Did you just eat a steak?"

Candy smiles and dips her head a little, biting her bottom lip. "When you want to attract a predator, would you use fruit or flesh?"

I laugh in the confines of the shower and pick her up by the waist, encouraging her to wrap her legs around me so I can get a nice grip on her firm ass. "I want to be inside you so badly, Candy. I don't think I can wait."

She smiles and tilts her hips, angling her wet pussy to accept the head of my engorged cock. "Who says you have to wait?" She circles her hips, forcing me in deeper. "Might be a little tight at first, but I bet you won't mind." The feel of her snug snatch covering the first two inches of my dick pushes my resolve and concentration past the breaking point. She rasps over the shower, "Do me hard and fast—then make it up to me on round two."

Relief over her simple acceptance of me races to the forefront, my heart burning in my chest. With an animal roar of lust, I squeeze that sweet little ass of hers in and thrust all the way home, feeling the walls of her hot pussy gripping my cock as I push deeper.

At our joining, her moan of pleasure matches my own, and she tosses her head back into the stream of water, letting the shower cascade over her chest and pretty little nipples. I spread my stance and change the grip of my hands to her hips, lifting the young woman off my length before sliding back into her waiting heat.

"Damn, Jon, you've got a nice thick prick," her passion-filled voice sounds husky and sexy in the acoustics of the shower.

I grumble low in my chest, the sound spilling like a low growl. "The better to fuck you with, my dear."

"Oh God, that's hot." She circles her hips on each thrust, working my prick inside her in a way I can't do from this angle on my own. "Oh yeah," she pants, "it's been so long. You have no idea."

I laugh, full and deep, while my cock plunges in her hot wet sheath. She truly has no idea the length of time since I've been with a woman like this...eight years or more.... I know I won't last much longer.

The world around us disappears into the steam as the clasp of her pussy forces every rational thought from my mind. The sole focus of my attention centers on my flesh pistoning in and out of this glorious woman, climbing higher and higher toward my release with every stroke.

A primal moan rips from Candy—her circling hips ratcheting up a notch, encouraging me to plunge harder and faster into her. My fingers dig into her slim hips, and there's a moment where I worry I'm gripping her too hard. She comes, her inner muscles rippling up and down my shaft. My own peak explodes with the added sensations, a guttural groan tearing from me to echo through the steam-filled shower.

I slow my pumping as my orgasm spills into her still-spasming flesh. Her upper body snaps forward, her mouth

Jonathan

open, a look of pure abandon in her expression. She latches onto the thick muscle of my shoulder and bites hard. Not enough to break the skin, but enough to leave a mark.

I laugh, taken by surprise at her actions. "What the hell was that?"

She licks the spot she bit, our bodies still firmly connected at our pelvises. Candy gazes at me with a sexually satisfied expression. "I've marked you with my intent."

The practice symbolizes the recent sexual joining was more than a physical release. That the Were is open to pursuing more if the other is willing.

At my look of shock she goes on. "Has no Were shown serious interest in you before?"

I reach behind me and turn off the water. My cock starts to regain its full firmness inside my new lover, eager to prove I'm good for more than one round. "No," I say and kiss her with a tenderness I don't think she expected after our passionate first encounter. "No one ever has."

"It was their loss, babe. Trust me." She disengages from my erection, a wistful look on her face, before sliding back to the floor. I let go of her with regret. God, it felt so good to cut loose and be myself with a woman... really be with a woman and not the farce I've attempted for years.

My feelings bubble up and out before I can analyze them to death and muzzle myself. "I'm glad you did." I smile to soften the intensity of the moment. "Now, I plan to do you again and 'mark' you 'til you can't walk."

Candy steps out of the shower and grabs a towel. With one sexy look over her shoulder she wraps the towel around herself. "You'll have to catch me first." She smirks and darts off toward the gym.

My heart sings as I leap after her, forgoing my own towel, eager to get my rigid cock between her silky folds again as fast as I possibly can.

Chapter Twenty-seven

Rafe

Over the course of the last few hours, I've seen the other two male vampires who originally were a part of my abduction, plus Coraline, and Lucas. The wizard has been curiously absent since he left my clothes. Cora wasn't too happy I had the garments on, but she wasn't willing to strip me down to my skivvies with no reason other than her own mean-spiritedness behind her.

While the numbers against me aren't in my favor, I have no doubt that with the right opening and enough surprise, I can get Dria free.

Playing weak has its advantages. Lucas and Coraline stand outside my cell door bickering about what to do with the other two vampires from Dria's seethe. Apparently, Paul and Drew walked right into a trap. I don't blame either of them for their failure. From what I understand, Drew has never dealt with anyone associated with the Tribunal before.

I stare at the stone wall of the cell, anger at myself being forefront in my mind. Now, I'll have to get their sorry asses out, too. Dria and I should have known better. *Beard the lions in their den.* Yes, indeed. That really worked out well.

Rafe

Then again, neither of us had any idea the depth of this conspiracy when we started.

Is there truly an organized group of manipulators against the Tribunal? Why would this band of torturers be so adamant if there wasn't some indication there was one? Dria's obviously not behind it all. So, who is?

The voices outside die down and one set of footsteps retreat down the hall. My wife's blond nemesis steps into the cold cell. I lay on the cot, curled on one side, waiting to see if she's here to deliver another round of her favorite question and beating game. Pretending to be under her compulsion wears thin, but I'll keep it up until I get the opportunity I need.

"I know you're awake," she says. "Might as well get up."

I push myself to a sitting position, moving slowly and feigning more pain than I feel. "I've told you everything I know."

An evil smile plays across her face. "Which has turned out to be very little, hasn't it?"

I look away, unwilling to provoke her if I can manage it. She looks like she's spun rather tightly and would probably enjoy a reason to beat me again.

Her high heels rap across the stone as she saunters to the cot. She's changed out of the drab black clothes she wore before and stands before me with a low-cut red blouse, and dark gray dress slacks. There's only one reason she'd come in here dressed in anything remotely attractive—to catch my eye.

I allow my gaze to linger longer than necessary on the exposed flesh at the opening of her shirt before I avert my eyes to the floor.

"Like what you see, Rafe?" A low, cruel laugh spills from her. "So ready to give up the love of your life?" I hunch my shoulders, letting her think I feel guilt over my actions, still refusing to look at her.

A cold hand grasps my chin and forces my head up. "Look at me, Rafe. I want to see what I've been missing."

Ahh... and there it is... exactly why I thought she came in here dressed to impress. I meet her eyes and permit her mental energy into the surface thoughts of my mind.

"You want me, Rafe." She presses her will forward. I conjure memories of Dria and me as we last made love, knowing she'll see them in my mind. "You think I'm Dria and want to make love to me."

A soft sigh slips from my mouth, and I relax my shoulders. I release the false tension in my muscles and soften the look on my face to one of love and adoration.

"Yes, liebling, I do." I reach my hands out to cup her cheeks, and widen my eyes, as if I'm finally becoming aware of our surroundings. "But, not here. You deserve better."

She leans in and places her lips to mine. Her hold slips from my mind, content she's placed enough compulsion on me to give herself over to the kiss. I grab the back of her head and pour an intensity into the union that can easily be mistaken for passion. She responds to my ploy with an eagerness that reveals her own hidden longing.

Cora pulls back, gasping for breath, her chest rising and falling with her sudden desires. She glances at the cot and grimace of distaste flashes across her face. "Yes, you're right. Let's move to a more comfortable place."

She takes my hand and pulls me up, staring into the soft adoring puppy dog face I'm wearing—and buying it lock, stock and barrel. We leave the cell. She leads down a narrow hall, past other doors marked for storage. We travel the empty corridor and into another, passing through areas I've never seen before.

Rafe

At the end of a hall, we climb a set of stairs to another level and stop at the third door on the right. She throws open the thick wood to reveal a well appointed room inside—a small fireplace to ward off the chill, a nicely made queen bed, and small writing desk with a chair against one wall.

"Much better, my dear." I slip my arms around the petite vampire and hug her from behind, kissing her neck once before letting go. I walk straight to the fireplace, worried that I might not be able to pull off the physical part of a man's arousal to convince her of my pretend interest. "It's cold in here. Let me get this fire going, so you don't catch a chill."

I hear the rustle of clothing behind me while I build the fire. I take my time, steeling myself for the woman waiting on the bed and what she expects from me. Catching her unawares and striking fast will be the only way I can pull this off.

I take a deep breath, relaxing my face and doing my best to look content and intrigued by what the evening holds.

"It looks good, darling." Cora whispers. "Come, join me."

I rise and turn toward her, a soft smile playing on my face. She's reclining on the bed, clad in a black bra and matching underwear, a look of longing clear on her expression. My fingers work the buttons on my shirt with deliberate care while I lock gazes with the bitch who'd see me dead the moment I ceased to amuse her.

Her dark blue eyes follow my hands, watching as I peel back the shirt and leisurely slip it off. The t-shirt underneath fits snug, pulling across the planes of my chest. I draw my hand across my pecs and down to my waist, deliberating teasing her with my slow movements.

If there's one thing I've learned in sixty-five years with Dria, it's how to heighten a woman's interest with slow seduction. A real smile spreads across my face as I recall exactly how much power I have over my wife by touching myself in a languid, non-sexual manner.

I pull up the hem of my shirt as I tighten my stomach, revealing the rippled muscles underneath. After a brief pause, I tug the fabric up higher and slip it over my head, casting it toward the desk. I've got her full attention as I unfasten my pants and push them over my hips to the floor, shoving them with my foot near the other discarded items. Realizing this next part could be my undoing, I close my eyes, blocking out the vision of the vampire before me and think of my wife.

Her pale skin and copper hair spill over the pillow as I thrust into her tight ass over and over again. My cock twitches at the memory of the rare pleasure, surging to life in my underwear. I rub my hand over my growing arousal, needing to make this farce as real as I can to get Cora where I need her.

In a burst of vampiric speed, Cora launches across the space between us to stand in front of me, brushing her breasts against the bottom of my ribs. My eyes open, desire for the replayed images with my wife showing for her to see.

The blond vampire stands on her toes with her fangs out, lust plain on her face. "Another kiss?"

I bend down to comply, placing my lips on hers in a tender touch. Her hot sucking mouth latches onto me as a groan of pure desire pushes up from her depths. The angle is wrong for what I need to do, so I pick her up and carry her to the bed, deepening the kiss with each step. I sit and place her across my lap, resting my hands softly on her hips to not alarm her to my intent.

She breaks the kiss and trails her mouth down my neck, lingering over the large, pulsing vein in my throat. I run my hands up and down her back, bringing them close to the base of her skull, like I'm cupping her head in passion, encouraging her to bite me.

"You smell so good," she whispers, awe in her voice. "I can hardly wait to taste you." She pulls back and opens her mouth wide, staring intently at my neck and nothing else.

I pull the tiny knob on my watch face. The razor wire whirs out in a flash, and I loop one hand around her neck as she plunges to bite me. The wire cuts through her flesh like butter, spraying blood over my face and torso. With one fierce tug, I pull the loop of the razor wire closed, decapitate the woman, and push her body to the floor.

It happened so fast—her dead face doesn't even register shock, still locked in a position to bite. Without wasting time, I scramble to the writing desk, searching for a letter opener or a pair of scissors. Instead, I find a silver dagger with blood dried at the hilt, even better for the task. I test the edge on my thumb and then move back to the headless body bleeding out on the floor.

I plunge the blade into her chest, hacking and forcing my way to the still beating heart. Cracking ribs with my bare hands, gore and flesh coat the skin on my forearm with red. The gruesome job pulls a wave of nausea from me, making me hesitate in a short flash of horror. Damn, it's so much easier when you don't have to cut out the heart.

I steel myself against the terror in my mind, focusing instead on the need to get to my wife before the same is done to her. Without a backward glance at the still warm body, I toss the heart into the fire and search for something to clean myself.

Using the bed coverings, I wipe off the worst of the blood, peel off the ruined underwear, and then clear the gore from the razor wire to force it back into its hidden case. I scoop up my clean clothes I striped out of earlier. I knew taking them off would be the only way I'd be able to walk out of here without looking like I committed murder.

Which is exactly what I did.

I ransack the room as fast as I can, searching for more weapons. The silver knife sits secure at my lower back in my waistband. I grab the heavy iron fire poker, holding it alongside my leg as I prepare to leave.

Coldness settles over me as I ease into the empty hallway, locking the inner handle and quietly pulling shut the door behind me. I don't care how many I have to kill before this day is over. I'll get to my wife, one way or another.

Or die trying.

Chapter Twenty-eight
Asa

I'm worried about Jon. He stormed out of the conference room hours ago when we needed to stay focused on the task at hand. Trying to avoid Cy inspired me to stop and visit with Paul's family for a little while, forgetting the kids would be asleep. I updated Bunny on what's been going on since I saw them last.

We haven't heard from Paul or Drew since they landed in Buenos Aires a little after midnight last night. Considering it's almost six a.m. down there now, we should have heard from them by now. And if we don't soon, I'll hold off on telling Bunny for a little while. We've got bigger fish to fry and stressing her out about her husband's possible danger thousands of miles away certainly won't help.

Do Paul and Drew stand a chance of breaching the Tribunal's security and finding out what is happening with Rafe and Vivian? I think back to the night Drew beheaded Ivan.

Drew stood over his wife's killer, hesitant on the next move. If Ivan hadn't taunted the bastard, Drew might not have had the courage to finish him. I stare at the concrete wall of the command center, tuning out the amused chatter of my brother and his friend.

How much action did the two young Weres see in Iraq? Are they comfortable with pulling the trigger or dropping the blade like I am? I'm not saying I enjoyed the war, but I did thrive on the action and the routine. The cares of the world melted away and your life spiraled down to fulfilling your job. You do the job, sometimes bored, sometimes with adrenaline pounding through your body as every sense is heightened to the max, then you go back to base and sleep. The next day you repeat... again and again... and again.

Weeks in the field didn't sap your grip on reality when you knew you had a solid country to go home to when your tour was up. The dreams of what you have waiting for you take on a life of their own, occasionally building a stronger meaning in your memory than that which really exists—but one simple fact remains: If you make it home, you'll be going home to *safety*. The people living in those war-ravaged countries *are* home.

They live day in and day out not knowing if soldiers will break down their doors while they sleep, if a car bomb will destroy all they own and love, or if an improvised explosive device will trigger as their children race across open ground.

The time I spent wandering Afghanistan, after I realized what I had become, seemed exactly like the hours I walked through a warzone holding a loaded rifle. I smelled every piece of refuse and rotting gore. I felt every grain of sand and grit that blew into me, heard the scratch of a stray dog in the next alley, and a family behind thin walls as they spoke softly in the night. A part of me deep inside sensed the energies around me, intuitively reading when danger was in the air.

Except, the sensations and experiences never lessened when I became a vampire. They never shut off when I went back to base—hell, there was no more base camp for me to go back to.

Being a newly changed vampire was the ultimate war high. Learning to live with the transformation and protect my sanity became my biggest challenge. A part of me wants to reach out and ask Eric and Pat what it means to be a werewolf. What do these two knuckle-heads next to me *feel*? What did they think of the war?

Should I tell them my time in Manhattan stretched the very fibers of my reality? That I worried I'd go insane and kill everyone around me? The constant bombardment of stimuli was almost enough to make me walk into the sun. Cy taught me how to center my mind and turn down my vampire senses. He may not have any military background, but he had a good grip on staying sane, helping me get through the worst. Which makes his blatant attempt to push into my head so out of character. What the hell is up with him?

I thump a fist into my thigh, unwilling to waste more time on Cy when I have no desire to confront him about it. Instead, as I sit here near the brother I thought I'd never see again, I allow the rush of my war senses to come forward like I did in the woods. I smell the soap residue clinging to both young men, the salt of the popcorn they're snacking on. I hear the rustle of their clothing as they shift in their seats. The low hum of the computers in the room sounds like a muted roar of static, drowning the other noises with its intensity. I feel footsteps above, the subtle vibrations carrying through the ceiling, the walls, and to my feet on the concrete floor.

This latest danger with supernatural hunters gunning for wolves may not be the same as war, but it is an attack on claimed territory, and a fight I intend to meet head on. Are the others as ready for battle as I am? If Drew and Paul survive, should I offer to train and make them stronger members of the seethe? Should we treat this isolated resort like a base and fortify it as strong as we can?

Assuming the seethe makes it out of Argentina alive, I intend to talk to Vivian and see what we can work out. She may want a peaceful existence living in the dark where no one can find her, but that dream is over and it's best we prepare.

Jon saunters into the command center, breaking my train of thought, looking like he's desperately trying not to smile. His step is lighter and the tension he's held ever since I've met him seems absent. The scent of sex wafts off the alpha, prompting me to shut my senses before I find out more than I'd like to about the man.

Paul and Eric lounge in the extra chairs, throwing popcorn across the room into each other's mouths—beaning each other in the face more than getting kernels in their open maws.

The evil smart-ass in me wants to tease them about making a dog work for his treats, but I hold back. Pat takes one look at his new alpha and chokes on a piece of popcorn he snagged off his shirt. His face turns red and then clears. "It's about freakin' time you got laid."

Eric sputters, managing to contain his burst of amusement before it gets out. He looks from one to man to the next, watching to see what Jon does—maybe wondering if he'll have to jump in and pull him off his obnoxious best friend. I smile at all of their reactions, my interest peaked.

When Jon finally answers Pat, a small grin quirks up one corner of his mouth. "I don't know what you're talking about, man."

"Uh-huh," Pat continues, unaware of stepping over lines that shouldn't be crossed. "So, if I start humming 'Dude Looks Like a Lady' you won't have any problem with it?"

Asa

Jon glances over his shoulder and shrugs. Candy steps into the room and now it's Pat's turn to sputter. He bolts up in the chair, taking his booted feet off the desk and straightens his face into one resembling sobriety. "Hey, there Candy," his voice squeaks. "How you doing?"

"I'm doing great, Pat," she answers while stepping around Jon and coming into the room. "What bothers you more—the fact I can make my dick bigger than yours?" She shifts before our eyes, lightning fast, into the form of Eric, her loose clothes stretching until she looks like a super-sized version of my brother. Eric's voice comes out of Candy's transformed body. "Or that I can turn into a beast...." She morphs into an albatross, the clothes dropping to the concrete floor, and flies at Pat's head, breaking off as he dives under the desk like a scared rat.

The huge, seagull-like bird squawks loudly and lands on Jon's shoulder, transforming back into the naked form of Candy, standing behind her new boyfriend. "Who can take your eye out before you knew what hit you?"

Pat looks at Jon, indignation and outrage fighting for dominance on his face. "Dude, you told her about my freak out over the *Birds* movie? So not cool." We all laugh as he climbs from under the desk and Candy puts her clothes on behind Jon. "Alright, alright. I'll hold my tongue." He shoots Candy one more glare, "Unless you dive bomb for my eyes, then all bets are off." He adjusts his shirt and mumbles "crazy bitch" under his breath.

An idea pops into my head, like there should be a big ole light bulb over me lit up like a halogen beam on high. "Candy, could you fly over the property to find the hunters' positions and tell us where they are?"

Jon opens his mouth, looking like he might object. "I'll do it," Candy says, no hesitation in her voice, no time needed to think about her answer.

"Wait a minute," Jon says. "I'm not so sure that's a good idea."

Cy picks that moment to join us from the hall, making me wonder if he was lurking there the entire time. "I think it sounds like a good plan, too." He leans against the doorjamb. "The cameras are all shot out. Asa and I had no luck. We need to pin down their location to capture them alive, right?"

Jon glances at his watch. "It's almost midnight, and it's well below freezing out there. Besides, birds don't fly at night."

Candy puts a hand on his arm. "No, but bats do. Echolocation might be just what we need to sniff out these wily bastards."

"I thought bats don't like the cold," Eric says.

"Well then," Candy smiles. "It's a good thing I'm not a born bat then, isn't it?"

The two Weres and I look to Jon, clearly acknowledging he's the deciding factor in this no matter how willing the young woman may be. Cy watches the interchange from the doorway, wisely keeping his mouth shut.

Jon looks reluctant, but agrees, giving a terse nod. "Alright, if you're sure that's what you want to do." He lets out a big sigh and wraps his arms around the slight woman. "I know you can keep yourself safe."

I rise from my chair, grabbing a stack of maps off an upper shelf over the desk, glad to be doing something and moving toward a common goal again. "Great. Let's go to the conference room and get you acquainted with the terrain. We'll need you to not only find them, but direct us when you get back."

"Okay." She rubs her hands together, looking eager for the challenge. "Let's get crackin'."

Drew

CHAPTER TWENTY-NINE

Drew

It's been hours since I was dragged into this room and left in a heap on the floor. My injuries healed while I searched every square inch of the dark space, seeking a way out. My labors proved fruitless, forcing me to sit and wait—wondering if the two men will come or leave me here to rot.

The only saving grace in our failed rescue attempt is I didn't endanger Chelly by bringing her here. Sure, the three in the hotel can't fly the jet home, but if they don't hear from us in a few days, they know to board a plane and get back to the safety of the inn.

By the feel deep in my bones, I can tell the sun has risen. The desire to fall into a restorative sleep calls like the warmth of a fire on a cold, wet night. Fear over what awaits when I shut my eyes drives me to bite my tongue to stay awake. Anyone could come in and stake me without my being able to stop them.

The hours run together until I'm no longer aware of the time I've been sitting here, resisting the peaceful lull of sleep. A shuffle sounds in the hall. A figure pauses by my door, and a soft knock breaks the silence. Would a captor knock, or just unlock the door and come in?

"Hello?" I call out, feeling stupid. Who the hell could be trying to rescue me?

For the next few minutes I hear metal scraping in the lock. I crawl toward the sound, waiting to see what happens next. The handle jiggles and the cold steel barrier swings inward. Bright light from the hall burns my eyes, blinding me as Rafe's familiar scent meets my nose.

"Rafe?" I ask, stumbling to my feet. "Is that you?"

"Shh, not so loud, you fool." He shoves some small metal pieces into his pocket. "Yes, it's me. Come out, quick."

I lunge for the door, adrenaline fueling me when my heavy muscles want to lie down and rest. My shoulder smacks into the doorjamb, and I stagger into the hall. Rafe looks cool and collected, the reek of fresh vampire blood coming off him in waves, despite his clean appearance.

"Holy shit," I whisper. "Who did you kill?"

Rafe shows no expression, his gaze intense, mouth set in a firm line. "Coraline." He darts a glance up and down the hall before marching along the long, winding corridor like he owns it. I lurch forward to follow, my movements becoming smoother with each step. "I've been searching for hours and have only found you." He glances back over his shoulder. "Tell me what happened."

I recount the events as briefly and quietly as I can, all too aware we're in enemy territory.

"How far did they drag you before placing you in there?" he asks when we get to a point where the hall splits two ways.

I stop dead in my tracks. "Good point." Rafe hears me halt and turns to face me. "They didn't take me far. Paul has got to be in one of the rooms nearby. Back the way we came."

We turn around, and I can't help but notice something feels different about Rafe. He's always been a big man, but he's never used his size before, if that makes sense. He stalks with purpose, whereas in the past he's held himself more aloof and in the background.

It's like he's purposely taken a back seat to Vivian's over-the-top, despotic-ruler ways. I'd assumed his deference was out of necessity rather than an actual choice on his part. The look in his eye and the way he's holding that iron poker next to his leg have me scrambling to reassess the laid back man.

The sound of footsteps approaching the corner spurns Rafe to act. The poker swings back and overhead in an arc, smashing into the vampire's skull as he comes into view, sending the man careening into a wall. Rafe tosses the poker, which I catch before it hits me. He kicks in the nearest door and drags the still form of the vampire inside.

"Get in!" he shouts. "Shut the door!"

Shock runs through me as I rush to obey, slapping on a light and closing the door as fast as I can. Rafe kneels over the vampire, ripping the fallen man's shirt open, buttons flying with enough force to sail across the storage room. He draws a dagger from behind his back and cuts into the man's chest as the vampire starts to stir.

Rafe holds him down and shouts, "Hit him again, dammit!"

The command in his voice holds a measure of compulsion, and I leap forward, no hesitation in my actions. The poker comes down and bashes the unknown man's head, the force splitting it like a melon.

Blood and gore pour onto the concrete and his struggles cease. The horror of what I've done pales when I glance down at Rafe, who is wrist deep in the man's chest. I backpedal, unsure what to do and unprepared for the quickness of this man's demise.

Rarely have I witnessed a vampire's death come so swiftly. No clash of power, no fighting, no warning, just wham—someone cracks you in the skull and you're dead.

Rafe remains emotionless as he works, his face a mask of stoic determination.

When he's done, he flings the heart across the room. It lands with a sickening splat and slides out of view. My stomach heaves as I struggle to swallow my disgust.

"We'll need to come back later to burn it." Rafe opens a box and rummages inside. He pulls out some stored napkin linens and proceeds to clean his arms. After a moment, he looks in my direction, not failing to see the shocked horror still on my face.

"He was one of the vampires who abducted us from our suite," he says.

I nod, not so sure his statement rings true. He took that swing before the man rounded the corner. "How did you know it was him?"

Rafe finishes his clean up and tosses the bloody rags to the floor. In two steps, he's in my space, staring down into my eyes. "I recognized his scent."

I nod and look away, wishing to God I could keep my mouth shut. Of course, with his enhanced strengths from Vivian he'd be more attuned in his senses.

Rafe gently takes the poker from my unresisting hands and steps toward the door. This is a side of Rafe I've never seen and I'm unsure how to proceed. He is undoubtedly the leader in the seethe without Vivian present, and we need to focus on getting to her, no matter the unpleasant tasks.

"Can you handle this, Drew?" he asks, no judgment in his tone, just a calm acceptance.

I straighten my spine, in for a penny, in for a pound. "Yeah. Sorry about that. The fight happened so fast, I wasn't prepared."

"I don't fight." Rafe looks over his shoulder and smiles, the humor not reaching his eyes. "I kill."

"Excuse me?"

Drew

"You don't fight an opponent stronger than you." His breathing appears even, despite the adrenaline he must have coursing through his body, and his eyes look steady. "The only way you'll win is with the element of surprise—which you lose in a straight fight. You strike first, go in hard, and make the kill. You may never get a second chance."

I nod, unused to the guerrilla-warfare train of thought. The sport of fencing I grew up with had rules and honor. Steps to follow and an understanding of how parties involved played the game.

The death laid out behind us is stark and horrible, cold and unyielding, swift and unmerciful. As Rafe slips into the hall, I can't help but make the comparison—he's all of those things, too.

And to think, all this time I thought Vivian was the one to fear the most.

Chapter Thirty

Jonathan

Candy returned thirty minutes after the sun rose. She arrived cold and exhausted, but full of information. The vampires are no help in the daylight, and Eric, Pat and I prepare to slip through the tunnels to track and capture the hunters. We're each armed with tazers and zip-cords to secure and bring them back for questioning.

Kotsana ranted to kill them on sight, and had to be sedated by the doctor in an upstairs guestroom. Romeo's pack isn't too thrilled with not being included on our upcoming venture, but since they can't access the tunnels or get past the sniper rifles it's a moot point.

Weak sunlight from a cloud-filled sky casts an odd half-light to the outdoors. Approaching these bastards like men, face-to-face, is the only way to subdue them without injury. Pat bitched the entire way here about wanting to put a cap in their asses, too. Shouting he'd like to see how they liked it. His complaining was more for our amusement than anything else.

I don't doubt his integrity. He'll stay the course. Besides, we aren't carrying guns. Despite the possible danger, I feel light-hearted and unafraid. We're on our land—frozen

Jonathan

tundra that it may be—and we're going to take it back from the demented bastards aiming to kill us.

As we approach the first location Candy showed us on the map, I signal for the other two to fan out. Adrenaline washes through my system, bringing my wolf senses and instincts closer to the forefront. The yearning to rip and kill runs just below the surface, like a caged beast eager for the slightest provocation to lunge.

Our steps through the brush are slow, measured, and quiet to not reveal our location. Ahead, behind a tall bush, I see the darker shadow of a man. He's covered on all sides by branches, and if I hadn't approached from the right angle, thanks to Candy's direction, I could have easily missed him.

I reach the edge of the scrub and whistle softly. The camouflaged man whips around at the noise, his rifle caught in the branches, a surprised look on his face. My fist snaps forward and cold clocks him once, hard. He goes down like a bag of rocks, as Eric and Pat rush forward, no pretense at stealth needed anymore.

We manhandle the guy out of the bush and roll him over, zipping together his wrists then ankles. Pat takes great glee in biting off a length of duct tape and slapping it over the man's slack mouth.

"That's one bitch down and two more to go. Boo-yah!" His fist pumps through the air.

We search his pockets and disarm him of all weapons, taking clips and knives with us. Eric smashes the hunter's radio and leaves it next to the man's former hiding spot.

"Hustle his body back to the cabin and put him face down on the floor," I say to Eric. "Pat and I will go to the next location, okay?"

"Yeah, sure. Meet you soon." He hefts the unconscious man over his shoulder and runs back the way we came.

"How 'bout letting me take point on this one?" Pat asks, the eager light of the chase in his eyes.

I open my mouth to agree, but something holds me back. The first catch may have been easy, but if anything happens with the next two, I don't want either pup in the direct line of fire. I shake my head. "Not this time. Let's stick to the plan for now."

"Yeah, fine. You're a fucking glory hound is all. Admit it." The crooked-nose bastard smiles and ducks into the woods before I can reply.

I laugh softly and move to catch up. We walk side-by-side, loping deep into the tundra to search for the next hunter. According to Candy, this one is hanging out in a deep fissure where the land pushed up on a frost upheaval.

Forty-five minutes pass before we work our way up behind the guy. The crack in the frozen ground he's hiding appears long and narrow. I step too close to the brittle edge and slip, sending a rock cascading down the interior.

The sound isn't loud, but it's enough to alert the man to our presence. He leaves his rifle on its secure mount and grabs his radio while turning to investigate. He's a mirror image of the first camouflaged guy, slightly bigger with a scraggily, brown beard. He spots me as I try to halt my slide.

One gloved finger punches the radio button and he screams, "Greg, they found me!" He drops the radio and fumbles for his sidearm.

I dive to the bottom of the shallow ravine, watching him take aim. Scrambling to stay moving, I launch myself to the opposite slopping dirt wall, right as the hunter squeezes off the first shot. The bullet misses by several feet and the steaming muzzle takes aim again.

Pat drops onto the hunter from above. The young Were shoves his tazer into the back of the man's neck, zapping him before another shot flies.

Jonathan

The big guy jerks and drops, proving no matter the size, a tazer makes a great equalizer. Eric runs up while we're securing the man's spasming limbs. The sharp, astringent scent of urine fills the air, and a dark, wet spot grows on the front of the unconscious man's pants.

I smile up at Pat. "You used the tazer, you haul the wet one."

He shrugs, unperturbed by the thought, still smiling from taking the man down.

"But it'll have to wait," I say. "You heard the guy. He's already informed the third man we're out here. The advantage is we know where he is and he doesn't know it. Let's get there—and be on the lookout for him heading this way."

The high from successfully stopping the first two hunters feels tight with tension. My slip on the stones almost earned me a slug. While I'd easily heal from a regular bullet that didn't hit my heart or head, I have no desire to test the werewolf ability against silver rounds.

As Jerry illustrated last fall when shooting Ivan, the silver bullets aren't accurate over long distance. If one of the Army's best snipers lands a shoulder wound at a hundred yards, instead of the headshot he was aiming for, you know the accuracy is lacking.

The young Weres run beside me across the tundra. Last night's freezing temperatures still hold, making the cold air burn our lungs with each breath. In a blur of brown and green, Pat breaks to the right and Eric to the left. I take the lead as we close in, under a mile from the last hunter's location.

The uneven terrain shifts day to day, often surprising those of us familiar with its quirks. I slow my pace when I spot the recent frost upheavals, unwilling to fall into one holding a steel trap like Naomi did. The dead grasses reach chest high in some patches, making it hard to discern the swift moving Weres flanking me.

A grunt off to the left pulls my attention, the soft noise dying away almost as quick as it sounded. This close to the third hunter, I don't want to risk calling out Eric's name, so I angle in the direction I last saw him, jogging silently over the terrain.

After about fifty yards, I find him. He lies on the ground, cradling his ankle in both hands. He looks up and motions to a deep hole near his feet. "Broke my ankle. Snapped like a dry twig."

"Stay down and stay quiet," I say, eyeing the bone sticking through his sock. Compound fractures hurt like a bitch, but the young man holds the pain in without complaint.

Eric nods, assuring me to go, and starts to collect twigs and grasses. "I'll brace it the best I can until the doc can get to it."

"We'll loop back and get you after we take down the last one." I get twenty feet when the familiar sound of a round being chambered in a rifle whips my head up.

The last lone hunter stands less than fifty feet away. Dressed like the other two in camouflage and cold weather hunting gear, he's holding a long-range rifle to his shoulder. His sites are set square on my chest. At this distance he could make a big hole in me.

I raise my hands to show I'm unarmed. "Hey man," I call out. "Do you know you're hunting on private property?" I casually walk to my left, away from Eric, drawing the man's aim with me.

"I know what you are," the hunter says.

I shrug, trying to stall as long as I can, hoping Pat hears our voices and flanks behind him. "I'm just a man out here walking."

Jonathan

"No, you're not. You're an abomination." He lowers his cheek to the stock preparing to squeeze the trigger.

I lunge to the side as the crack of the large caliber ricochets across the tundra. Fire blooms in my shoulder, the force of the bullet spinning me around. The burning pain associated with silver courses through my veins, ripping an involuntary scream from my lungs. As I fall to the ground, I hear scuffles from the direction the hunter stood. Blackness creeps in, obscuring my vision as the sucking agony steals my consciousness.

Chapter Thirty-one

Paul

I huddle in a corner, crying softly. Afraid if I close my eyes to the darkness I'll never wake again. Remembering all I'll lose if I pass out works as a good motivator, but as the sun creeps higher in the sky, I'm not so sure how much longer I'll last.

Hugging my legs to my chest, I begin to rock, replaying the past few days in my mind. The horrors of the week came at us fast and furious. I think over every choice, wondering what went wrong, when did this trip slip so far out of control.

Was it our impulsive decision to rent a plane and fly here? Would staying on an island with humans mind-altered by Vivian's enemies be any better? The rhythm of the small back and forth motion offers a lull to my scattered thoughts, steering my mind to a time I rocked my son in my arms, soothing him when he woke with a fever one night.

Will I see him again? Will I hold either child again, or will I die in this stinky hellhole underground? I dry my eyes with the back of one hand, disgusted by my emotional breakdown, but still unable to shake the feelings of despair.

Paul

Steps sound in the hall outside, pausing when they reach my door. "I hear him crying behind this one," Drew's hushed tone comes through the dark.

"I'm in here!" I scramble to my feet and follow the wall to the door, avoiding the broken furniture.

The door crashes against the opposite wall and Rafe's scent spills in with the light. "Come on, Paul. Let's go."

I trip as I cross the threshold, my tiredness making me clumsy. Drew catches me and draws me to his side, away from the hard visage of our master's husband. I nod my thanks while staring at Rafe. His rugged, good looks have transformed into a face that sparks pure terror into my soul.

His blue eyes glint like chips of ice, his clenched jaw makes the muscles of his neck stand out, and a hollowness in his cheeks lends an air of madness to him. I've never experienced the self-assured and relaxed man do more than raise his voice, and yet, right now he appears like a person comfortable with murder.

I pull back, shocked at what I see. I glance at Drew, and he looks away, discouraging any questions on my part. Without a word, Rafe kicks in the next door.

"She's here somewhere." He flicks on the light and looks around before marching to the next door. "I'm not stopping until I find her."

He carries on like this along the entire hallway. At the last door, he rushes in and hope blooms within me. Drew and I race to the doorway. He gets there first and holds up an arm to keep me back. Rafe straddles the sleeping form of a black haired vampire, the greasy strands sticking against the golden skin of the man's forehead. Rafe raises a dagger and plunges it straight into the unresisting vampire.

Drew shoves me into the hall, whispering, "You don't want to see this, Paul."

I land against the far wall, staring back at Drew, my mouth hanging open. "What the hell is going on?"

The sickening sounds of hacking flesh and the scent of vampire blood billow from the room. A wave of nausea hits me, forcing me to double over and wrap my arms around my middle.

"Dear God," I choke out. "Has he gone mad?"

All of a sudden I wonder if I'm dreaming. There's no way Rafe is on the other side of that wall butchering a vampire while the creature sleeps, is there? Aside from the moment in the hangar when I attacked Emiko, I've never fought anyone, even in self-defense. I haven't been dead long enough that the thought of butchering someone in cold blood appeals to me, either.

Drew steps away from the door and slides down the wall —the shock of fighting exhaustion and the call to sleep clearly plague the other man, too. "He's a demon possessed, searching for Vivian."

"Is there a chance she's still alive?" I ask.

Rafe looms in the doorway, staring down the hall, not looking at us. "Of course she's alive. I would know if she wasn't." He strides through the corridor, heading for the stairs. "Keep up or I'll leave you behind."

Drew and I lurch to our feet, the weight of the sun and our recent healing from the fall through the trap door taking its toll. Our staggering steps give Rafe pause and a flash of the man I knew flicks across his face and disappears. "You two move like zombies," he says, a trace of humor in his voice.

"Good," Drew quips back, his exhaustion making him reckless. "Glad we fucking amuse you, you ruthless bastard."

Rafe gets in Drew's face. "Do you have a problem with how I'm handling the situation?" There's no fear on the larger man's expression as he stands toe to toe with the smaller, hundred and fifty year old vampire.

"If by a *problem* you mean watching you hack out the hearts of vampires like you're carving a Sunday ham?" Drew asks. "Then yeah, I may have a problem."

A stillness comes over Rafe, making his earlier quip about zombies seem like it didn't happen. "What do you think they're doing to my wife? Calmly questioning her to reveal what she knows about manipulators?" His eyes cut to me, and I gasp. "Do you think she'd give up Paul no matter what they did to her?" He steps closer and Drew retreats. "Or do you think they're torturing her beyond all she can handle, to the point when her own sanity may break?"

The stiffness in Drew's spine deflates, and he slumps against the wall. "I'm sorry, Rafe. You're right. I'm stretched beyond all I can handle." He runs a hand over his face. "I don't know what good we are. And frankly, you're scaring the crap out of me."

Rafe punches him lightly in the shoulder. "Buck up. Let's get you two closer to the surface and hide you someplace while I continue on."

"If you waited 'til after we slept," I say. "We'd be able to help."

He snorts and climbs the stairs two at a time. "Yeah, and everyone would be awake, too. Think, man—the best time to strike is when they are very weak or sleeping. Anything else is suicide."

The logic of what he says sinks in, but I'm no help, dragging one foot after another, hoping like hell I can stay upright long enough to do as he bids.

We climb two flights of stairs, not encountering anyone in the elaborate underground warren. No surprise, since the time is well past noon and any smart vampires are tucked in their beds.

This floor looks different from the others. The ceilings are higher, and the lighting is better. The man Drew accused of being a wizard steps into the hall, stopping Rafe with his sudden appearance. "It'll be easier if I tell you where she is," he says and looks away, perhaps not liking what he sees on Rafe's face.

"Why would you help us?" Rafe asks, clenching his fists, looking like he's going to leap on the man and beat the information out of him if the wizard changes his mind.

The young man meets his gaze. "Because I was hired to place security wards on the Tribunal property. Elaborate work, acting like an early warning system. I was apprehensive when Cora approached me to cast a binding spell. If I had known where it was going to lead, I would have refused the extra money." He squares his shoulders and raises his head. "I've no desire to get in the middle of a vampire feud."

"Well, bully for you, Justin." Rafe steps closer and draws his knife. "You're in the middle of it, now."

Justin shrugs. "Yeah, well, maybe telling you where she is will matter for something when the shit hits the fan." He smiles a crooked grin, slow and sure of himself, with a measure of respect showing in his eyes toward Rafe. "And trust me, I'd bet my bottom dollar when the head honchos wake up tonight there's going to be hell to pay."

Rafe nods, accepting his explanation of self-preservation. "Lead on."

The two move down the hall, and I fall to the floor, my exhaustion finally getting the better of me. Drew trips on my foot and crashes on top of me.

"Crap," Rafe says. "This is as far as they go. Help me drag them into a closet and then let's get going."

I hear their steps toward us... and then nothing.

Chapter Thirty-Two

Asa

Over an hour ago, Pat raced down to the basement with Jon's bloody form draped over his shoulders. Dr. Cook was already on the premises and began working on his wound immediately. Candy paced the halls, unwilling to be too far from her new lover's side.

The delectable scent of werewolf blood filled the lower level, prompting Cy to leave, getting out of temptation's way by locking himself in Paul's room. I would have thought being married to a werewolf meant he'd have his fill of their potent brew, but maybe the opposite has occurred and he's been too long from his wife.

Romeo and Elsa left with a few of their pack to help Pat retrieve the captured hunters and Eric. The hunter who shot Jon, the one called Greg, turned out to be the man who organized the expedition. We had to hold his questioning until Jon could attend. While everyone wants to know what's going on, it's been agreed only Romeo, Jon and I will interview the man.

I sit in the conference room, sipping my bloodcoffee and glance at the clock. It's almost ten a.m. and I'll not be much good at mesmerizing the dude if Jon doesn't hurry. The pale

Were staggers into the conference room, swathed in bandages and rolling an IV drip alongside.

Candy helps him with the IV pole then leaves, respecting the privacy we've requested.

"I'm here," Jon says. "Let's get this over with."

Before the door closes, we hear Eric bellow as the doctor sets his broken ankle. I wince at the sound, pity for my brother welling up.

"Wipe that sad sap look off your face, man," Jon directs my way. "I'm the one who got shot."

I smile at the bloody alpha. He didn't even shower off the dried blood before coming in. The bastard is tough, I'll give him that. "Yeah, whatever, Jon. I'm not related to you."

Romeo drags in the hunter, throwing his cuffed form in a chair and placing his hands on his shoulders to keep him in place.

"You freakin' animals!" Greg screams, spittle flying in his rage. "I'm gonna—"

I place my hands on the table and lean forward, pressing my will to voice while saying, "You're gonna be quiet." The man's jaw snaps shut and a glassy look overtakes over his eyes. "Now, you're going to truthfully answer every question we ask."

There's a hushed expectance in the air as the group waits for Greg to nod. Once he does, Jon launches in. "What brought you here to hunt werewolves?"

Romeo no longer needs to hold the man in his chair, and walks to the other side of the table to sit down and join in the questioning.

"One of you killed my sister," Greg says, the pain clear in his voice.

I look at Jon, raising an eyebrow. "Dude," he says. "It wasn't me. I told you I've been here."

Asa

I direct my attention back to the hunter. "What made you think it was a werewolf?"

"I tracked the prints for hours after the incident. They eventually led to a large clearing where only human footprints led away." He shrugs, the anger in his posture making him stiff. "It was easy to track cars into the park via the cameras at the entrances."

Romeo clears his throat. "Where did your sister die?"

"North of Winnipeg, we were camping off season where I'm a ranger."

A look of sorrow passes over the Manitoba Alpha's face. "When?"

"Last fall, late October. The cops closed the investigation, no matter what I said. Saying she was mauled by wolves—but I knew better."

"What made you think they were wrong?" Jon asks.

"Because I was there at the end. I'd returned from showering and saw the creature leaving the campsite. It was too big to be a regular wolf." Greg appears drained, remembering the incident. "I called for help but it was too late. After the cops investigated, I did a little searching of my own."

Romeo's face collapses and a heavy sadness fills the Were. "I know the accident he's talking about."

Greg looks ready to leap out of his chair. "You call killing my sister a fucking accident?"

One glance from me has him lowering back down.

"What happened?" Jon asks Romeo.

Romeo looks toward me, pain in his eyes before he looks away. "He doesn't know he did it."

A cold steals down my spine, and suddenly I'm very afraid for my brother, and not because he's moaning down the hall over his fractured ankle. "Spill it, man."

A sigh escapes the stocky alpha and his shoulders hunch. "It was Eric's first change. Freezing rain came down heavy that night, making it hard to keep on top of both him and Pat. He broke away from the pack and it took us hours to track him. By then it was too late. He'd ripped the girl to shreds."

I sit in shock, listening to the recounting of how Eric killed an innocent woman.

"Asa," Jon says, pulling my gaze to him. "It wasn't his fault."

"Oh yeah?" says Greg. "Then who's fucking fault was it?"

"Mine," says Romeo, he looks at me with steel in his gaze. "And Eric doesn't need to know what he did. He was too out of it—like a lot of new werewolves, the animal side had almost complete control during that first shift. When he remembered some of the details, I told him the girl lived. Reassured him she didn't contract the disease since he hadn't been a wolf long enough to spread it."

I nod and lean toward the hunter, ready to wipe all their minds of what they know and block out the secret I've learned of my little brother. "Now, who else knows you're here?"

Chapter Thirty-three

Vivian

The stink of death hangs over Rome like thick smoke on a day with no wind. Less than an hour after my arrival, my senses became overwhelmed with the rotting bodies of plague victims clogging the cobblestone streets.

Young, old, women, and children stacked up like wood, waiting to be hauled away. I've seen this before when death ravages a city—there are not enough people to do the work. Having a rogue vampire preying on anything healthy doesn't help, either.

The council sent me when other vampires fled the city, reporting the plague wasn't the only thing sweeping through the population, killing with abandon. From what I was told, this same scenario has happened in the past—a high death count triggers something deep in a vampire's psyche, destroying the tenuous hold they have on their inner monster, pushing them rogue.

A few conceal their insanity, walking the fine line of hiding their many kills from society and their brethren for decades, while others snap and slaughter blindly until caught and eliminated.

The moist heat of the Italian summer wraps a suffocating hold around me as I slip through the darkened, deserted streets. I'm dressed like a nobleman in hose, breeches, a linen shirt, and a sleeveless doublet—with my sword in a scabbard at my side. My long hair is bound under a hat, my face darkened with coal to look like facial hair.

I searched for days to discover where the rogue hunted. The residences of the city's merchant families don't have many bodies outside, indicating they've shut themselves off from the lower classes whom the sickness often hits first. I came across three separate piles of sheet-wrapped victims, none of them reeking of disease.

Tonight, I wander those same streets, listening for any movement in the darkness, pausing next to posts... waiting to see what the evening may bring. As midnight looms closer a lone figure roams the cobblestones, his head swiveling back and forth scanning for signs of prey.

He strolls past piles of garbage, then hesitates outside a dwelling where a candle flickers inside. The sound of a baby crying for a midnight feeding rouses the home's occupants —perfect preoccupied targets for a deranged murderer. I sneeze, turning the simple noise into a loud hoot of air to draw the vampire's attention, and step away from the post, walking straight toward the beast.

I keep my head down, looking through my lashes, watching to see what he'll do. He glances from the house to me, then settles on the meal coming at him—can't get much easier than that.

The rogue's unwashed stench hits me from fifteen feet away, a sign his madness might have progressed past the ability to blend into society. My powers are locked down tightly and the illusion of a healthy human pulses around me like a second skin.

Vivian

Halfway across the street, I drop my coin purse, making a big show of retrieving it and displaying my neck as an effortless target. The insane vampire can't resist, and lunges, covering the distance between us in the blink of an eye. Anticipating his move, I draw the sword from my side, sweeping my arm up in an underhanded strike.

The blow guts the advancing vampire from stomach to chest. Wobbling on his feet, his innards spill onto the stones. The rush of his released power fills me, the high of killing coating my mind, urging me to finish the kill.

A shocked scream of outrage spills into the night, but I pay it no mind. I step to the side, gripping the blade with both hands, and slice his head from his neck. Blood spurts into the hot night as the body crumples to the ground.

My instincts race to the surface, driving me to follow custom, and drink. Spoils to the victor.

The hot liquid flows down my throat, instantly changing from the acidic taste of the crazed to the rare flavor of love. Memories flood my mind as I spiral into the darkness, gulping down the blood like my very existence depends on it.

Passionate kisses, loving embraces... sweaty, frantic coupling with the man I love... the memory of a life I thought would be forever denied me, calling me back... my hands latch onto a warm wrist and the smell of my husband fills my senses.

"That's it, liebling... drink. I have you now."

I drink for several minutes, afraid to open my eyes and see he might not be real. The burning in my body lessens with every pull. I stop when I hear a change in the heartbeat under my ear, telling me I've taken enough from my willing donor.

A rough hand travels up and down my shoulder, soothing me while I'm rocked gently on a warm lap. If this is a dream my mind has created to escape the torture I don't want to wake up.

"Dria? Can you hear me?" The ragged whisper breaks through my haze, the pain in the voice unmistakable. Small drops hit my face as lips press to my mouth in a brief kiss. "Come back to me. Fight the dark and come back to me."

Unable to put off the agony of not knowing any longer, I open my eyes, unsure what I'll do if I see the taunting forms of Lucas and Cora standing over me again. But they're not.

The only link to my remaining humanity looks down at me, the soft smile on his face full of love. "I'd thought I lost you there for a while," Rafe says.

My husband stands, carrying my battered body and steps over the decapitated body of Lucas on his way to the door. The aroma of death lingers on him, the scents too many for me to discern at once.

Tears sting my eyes, mingling with Rafe's, as they course down my cheeks. "I thought I'd already lost you."

His smile grows, easing the ragged lines of exhaustion carved into his face. "You should know by now—I will never give up."

The mental wall I hold close crumbles and sobs wrack my body. I hug the man I love more than anything in the world—clinging to him with a ferocity born from the desperation of my own insanity. I was there. I was locked inside of the killing.

I didn't want to come back.

Without him, there would be no coming back.

The rest of the afternoon zips by in a blur. Rafe hustles me, and the covered forms of Drew and Paul, out to a waiting car. He says it's borrowed from someone named Justin, but I have no idea who that is, nor do I particularly care.

Vivian

We're unloaded in the garage of a hotel downtown and transported upstairs to a suite of rooms with Chelly, Bob, and Tommy waiting for us. Rafe force feeds me two bags of Jon's blood, then cleans my limp, healing body in the shower and bundles me in a fluffy robe.

The horrors of my torture still linger close to the surface, and I'm grateful we're alone in the bedroom. I don't think I can take the curious stares and questions.

My strength is returning, drinking Jon's blood really helped, but mentally I'm not quite myself, nor has the silver poisoning worked its way through my system yet. I crave a deep restorative sleep for the first time in years, and yet, a part of my mind fears letting go... of what I'll see lurking in the dark when I'm weak. As I lie on the bed and hold my husband's hand, a tingle presses against my mind.

"I need to call Jon," I say, pushing myself to lean against the headboard.

Rafe nods, looking for the world like he's about to drop. "Call this satellite number." He rumbles off the numbers of one of the phones I keep in the tunnels.

"Why? Has something happened?"

He nods and closes his eyes, putting his head in my lap and wrapping an arm over my thighs. "Yes, but they handled it."

I pick up the phone on the bedside table and dial the number while sending out a mental push of *Answer your phone* through the mental link I have with Jon.

The phone rings six or seven times before the breathless Were picks up. "Hello? Dria, is it you?"

I smile at his use of my real name, an intimacy he rarely allows himself. "Yes."

A heavy sigh comes over the line. "What the hell happened? I couldn't feel you in my mind."

"It's a long story..." I relay everything that happened—not lingering over the bad parts like my torture and temporary loss of sanity—and answer his questions when he butts in.

He fills me in on what happened in Alaska, including the mind wipe of the three hunters, and the implanted story that a rabid wolf really killed the girl, a wolf they followed all the way to Alaska to hunt down and kill. Sticking as close to the story as possible always helps the new memories stick.

I chuckle when he gets to the end. Apparently, the likelihood of a rabid wolf traveling from Manitoba to Alaska didn't seem too far-fetched to the men when they thought up the idea.

I try to end the call when the exhaustion gets to be too much. Jon's voice takes on a note of panic when he hears my voice trail off for the third time. Before he'll let me hang up, I have to promise to call back after resting.

Despite my earlier fears of what might await me, I wrap my arms around my snoozing husband, and lean back on the pillows, letting myself go.

We wake after midnight and everyone gathers in the living room of the large multi-bedroom suite. Drew and Paul informed Chelly, Bob, and Tommy of what happened at the Tribunal before Rafe and I join them, which is fine by me. I'd rather not have to discuss the details again, if I don't have to.

Drew shares his thoughts on what was happening on the island, and we agree to fly back tomorrow to check out everyone and correct any vampire mind meddling that may have occurred.

Later, in the privacy of our bedroom, Rafe tells me about the wizard Justin. How the man was hired to place protective wards around the Tribunal and paid extra for the binding spell. Now that I think about it, both spells had a similar feel

Vivian

to them. That certainly explains the apprehension I felt when we stepped out of the limo that first night, and again in the bathroom suite before they slipped the hood over me.

Rafe relays his own plight after we were abducted, and how they questioned him about other Manipulators.

I sigh and snuggle into the bed. "I never would have expected Rolando to be involved."

A heavy sigh issues from my husband as he sits up. "I've got some bad news. I didn't cross paths with Rolando when searching for you."

A cold chill spirals down my back. "I thought you got them all. You told me you killed everyone who was in on the abduction."

Rafe runs a hand over his face, squeezing the bridge of his nose like he's trying to ward off a headache. "I killed Cora, then the two guys who held me, then Lucas. I'm sorry, I missed Rolando."

I nod, my thoughts turning inward as I contemplate our next move. "He wanted me to name who I had turned over the centuries."

"I know that look, Dria." Rafe's face pinches. "You can't confront him, right now. You need to heal and get stronger."

I look at my husband—the man who'd slaughter anyone who stood between us without batting an eye—and run my hand down his chest to his flat stomach. "You're exactly right." My hand dips lower to cup and tease, rousing what I need almost as much as blood. "And when we come back, we'll get him off Tribunal property to find out exactly what in the hell is going on."

With a growl, Rafe pins me to the bed and plants kisses down my neck, nudging open my robe in the process. "Not for a very long while." His attentions move lower, where he nips a breast, then licks the skin. "Not if I can help it."

C.J. Ellisson

~~*~~

The release date of this book, April 23rd, 2012, marks the two year anniversary of my nephew Eric's fatal accident on a motorcycle. He was 21 and recently back from his first tour in Iraq. A portion of the book's proceeds will be donated to a group dedicated to increasing motorcycle awareness in motorists. Stay off your phone, never text when driving, and be aware of bikers—they have every right to the road as you.

About the Author: C.J. Ellisson lives in northern Virginia with her husband, two children, two dogs, and a fluffy black cat who makes her sneeze. She writes contemporary fantasy and erotica, as well as non-fiction and middle grade fiction (under the pen name C.J. Stern, titles to be released soon).

Big Game is the third book in the *V V Inn* series and there are currently five novels and two novellas planned, with more to be added if there is enough reader interest.

Please, stop by the author's website: (http://www.cjellisson.com) to sign up for her email distribution or "friendship rate" list to find out when the next book will be available for three days only at 99 cents.

You can also visit her on Facebook at: (http://www.facebook.com/c.j.ellissonfanpage)

Glossary

Glossary of Terms and Characters:

Asa - the fledgling vampire sent by Cy, who was turned in Afghanistan while serving in the Army.
Angie - a human guest who stayed at the inn eight years ago with her first husband, Ivan.
Bloodcoffee - a mixture of half-blood and half-coffee, favored by undead everywhere.
Bloodwine - same principal as bloodcoffee, but half-blood and half-wine.
Blood Bond - a term used to describe the exchange of blood between either a human and a vampire, both ways, or a master vampire and a member of their seethe. It enables telepathic communication between them through the bond, if desired.
Bob - an employee, he works on the grounds-keeping crew.
Bonded Mate - a deeper connection than a servant, this bond allows the non-vampire to stop aging and share a significant amount of power associated with the bonded vampire. A complex ritual and exchange of large amounts of blood must take place for this bond to occur. The only way to break the bond is through death or a rare deep mind manipulation severing the link.
Bunny - Paul's wife.
Cali - Cy's bonded mate, and a werewolf. She's also Asa's aunt.
Carmella & Carmina (Mina) - Flavia's twin sisters, working on the island as maids this season.
Chelly - see Michelle.
Coraline - a member of the Inner Circle who cares for and guards the Tribunal of Ancients.

Companion - a human who has donated blood to a vampire and been accepted into the vampire's care for future feedings.
Cy - Vivian's contact in New York, whom she turned when she discovered him close to death in an alley outside his bar over forty-five years ago.
Dalton - the caretaker on the Argentine island.
Daniel - old vampire fling of Vivian's.
Deneishia - married to Kotsana and a member of Romeo's pack.
Diane - Dr. Cook's adult daughter and a witch.
Donald Swanson - one of the vampire hunters.
Donor - a human who donates blood to a vampire, willingly, with no connections.
Dr. Margery Cook - the onsite doctor on the property should a problem with a human arise.
Drew - one of the new member's of Vivian's seethe.
Dria - the master vampire who narrates the first book, aka Vivian and Alexandria.
Eric - a new werewolf from Romeo's pack.
Elsa - Romeo's werewolf mate.
Emiko - the rogue designated by the Tribunal to be hunted at the resort (book two).
Enforcer - a highly skilled vampire assassin, used as an instrument of justice by the tribunal.
Flavia - Dalton's wife and a fellow caretaker on the Argentine island.
Fledgling - term used for a vampire under the age of five years.
George - Security at the Tribunal of Ancients.
Ivan - Angie's first husband and bonded mate (book one).
Jerry - an engineer and sharp shooter employed twenty years on the property.

Glossary

Jonathan - Vivian's werewolf servant and the head groundskeeper on the property.
Justin - The wizard hired by the Tribunal to set up early warning wards around the property.
Kotsana - one of Romeo's pack, married to Deneishia.
Liebling - German endearment, meaning darling.
Lori - a werewolf in Romeo's pack.
Lucas - a vampire in Argentia who hates Vivian for killing his old lover.
Manipulator - a rare breed of vampire able to mind control other vampires. Usually hunted down and killed by their own kind to ensure they do not gain power over their fellow vampires.
Master Vampire - a vampire who heads their own seethe, or is independent of a seethe. One not requiring the blood of a master to gain in power, but has accumulated enough strength to hold their own in a battle where an older vampire may try to drain a younger one for their blood.
Mate - see Bonded Mate.
Michelle - aka "Chelly", an employee at the inn, who also doubles as a blood donor.
Naomi - one of Romeo's wolves.
Old Blood - a term used to describe the blood a seethe member gets from a master to increase their own power. Contains the added benefit of increasing a vampire's perceived undead age if the blood is strong enough and consumed regularly.
Pat - a new werewolf from Romeo's pack.
Paul - a gourmet chef imported from the lower forty-eight, married to Bunny and a newly turned vampire who is also part of Vivian's seethe.

Rafe - Vivian's bonded mate for sixty-five years, and co-owner to the inn.
Rolando - part of the tribunal of Ancients, located in Argentina.
Romeo - Jonathan's old Alpha, but not the Were who infected him.
Rosia - Flavia and Dalton's daughter.
Seethe - A vampire family, or group of vampires, with a master vampire at its head.
Servant - see Vampire Servant
Spike - A member of Romeo's pack.
Stephanie - one of the chefs at the inn.
Tommy - an employee, originally from Australia, who mainly works the front desk and organizes the blood donor list for the guests.
Tribunal of Ancients - the governing body of ruling ancient vampires, entrusted with maintaining the secrecy of the existence of vampires from the human race.
Turning - term used for when a human has been changed into a vampire.
Vivian - the nickname for Dria, a play on words from The V V Inn.
Were - shorthand for werewolf.
Vampire Servant - a human, or Were, who has donated to and ingested the blood of a vampire. A mind connection can be established (and broken), allowing telepathic communication. The servant feels a desire to protect and serve the vampire above his or her own needs.
Vikram - A vampire from Sanji's seethe, but not participating in the hunt (book two).